THE TALES OF CHEKHOV
VOLUME 10

THE HORSE-STEALERS
AND OTHER STORIES

THE TALES OF CHEKHOV

Volume 1   *The Darling and Other Stories*

Volume 2   *The Duel and Other Stories*

Volume 3   *The Lady with the Dog and Other Stories*

Volume 4   *The Party and Other Stories*

Volume 5   *The Wife and Other Stories*

Volume 6   *The Witch and Other Stories*

Volume 7   *The Bishop and Other Stories*

Volume 8   *The Chorus Girl and Other Stories*

Volume 9   *The Schoolmistress and Other Stories*

Volume 10   *The Horse-Stealers and Other Stories*

Volume 11   *The Schoolmaster and Other Stories*

Volume 12   *The Cook's Wedding and Other Stories*

Volume 13   *Love and Other Stories*

THE
HORSE-STEALERS

AND OTHER STORIES

By
ANTON CHEKHOV

Translated By
CONSTANCE GARNETT

The Ecco Press
New York

Library of Congress Cataloging in Publication Data
Chekhov, Anton Pavlovich, 1860–1904.
The horse-stealers and other stories.
(The Tales of Chekhov; vol. 10)
Reprint. Originally published: New York: Macmillan, 1921.
Contents: The horse-stealers–Ward no.6–The petchenyeg–[etc.]
1. Chekhov, Anton Pavlovich, 1860–1904–Translations, English.
I. Title. II. Series: Chekhov, Anton Pavlovich, 1860–1904.
Short stories. English; vol. 10
PG3456.A15G3   1986   vol. 10   891.73′3s [891.73′3]   85-16218
ISBN 0-88001-057-6   (pbk.)

CONTENTS

	PAGE
THE HORSE-STEALERS	3
WARD No. 6	29
THE PETCHENYEG	113
A DEAD BODY	131
A HAPPY ENDING	141
THE LOOKING-GLASS	151
OLD AGE	161
DARKNESS	171
THE BEGGAR	179
A STORY WITHOUT A TITLE	189
IN TROUBLE	197
FROST	209
A SLANDER	221
MINDS IN FERMENT	229
GONE ASTRAY	237
AN AVENGER	245
THE JEUNE PREMIER	255
A DEFENCELESS CREATURE	265
AN ENIGMATIC NATURE	275
A HAPPY MAN	281
A TROUBLESOME VISITOR	291
AN ACTOR'S END	303

THE TALES OF CHEKHOV
VOLUME 10

THE HORSE-STEALERS
AND OTHER STORIES

THE HORSE-STEALERS
AND OTHER STORIES

THE HORSE-STEALERS

A HOSPITAL assistant, called Yergunov, an empty-headed fellow, known throughout the district as a great braggart and drunkard, was returning one evening in Christmas week from the hamlet of Ryepino, where he had been to make some purchases for the hospital. That he might get home in good time and not be late, the doctor had lent him his very best horse.

At first it had been a still day, but at eight o'clock a violent snow-storm came on, and when he was only about four miles from home Yergunov completely lost his way.

He did not know how to drive, he did not know the road, and he drove on at random, hoping that the horse would find the way of itself. Two hours passed; the horse was exhausted, he himself was chilled, and already began to fancy that he was not going home, but back towards Ryepino. But at last above the uproar of the storm he heard the far-away barking of a dog, and a murky red blur came into sight ahead of him: little by little, the outlines of a high gate could be discerned, then a long fence on which there were nails with their points uppermost,

3

and beyond the fence there stood the slanting crane of a well. The wind drove away the mist of snow from before the eyes, and where there had been a red blur, there sprang up a small, squat little house with a steep thatched roof. Of the three little windows one, covered on the inside with something red, was lighted up.

What sort of place was it? Yergunov remembered that to the right of the road, three and a half or four miles from the hospital, there was Andrey Tchirikov's tavern. He remembered, too, that this Tchirikov, who had been lately killed by some sledge-drivers, had left a wife and a daughter called Lyubka, who had come to the hospital two years before as a patient. The inn had a bad reputation, and to visit it late in the evening, and especially with someone else's horse, was not free from risk. But there was no help for it. Yergunov fumbled in his knapsack for his revolver, and, coughing sternly, tapped at the window-frame with his whip.

" Hey! who is within? " he cried. " Hey, granny! let me come in and get warm! "

With a hoarse bark a black dog rolled like a ball under the horse's feet, then another white one, then another black one—there must have been a dozen of them. Yergunov looked to see which was the biggest, swung his whip and lashed at it with all his might. A small, long-legged puppy turned its sharp muzzle upwards and set up a shrill, piercing howl.

Yergunov stood for a long while at the window, tapping. But at last the hoar-frost on the trees near the house glowed red, and a muffled female figure appeared with a lantern in her hands.

" Let me in to get warm, granny," said Yergunov. " I was driving to the hospital, and I have lost my way. It's such weather, God preserve us. Don't be afraid; we are your own people, granny."

" All my own people are at home, and we didn't invite strangers," said the figure grimly. " And what are you knocking for? The gate is not locked."

Yergunov drove into the yard and stopped at the steps.

" Bid your labourer take my horse out, granny," said he.

" I am not granny."

And indeed she was not a granny. While she was putting out the lantern the light fell on her face, and Yergunov saw black eyebrows, and recognized Lyubka.

" There are no labourers about now," she said as she went into the house. " Some are drunk and asleep, and some have been gone to Ryepino since the morning. It's a holiday. . . ."

As he fastened his horse up in the shed, Yergunov heard a neigh, and distinguished in the darkness another horse, and felt on it a Cossack saddle. So there must be someone else in the house besides the woman and her daughter. For greater security Yergunov unsaddled his horse, and when he went into the house, took with him both his purchases and his saddle.

The first room into which he went was large and very hot, and smelt of freshly washed floors. A short, lean peasant of about forty, with a small, fair beard, wearing a dark blue shirt, was sitting at the table under the holy images. It was Kalashnikov, an arrant scoundrel and horse-stealer, whose father and uncle kept a tavern in Bogalyovka, and disposed of the stolen horses where they could. He too had been to the hospital more than once, not for medical treatment, but to see the doctor about horses —to ask whether he had not one for sale, and whether his honour would not like to swop his bay mare for a dun-coloured gelding. Now his head was pomaded and a silver ear-ring glittered in his ear, and altogether he had a holiday air. Frowning and dropping his lower lip, he was looking intently at a big dog's-eared picture-book. Another peasant lay stretched on the floor near the stove; his head, his shoulders, and his chest were covered with a sheepskin—he was probably asleep; beside his new boots, with shining bits of metal on the heels, there were two dark pools of melted snow.

Seeing the hospital assistant, Kalashnikov greeted him.

" Yes, it is weather," said Yergunov, rubbing his chilled knees with his open hands. " The snow is up to one's neck; I am soaked to the skin, I can tell you. And I believe my revolver is, too. . . ."

He took out his revolver, looked it all over, and put it back in his knapsack. But the revolver made no impression at all; the peasant went on looking at the book.

" Yes, it is weather. . . . I lost my way, and if it had not been for the dogs here, I do believe it would have been my death. There would have been a nice to-do. And where are the women? "

" The old woman has gone to Ryepino, and the

girl is getting supper ready . . ." answered Kalashnikov.

Silence followed. Yergunov, shivering and gasping, breathed on his hands, huddled up, and made
a show of being very cold and exhausted. The still
angry dogs could be heard howling outside. It
was dreary.

"You come from Bogalyovka, don't you?" he
asked the peasant sternly.

"Yes, from Bogalyovka."

And to while away the time Yergunov began to
think about Bogalyovka. It was a big village and
it lay in a deep ravine, so that when one drove along
the highroad on a moonlight night, and looked down
into the dark ravine and then up at the sky, it
seemed as though the moon were hanging over a
bottomless abyss and it were the end of the world.
The path going down was steep, winding, and so
narrow that when one drove down to Bogalyovka
on account of some epidemic or to vaccinate the
people, one had to shout at the top of one's voice,
or whistle all the way, for if one met a cart coming
up one could not pass. The peasants of Bogalyovka
had the reputation of being good gardeners and
horse-stealers. They had well-stocked gardens. In
spring the whole village was buried in white cherry-
blossom, and in the summer they sold cherries at
three kopecks a pail. One could pay three kopecks
and pick as one liked. Their women were handsome and looked well fed, they were fond of finery,
and never did anything even on working-days, but
spent all their time sitting on the ledge in front of
their houses and searching in each other's heads.

But at last there was the sound of footsteps. Lyubka, a girl of twenty, with bare feet and a red dress, came into the room. . . . She looked sideways at Yergunov and walked twice from one end of the room to the other. She did not move simply, but with tiny steps, thrusting forward her bosom; evidently she enjoyed padding about with her bare feet on the freshly washed floor, and had taken off her shoes on purpose.

Kalashnikov laughed at something and beckoned her with his finger. She went up to the table, and he showed her a picture of the Prophet Elijah, who, driving three horses abreast, was dashing up to the sky. Lyubka put her elbow on the table; her plait fell across her shoulder—a long chestnut plait tied with red ribbon at the end—and it almost touched the floor. She, too, smiled.

"A splendid, wonderful picture," said Kalashnikov. "Wonderful," he repeated, and motioned with his hand as though he wanted to take the reins instead of Elijah.

The wind howled in the stove; something growled and squeaked as though a big dog had strangled a rat.

"Ugh! the unclean spirits are abroad!" said Lyubka.

"That's the wind," said Kalashnikov; and after a pause he raised his eyes to Yergunov and asked: "And what is your learned opinion, Osip Vassilyitch —are there devils in this world or not?"

"What's one to say, brother?" said Yergunov, and he shrugged one shoulder. "If one reasons from science, of course there are no devils, for it's

a superstition; but if one looks at it simply, as you
and I do now, there are devils, to put it shortly. . . .
I have seen a great deal in my life. . . . When I
finished my studies I served as medical assistant in
the army in a regiment of the dragoons, and I have
been in the war, of course. I have a medal and a
decoration from the Red Cross, but after the treaty
of San Stefano I returned to Russia and went into
the service of the Zemstvo. And in consequence of
my enormous circulation about the world, I may say
I have seen more than many another has dreamed
of. It has happened to me to see devils, too; that
is, not devils with horns and a tail—that is all
nonsense—but just, to speak precisely, something of
the sort."

" Where? " asked Kalashnikov.

" In various places. There is no need to go far.
Last year I met him here—speak of him not at
night—near this very inn. I was driving, I remember, to Golyshino; I was going there to vaccinate. Of course, as usual, I had the racing droshky
and a horse, and all the necessary paraphernalia,
and, what's more, I had a watch and all the rest of
it, so I was on my guard as I drove along, for fear
of some mischance. There are lots of tramps of all
sorts. I came up to the Zmeinoy Ravine—damnation
take it—and was just going down it, when all at
once somebody comes up to me—such a fellow!
Black hair, black eyes, and his whole face looked
smutted with soot. . . . He comes straight up to
the horse and takes hold of the left rein: ' Stop! '
He looked at the horse, then at me, then dropped
the reins, and without saying a bad word, ' Where

are you going?' says he. And he showed his teeth in a grin, and his eyes were spiteful-looking. . . . 'Ah,' thought I, 'you are a queer customer!' 'I am going to vaccinate for the smallpox,' said I. 'And what is that to you?' 'Well, if that's so,' says he, 'vaccinate me.' He bared his arm and thrust it under my nose. Of course, I did not bandy words with him; I just vaccinated him to get rid of him. Afterwards I looked at my lancet and it had gone rusty."

The peasant who was asleep near the stove suddenly turned over and flung off the sheepskin; to his great surprise, Yergunov recognized the stranger he had met that day at Zmeinoy Ravine. This peasant's hair, beard, and eyes were black as soot; his face was swarthy; and, to add to the effect, there was a black spot the size of a lentil on his right cheek. He looked mockingly at the hospital assistant and said:

"I did take hold of the left rein—that was so; but about the smallpox you are lying, sir. And there was not a word said about the smallpox between us."

Yergunov was disconcerted.

"I'm not talking about you," he said. "Lie down, since you are lying down."

The dark-skinned peasant had never been to the hospital, and Yergunov did not know who he was or where he came from; and now, looking at him, he made up his mind that the man must be a gypsy. The peasant got up and, stretching and yawning loudly, went up to Lyubka and Kalashnikov, and sat down beside them, and he, too, began looking at the book. His sleepy face softened and a look of envy came into it.

"Look, Merik," Lyubka said to him; "get me such horses and I will drive to heaven."

"Sinners can't drive to heaven," said Kalashnikov. "That's for holiness."

Then Lyubka laid the table and brought in a big piece of fat bacon, salted cucumbers, a wooden platter of boiled meat cut up into little pieces, then a frying-pan, in which there were sausages and cabbage spluttering. A cut-glass decanter of vodka, which diffused a smell of orange-peel all over the room when it was poured out, was put on the table also.

Yergunov was annoyed that Kalashnikov and the dark fellow Merik talked together and took no notice of him at all, behaving exactly as though he were not in the room. And he wanted to talk to them, to brag, to drink, to have a good meal, and if possible to have a little fun with Lyubka, who sat down near him half a dozen times while they were at supper, and, as though by accident, brushed against him with her handsome shoulders and passed her hands over her broad hips. She was a healthy, active girl, always laughing and never still: she would sit down, then get up, and when she was sitting down she would keep turning first her face and then her back to her neighbour, like a fidgety child, and never failed to brush against him with her elbows or her knees.

And he was displeased, too, that the peasants drank only a glass each and no more, and it was awkward for him to drink alone. But he could not refrain from taking a second glass, all the same, then a third, and he ate all the sausage. He brought himself to flatter the peasants, that they might accept him as one of the party instead of holding him at arm's length.

"You are a fine set of fellows in Bogalyovka!" he said, and wagged his head.

"In what way fine fellows?" enquired Kalashnikov.

"Why, about horses, for instance. Fine fellows at stealing!"

"H'm! fine fellows, you call them. Nothing but thieves and drunkards."

"They have had their day, but it is over," said Merik, after a pause. "But now they have only Filya left, and he is blind."

"Yes, there is no one but Filya," said Kalashnikov, with a sigh. "Reckon it up, he must be seventy; the German settlers knocked out one of his eyes, and he does not see well with the other. It is cataract. In old days the police officer would shout as soon as he saw him: 'Hey, you Shamil!' and all the peasants called him that—he was Shamil all over the place; and now his only name is One-eyed Filya. But he was a fine fellow! Lyuba's father, Andrey Grigoritch, and he stole one night into Rozhnovo—there were cavalry regiments stationed there—and carried off nine of the soldiers' horses, the very best of them. They weren't frightened of the sentry, and in the morning they sold all the horses for twenty roubles to the gypsy Afonka. Yes! But nowadays a man contrives to carry off a horse whose rider is drunk or asleep, and has no fear of God, but

will take the very boots from a drunkard, and then
slinks off and goes away a hundred and fifty miles
with a horse, and haggles at the market, haggles like
a Jew, till the policeman catches him, the fool.
There is no fun in it; it is simply a disgrace! A
paltry set of people, I must say."

"What about Merik?" asked Lyubka.

"Merik is not one of us," said Kalashnikov.
"He is a Harkov man from Mizhiritch. But that
he is a bold fellow, that's the truth; there's no gainsaying that he is a fine fellow."

Lyubka looked slily and gleefully at Merik, and
said:

"It wasn't for nothing they dipped him in a hole
in the ice."

"How was that?" asked Yergunov.

"It was like this . . ." said Merik, and he
laughed. "Filya carried off three horses from the
Samoylenka tenants, and they pitched upon me.
There were ten of the tenants at Samoylenka, and
with their labourers there were thirty altogether,
and all of them Molokans. . . . So one of them
says to me at the market: 'Come and have a look.
Merik; we have brought some new horses from the
fair.' I was interested, of course. I went up to
them, and the whole lot of them, thirty men, tied
my hands behind me and led me to the river. 'We'll
show you fine horses,' they said. One hole in the ice
was there already; they cut another beside it seven
feet away. Then, to be sure, they took a cord and
put a noose under my armpits, and tied a crooked
stick to the other end, long enough to reach both
holes. They thrust the stick in and dragged it

through. I went plop into the ice-hole just as I was, in my fur coat and my high boots, while they stood and shoved me, one with his foot and one with his stick, then dragged me under the ice and pulled me out of the other hole."

Lyubka shuddered and shrugged.

" At first I was in a fever from the cold," Merik went on, " but when they pulled me out I was helpless, and lay in the snow, and the Molokans stood round and hit me with sticks on my knees and my elbows. It hurt fearfully. They beat me and they went away . . . and everything on me was frozen, my clothes were covered with ice. I got up, but I couldn't move. Thank God, a woman drove by and gave me a lift."

Meanwhile Yergunov had drunk five or six glasses of vodka; his heart felt lighter, and he longed to tell some extraordinary, wonderful story too, and to show that he, too, was a bold fellow and not afraid of anything.

" I'll tell you what happened to us in Penza Province . . ." he began.

Either because he had drunk a great deal and was a little tipsy, or perhaps because he had twice been detected in a lie, the peasants took not the slightest notice of him, and even left off answering his questions. What was worse, they permitted themselves a frankness in his presence that made him feel uncomfortable and cold all over, and that meant that they took no notice of him.

Kalashnikov had the dignified manners of a sedate and sensible man; he spoke weightily, and made the sign of the cross over his mouth every time he

yawned, and no one could have supposed that this
was a thief, a heartless thief who had stripped poor
creatures, who had already been twice in prison, and
who had been sentenced by the commune to exile in
Siberia, and had been bought off by his father and
uncle, who were as great thieves and rogues as he
was. Merik gave himself the airs of a bravo. He
saw that Lyubka and Kalashnikov were admiring
him, and looked upon himself as a very fine fellow,
and put his arms akimbo, squared his chest, or
stretched so that the bench creaked under him. . . .

After supper Kalashnikov prayed to the holy
image without getting up from his seat, and shook
hands with Merik; the latter prayed too, and shook
Kalashnikov's hand. Lyubka cleared away the supper, shook out on the table some peppermint bis-
cuits, dried nuts, and pumpkin seeds, and placed two
bottles of sweet wine.

"The kingdom of heaven and peace everlasting
to Andrey Grigoritch," said Kalashnikov, clinking
glasses with Merik. "When he was alive we used
to gather together here or at his brother Martin's,
and—my word! my word! what men, what talks!
Remarkable conversations! Martin used to be here,
and Filya, and Fyodor Stukotey. . . . It was all
done in style, it was all in keeping. . . . And what
fun we had! We did have fun, we did have fun!"

Lyubka went out and soon afterwards came back
wearing a green kerchief and beads.

"Look, Merik, what Kalashnikov brought me
to-day," she said.

She looked at herself in the looking-glass, and
tossed her head several times to make the beads

jingle. And then she opened a chest and began taking out, first, a cotton dress with red and blue flowers on it, and then a red one with flounces which rustled and crackled like paper, then a new kerchief, dark blue, shot with many colours—and all these things she showed and flung up her hands, laughing as though astonished that she had such treasures.

Kalashnikov tuned the balalaika and began playing it, but Yergunov could not make out what sort of song he was singing, and whether it was gay or melancholy, because at one moment it was so mournful he wanted to cry, and at the next it would be merry. Merik suddenly jumped up and began tapping with his heels on the same spot, then, brandishing his arms, he moved on his heels from the table to the stove, from the stove to the chest, then he bounded up as though he had been stung, clicked the heels of his boots together in the air, and began going round and round in a crouching position. Lyubka waved both her arms, uttered a desperate shriek, and followed him. At first she moved sideways, like a snake, as though she wanted to steal up to someone and strike him from behind. She tapped rapidly with her bare heels as Merik had done with the heels of his boots, then she turned round and round like a top and crouched down, and her red dress was blown out like a bell. Merik, looking angrily at her, and showing his teeth in a grin, flew towards her in the same crouching posture as though he wanted to crush her with his terrible legs, while she jumped up, flung back her head, and waving her arms as a big bird does its wings, floated across the room scarcely touching the floor. . . .

"What a flame of a girl!" thought Yergunov, sitting on the chest, and from there watching the dance. "What fire! Give up everything for her, and it would be too little. . . ."

And he regretted that he was a hospital assistant, and not a simple peasant, that he wore a reefer coat and a chain with a gilt key on it instead of a blue shirt with a cord tied round the waist. Then he could boldly have sung, danced, flung both arms round Lyubka as Merik did. . . .

The sharp tapping, shouts, and whoops set the crockery ringing in the cupboard and the flame of the candle dancing.

The thread broke and the beads were scattered all over the floor, the green kerchief slipped off, and Lyubka was transformed into a red cloud flitting by and flashing black eyes, and it seemed as though in another second Merik's arms and legs would drop off.

But finally Merik stamped for the last time, and stood still as though turned to stone. Exhausted and almost breathless, Lyubka sank on to his bosom and leaned against him as against a post, and he put his arms round her, and looking into her eyes, said tenderly and caressingly, as though in jest:

"I'll find out where your old mother's money is hidden, I'll murder her and cut your little throat for you, and after that I will set fire to the inn. . . . People will think you have perished in the fire, and with your money I shall go to Kuban. I'll keep droves of horses and flocks of sheep. . . ."

Lyubka made no answer, but only looked at him with a guilty air, and asked:

" And is it nice in Kuban, Merik? "

He said nothing, but went to the chest, sat down, and sank into thought; most likely he was dreaming of Kuban.

" It's time for me to be going," said Kalashnikov, getting up. " Filya must be waiting for me. Goodbye, Lyuba."

Yergunov went out into the yard to see that Kalashnikov did not go off with his horse. The snowstorm still persisted. White clouds were floating about the yard, their long tails clinging to the rough grass and the bushes, while on the other side of the fence in the open country huge giants in white robes with wide sleeves were whirling round and falling to the ground, and getting up again to wave their arms and fight. And the wind, the wind! The bare birches and cherry-trees, unable to endure its rude caresses, bowed low down to the ground and wailed: " God, for what sin hast Thou bound us to the earth and will not let us go free? "

" Wo! " said Kalashnikov sternly, and he got on his horse; one half of the gate was opened, and by it lay a high snowdrift. " Well, get on! " shouted Kalashnikov. His little short-legged nag set off, and sank up to its stomach in the drift at once. Kalashnikov was white all over with the snow, and soon vanished from sight with his horse.

When Yergunov went back into the room, Lyubka was creeping about the floor picking up her beads; Merik was not there.

" A splendid girl! " thought Yergunov, as he lay down on the bench and put his coat under his head. " Oh, if only Merik were not here." Lyubka ex-

cited him as she crept about the floor by the bench,
and he thought that if Merik had not been there he
would certainly have got up and embraced her, and
then one would see what would happen. It was
true she was only a girl, but not likely to be chaste;
and even if she were—need one stand on ceremony
in a den of thieves? Lyubka collected her beads and
went out. The candle burnt down and the flame
caught the paper in the candlestick. Yergunov laid
his revolver and matches beside him, and put out
the candle. The light before the holy images flickered so much that it hurt his eyes, and patches of
light danced on the ceiling, on the floor, and on the
cupboard, and among them he had visions of Lyubka,
buxom, full-bosomed: now she was turning round
like a top, now she was exhausted and breathless. . . .

"Oh, if the devils would carry off that Merik,"
he thought.

The little lamp gave a last flicker, spluttered, and
went out. Someone, it must have been Merik, came
into the room and sat down on the bench. He puffed
at his pipe, and for an instant lighted up a dark
cheek with a patch on it. Yergunov's throat was
irritated by the horrible fumes of the tobacco
smoke.

"What filthy tobacco you have got—damnation
take it!" said Yergunov. "It makes me positively
sick."

"I mix my tobacco with the flowers of the oats,"
answered Merik after a pause. "It is better for
the chest."

He smoked, spat, and went out again. Half an
hour passed, and all at once there was the gleam of

a light in the passage. Merik appeared in a coat and cap, then Lyubka with a candle in her hand.

" Do stay, Merik," said Lyubka in an imploring voice.

" No, Lyuba, don't keep me."

" Listen, Merik," said Lyubka, and her voice grew soft and tender. " I know you will find mother's money, and will do for her and for me, and will go to Kuban and love other girls; but God be with you. I only ask you one thing, sweetheart: do stay! "

" No, I want some fun . . ." said Merik, fastening his belt.

" But you have nothing to go on. . . . You came on foot; what are you going on? "

Merik bent down to Lyubka and whispered something in her ear; she looked towards the door and laughed through her tears.

" He is asleep, the puffed-up devil . . ." she said.

Merik embraced her, kissed her vigorously, and went out. Yergunov thrust his revolver into his pocket, jumped up, and ran after him.

" Get out of the way! " he said to Lyubka, who hurriedly bolted the door of the entry and stood across the threshold. " Let me pass! Why are you standing here? "

" What do you want to go out for? "

" To have a look at my horse."

Lyubka gazed up at him with a sly and caressing look.

" Why look at it? You had better look at me . . ." she said, then she bent down and touched with her finger the gilt watch-key that hung on his chain.

" Let me pass, or he will go off on my horse," said

Yergunov. "Let me go, you devil!" he shouted, and giving her an angry blow on the shoulder, he pressed his chest against her with all his might to push her away from the door, but she kept tight hold of the bolt, and was like iron.

"Let me go!" he shouted, exhausted; "he will go off with it, I tell you."

"Why should he? He won't." Breathing hard and rubbing her shoulder, which hurt, she looked up at him again, flushed a little and laughed. "Don't go away, dear heart," she said; "I am dull alone."

Yergunov looked into her eyes, hesitated, and put his arms round her; she did not resist.

"Come, no nonsense; let me go," he begged her. She did not speak.

"I heard you just now," he said, "telling Merik that you love him."

"I dare say. . . . My heart knows who it is I love."

She put her finger on the key again, and said softly: "Give me that."

Yergunov unfastened the key and gave it to her. She suddenly craned her neck and listened with a grave face, and her expression struck Yergunov as cold and cunning; he thought of his horse, and now easily pushed her aside and ran out into the yard. In the shed a sleepy pig was grunting with lazy regularity and a cow was knocking her horn. Yergunov lighted a match and saw the pig, and the cow, and the dogs, which rushed at him on all sides at seeing the light, but there was no trace of the horse. Shouting and waving his arms at the dogs, stumbling over the drifts and sticking in the snow, he ran out at the gate and fell to gazing into the darkness. He strained his eyes to the utmost, and saw only the snow flying and the snowflakes distinctly forming into all sorts of shapes; at one moment the white, laughing face of a corpse would peep out of the darkness, at the next a white horse would gallop by with an Amazon in a muslin dress upon it, at the next a string of white swans would fly overhead. . . . Shaking with anger and cold, and not knowing what to do, Yergunov fired his revolver at the dogs, and did not hit one of them; then he rushed back to the house.

When he went into the entry he distinctly heard someone scurry out of the room and bang the door. It was dark in the room. Yergunov pushed against the door; it was locked. Then, lighting match after match, he rushed back into the entry, from there into the kitchen, and from the kitchen into a little room where all the walls were hung with petticoats and dresses, where there was a smell of cornflowers and fennel, and a bedstead with a perfect mountain of pillows, standing in the corner by the stove; this must have been the old mother's room. From there he passed into another little room, and here he saw Lyubka. She was lying on a chest, covered with a gay-coloured patchwork cotton quilt, pretending to be asleep. A little ikon-lamp was burning in the corner above the pillow.

" Where is my horse? " Yergunov asked.

Lyubka did not stir.

" Where is my horse, I am asking you? " Yergunov repeated still more sternly, and he tore the quilt off her. " I am asking you, she-devil! " he shouted.

She jumped up on her knees, and with one hand
holding her shift and with the other trying to clutch
the quilt, huddled against the wall. . . . She looked
at Yergunov with repulsion and terror in her eyes,
and, like a wild beast in a trap, kept cunning watch
on his faintest movement.

"Tell me where my horse is, or I'll knock the
life out of you," shouted Yergunov.

"Get away, dirty brute!" she said in a hoarse
voice.

Yergunov seized her by the shift near the neck
and tore it. And then he could not restrain himself,
and with all his might embraced the girl. But hissing with fury, she slipped out of his arms, and free-
ing one hand—the other was tangled in the torn
shift—hit him a blow with her fist on the skull.

His head was dizzy with the pain, there was a
ringing and rattling in his ears, he staggered back,
and at that moment received another blow—this
time on the temple. Reeling and clutching at the
doorposts, that he might not fall, he made his way
to the room where his things were, and lay down on
the bench; then after lying for a little time, took the
matchbox out of his pocket and began lighting match
after match for no object: he lit it, blew it out, and
threw it under the table, and went on till all the
matches were gone.

Meanwhile the air began to turn blue outside, the
cocks began to crow, but his head still ached, and
there was an uproar in his ears as though he were
sitting under a railway bridge and hearing the trains
passing over his head. He got, somehow, into his
coat and cap; the saddle and the bundle of his pur-

chases he could not find, his knapsack was empty: it was not for nothing that someone had scurried out of the room when he came in from the yard.

He took a poker from the kitchen to keep off the dogs, and went out into the yard, leaving the door open. The snow-storm had subsided and it was calm outside. . . . When he went out at the gate, the white plain looked dead, and there was not a single bird in the morning sky. On both sides of the road and in the distance there were bluish patches of young copse.

Yergunov began thinking how he would be greeted at the hospital and what the doctor would say to him; it was absolutely necessary to think of that, and to prepare beforehand to answer questions he would be asked, but this thought grew blurred and slipped away. He walked along thinking of nothing but Lyubka, of the peasants with whom he had passed the night; he remembered how, after Lyubka struck him the second time, she had bent down to the floor for the quilt, and how her loose hair had fallen on the floor. His mind was in a maze, and he wondered why there were in the world doctors, hospital assistants, merchants, clerks, and peasants instead of simple free men? There are, to be sure, free birds, free beasts, a free Merik, and they are not afraid of anyone, and don't need anyone! And whose idea was it, who had decreed that one must get up in the morning, dine at midday, go to bed in the evening; that a doctor takes precedence of a hospital assistant; that one must live in rooms and love only one's wife? And why not the contrary—dine at night and sleep in the day? Ah, to jump on a horse without enquiring whose it is, to ride races with the wind like a devil, over fields and forests and ravines, to make love to girls, to mock at everyone. . . .

Yergunov thrust the poker into the snow, pressed his forehead to the cold white trunk of a birch-tree, and sank into thought; and his grey, monotonous life, his wages, his subordinate position, the dispensary, the everlasting to-do with the bottles and blisters, struck him as contemptible, sickening.

" Who says it's a sin to enjoy oneself? " he asked himself with vexation. " Those who say that have never lived in freedom like Merik and Kalashnikov, and have never loved Lyubka; they have been beggars all their lives, have lived without any pleasure, and have only loved their wives, who are like frogs."

And he thought about himself that he had not hitherto been a thief, a swindler, or even a brigand, simply because he could not, or had not yet met with a suitable opportunity.

*　　　*　　　*　　　*

A year and a half passed. In spring, after Easter, Yergunov, who had long before been dismissed from the hospital and was hanging about without a job, came out of the tavern in Ryepino and sauntered aimlessly along the street.

He went out into the open country. Here there was the scent of spring, and a warm caressing wind was blowing. The calm, starry night looked down from the sky on the earth. My God, how infinite the depth of the sky, and with what fathomless immensity it stretched over the world! The world is created well enough, only why and with what right do people, thought Yergunov, divide their fellows into the sober and the drunken, the employed and the dismissed, and so on. Why do the sober and well fed sleep comfortably in their homes while the drunken and the hungry must wander about the country without a refuge? Why was it that if anyone had not a job and did not get a salary he had to go hungry, without clothes and boots? Whose idea was it? Why was it the birds and the wild beasts in the woods did not have jobs and get salaries, but lived as they pleased?

Far away in the sky a beautiful crimson glow lay quivering, stretched wide over the horizon. Yergunov stopped, and for a long time he gazed at it, and kept wondering why was it that if he had carried off someone else's samovar the day before and sold it for drink in the taverns it would be a sin? Why was it?

Two carts drove by on the road; in one of them there was a woman asleep, in the other sat an old man without a cap on. . . .

" Grandfather, where is that fire? " asked Yergunov.

" Andrey Tchirikov's inn," answered the old man.

And Yergunov recalled what had happened to him eighteen months before in the winter, in that very inn, and how Merik had boasted; and he imagined the old woman and Lyubka, with their throats cut, burning, and he envied Merik. And when he walked back to the tavern, looking at the houses of the rich publicans, cattle-dealers, and blacksmiths, he reflected how nice it would be to steal by night into some rich man's house!

1890

WARD NO. 6

WARD NO. 6

I

In the hospital yard there stands a small lodge surrounded by a perfect forest of burdocks, nettles, and wild hemp. Its roof is rusty, the chimney is tumbling down, the steps at the front-door are rotting away and overgrown with grass, and there are only traces left of the stucco. The front of the lodge faces the hospital; at the back it looks out into the open country, from which it is separated by the grey hospital fence with nails on it. These nails, with their points upwards, and the fence, and the lodge itself, have that peculiar, desolate, God-forsaken look which is only found in our hospital and prison buildings.

If you are not afraid of being stung by the nettles, come by the narrow footpath that leads to the lodge, and let us see what is going on inside. Opening the first door, we walk into the entry. Here along the walls and by the stove every sort of hospital rubbish lies littered about. Mattresses, old tattered dressing-gowns, trousers, blue striped shirts, boots and shoes no good for anything—all these remnants are piled up in heaps, mixed up and crumpled, mouldering and giving out a sickly smell.

The porter, Nikita, an old soldier wearing rusty

good-conduct stripes, is always lying on the litter with a pipe between his teeth. He has a grim, surly, battered-looking face, overhanging eyebrows which give him the expression of a sheep-dog of the steppes, and a red nose; he is short and looks thin and scraggy, but he is of imposing deportment and his fists are vigorous. He belongs to the class of simple-hearted, practical, and dull-witted people, prompt in carrying out orders, who like discipline better than anything in the world, and so are convinced that it is their duty to beat people. He showers blows on the face, on the chest, on the back, on whatever comes first, and is convinced that there would be no order in the place if he did not.

Next you come into a big, spacious room which fills up the whole lodge except for the entry. Here the walls are painted a dirty blue, the ceiling is as sooty as in a hut without a chimney—it is evident that in the winter the stove smokes and the room is full of fumes. The windows are disfigured by iron gratings on the inside. The wooden floor is grey and full of splinters. There is a stench of sour cabbage, of smouldering wicks, of bugs, and of ammonia, and for the first minute this stench gives you the impression of having walked into a menagerie. . . .

There are bedsteads screwed to the floor. Men in blue hospital dressing-gowns, and wearing nightcaps in the old style, are sitting and lying on them. These are the lunatics.

There are five of them in all here. Only one is of the upper class, the rest are all artisans. The one nearest the door—a tall, lean workman with

shining red whiskers and tear-stained eyes—sits
with his head propped on his hand, staring at the
same point. Day and night he grieves, shaking his
head, sighing and smiling bitterly. He rarely takes
a part in conversation and usually makes no answer
to questions; he eats and drinks mechanically when
food is offered him. From his agonizing, throbbing
cough, his thinness, and the flush on his cheeks, one
may judge that he is in the first stage of consumption. Next him is a little, alert, very lively old man,
with a pointed beard and curly black hair like a
negro's. By day he walks up and down the ward
from window to window, or sits on his bed, cross-
legged like a Turk, and, ceaselessly as a bullfinch
whistles, softly sings and titters. He shows his
childish gaiety and lively character at night also
when he gets up to say his prayers—that is, to beat
himself on the chest with his fists, and to scratch
with his fingers at the door. This is the Jew Moiseika, an imbecile, who went crazy twenty years ago
when his hat factory was burnt down.

And of all the inhabitants of Ward No. 6, he is
the only one who is allowed to go out of the lodge,
and even out of the yard into the street. He has
enjoyed this privilege for years, probably because
he is an old inhabitant of the hospital—a quiet, harm-
less imbecile, the buffoon of the town, where people
are used to seeing him surrounded by boys and dogs.
In his wretched gown, in his absurd night-cap, and
in slippers, sometimes with bare legs and even without trousers, he walks about the streets, stopping at
the gates and little shops, and begging for a copper.
In one place they will give him some kvass, in an-

other some bread, in another a copper, so that he generally goes back to the ward feeling rich and well fed. Everything that he brings back Nikita takes from him for his own benefit. The soldier does this roughly, angrily turning the Jew's pockets inside out, and calling God to witness that he will not let him go into the street again, and that breach of the regulations is worse to him than anything in the world.

Moiseika likes to make himself useful. He gives his companions water, and covers them up when they are asleep; he promises each of them to bring him back a kopeck, and to make him a new cap; he feeds with a spoon his neighbour on the left, who is paralyzed. He acts in this way, not from compassion nor from any considerations of a humane kind, but through imitation, unconsciously dominated by Gromov, his neighbour on the right hand.

Ivan Dmitritch Gromov, a man of thirty-three, who is a gentleman by birth, and has been a court usher and provincial secretary, suffers from the mania of persecution. He either lies curled up in bed, or walks from corner to corner as though for exercise; he very rarely sits down. He is always excited, agitated, and overwrought by a sort of vague, undefined expectation. The faintest rustle in the entry or shout in the yard is enough to make him raise his head and begin listening: whether they are coming for him, whether they are looking for him. And at such times his face expresses the utmost uneasiness and repulsion.

I like his broad face with its high cheek-bones, always pale and unhappy, and reflecting, as though in a mirror, a soul tormented by conflict and long-continued terror. His grimaces are strange and abnormal, but the delicate lines traced on his face by profound, genuine suffering show intelligence and sense, and there is a warm and healthy light in his eyes. I like the man himself, courteous, anxious to be of use, and extraordinarily gentle to everyone except Nikita. When anyone drops a button or a spoon, he jumps up from his bed quickly and picks it up; every day he says good-morning to his companions, and when he goes to bed he wishes them good-night.

Besides his continually overwrought condition and his grimaces, his madness shows itself in the following way also. Sometimes in the evenings he wraps himself in his dressing-gown, and, trembling all over, with his teeth chattering, begins walking rapidly from corner to corner and between the bedsteads. It seems as though he is in a violent fever. From the way he suddenly stops and glances at his companions, it can be seen that he is longing to say something very important, but, apparently reflecting that they would not listen, or would not understand him, he shakes his head impatiently and goes on pacing up and down. But soon the desire to speak gets the upper hand of every consideration, and he will let himself go and speak fervently and passionately. His talk is disordered and feverish like delirium, disconnected, and not always intelligible, but, on the other hand, something extremely fine may be felt in it, both in the words and the voice. When he talks you recognize in him the lunatic and the man. It is difficult to reproduce on paper his insane talk.

He speaks of the baseness of mankind, of violence trampling on justice, of the glorious life which will one day be upon earth, of the window-gratings, which remind him every minute of the stupidity and cruelty of oppressors. It makes a disorderly, incoherent potpourri of themes old but not yet out of date.

II

Some twelve or fifteen years ago an official called Gromov, a highly respectable and prosperous person, was living in his own house in the principal street of the town. He had two sons, Sergey and Ivan. When Sergey was a student in his fourth year he was taken ill with galloping consumption and died, and his death was, as it were, the first of a whole series of calamities which suddenly showered on the Gromov family. Within a week of Sergey's funeral the old father was put on his trial for fraud and misappropriation, and he died of typhoid in the prison hospital soon afterwards. The house, with all their belongings, was sold by auction, and Ivan Dmitritch and his mother were left entirely without means.

Hitherto in his father's lifetime, Ivan Dmitritch, who was studying in the University of Petersburg, had received an allowance of sixty or seventy roubles a month, and had had no conception of poverty; now he had to make an abrupt change in his life. He had to spend his time from morning to night giving lessons for next to nothing, to work at copying, and with all that to go hungry, as all his earnings were sent to keep his mother. Ivan Dmitritch could not stand such a life; he lost heart and strength, and, giving up the university, went home.

Here, through interest, he obtained the post of teacher in the district school, but could not get on with his colleagues, was not liked by the boys, and soon gave up the post. His mother died. He was for six months without work, living on nothing but bread and water; then he became a court usher. He kept this post until he was dismissed owing to his illness.

He had never even in his young student days given the impression of being perfectly healthy. He had always been pale, thin, and given to catching cold; he ate little and slept badly. A single glass of wine went to his head and made him hysterical. He always had a craving for society, but, owing to his irritable temperament and suspiciousness, he never became very intimate with anyone, and had no friends. He always spoke with contempt of his fellow-townsmen, saying that their coarse ignorance and sleepy animal existence seemed to him loathsome and horrible. He spoke in a loud tenor, with heat, and invariably either with scorn and indignation, or with wonder and enthusiasm, and always with perfect sincerity. Whatever one talked to him about he always brought it round to the same subject: that life was dull and stifling in the town; that the townspeople had no lofty interests, but lived a dingy, meaningless life, diversified by violence, coarse profligacy, and hypocrisy; that scoundrels were well fed and clothed, while honest men lived from hand to mouth; that they needed schools, a progressive local paper, a theatre, public lectures,

the co-ordination of the intellectual elements; that
society must see its failings and be horrified.   In
his criticisms of people he laid on the colours thick,
using only black and white, and no fine shades; mankind was divided for him into honest men and scoundrels: there was nothing in between.   He always
spoke with passion and enthusiasm of women and
of love, but he had never been in love.

In spite of the severity of his judgments and his
nervousness, he was liked, and behind his back was
spoken of affectionately as Vanya.   His innate re-
finement and readiness to be of service, his good
breeding, his moral purity, and his shabby coat, his
frail appearance and family misfortunes, aroused a
kind, warm, sorrowful feeling.   Moreover, he was
well educated and well read; according to the townspeople's notions, he knew everything, and was in
their eyes something like a walking encyclopædia.

He had read a great deal.   He would sit at the
club, nervously pulling at his beard and looking
through the magazines and books; and from his
face one could see that he was not reading, but
devouring the pages without giving himself time to
digest what he read.   It must be supposed that
reading was one of his morbid habits, as he fell upon
anything that came into his hands with equal avidity,
even last year's newspapers and calendars.   At home
he always read lying down.

III.

One autumn morning Ivan Dmitritch, turning up
the collar of his greatcoat and splashing through the

mud, made his way by side-streets and back lanes to
see some artisan, and to collect some payment that
was owing. He was in a gloomy mood, as he always
was in the morning. In one of the side-streets he
was met by two convicts in fetters and four soldiers
with rifles in charge of them. Ivan Dmitritch had
very often met convicts before, and they had always
excited feelings of compassion and discomfort in
him; but now this meeting made a peculiar, strange
impression on him. It suddenly seemed to him for
some reason that he, too, might be put into fetters
and led through the mud to prison like that. After
visiting the artisan, on the way home he met near
the post office a police superintendent of his acquaintance, who greeted him and walked a few paces along
the street with him, and for some reason this seemed
to him suspicious. At home he could not get the
convicts or the soldiers with their rifles out of his
head all day, and an unaccountable inward agitation
prevented him from reading or concentrating his
mind. In the evening he did not light his lamp, and
at night he could not sleep, but kept thinking that he
might be arrested, put into fetters, and thrown into
prison. He did not know of any harm he had done,
and could be certain that he would never be guilty
of murder, arson, or theft in the future either; but
was it not easy to commit a crime by accident, unconsciously, and was not false witness always possible,
and, indeed, miscarriage of justice? It was not without good reason that the agelong experience of the
simple people teaches that beggary and prison are ills
none can be safe from. A judicial mistake is very
possible as legal proceedings are conducted nowa-

days, and there is nothing to be wondered at in it. People who have an official, professional relation to other men's sufferings—for instance, judges, police officers, doctors—in course of time, through habit, grow so callous that they cannot, even if they wish it, take any but a formal attitude to their clients; in this respect they are not different from the peasant who slaughters sheep and calves in the back-yard, and does not notice the blood. With this formal, soulless attitude to human personality the judge needs but one thing—time—in order to deprive an innocent man of all rights of property, and to condemn him to penal servitude. Only the time spent on performing certain formalities for which the judge is paid his salary, and then—it is all over. Then you may look in vain for justice and protection in this dirty, wretched little town a hundred and fifty miles from a railway station! And, indeed, is it not absurd even to think of justice when every kind of violence is accepted by society as a rational and consistent necessity, and every act of mercy—for instance, a verdict of acquittal—calls forth a perfect outburst of dissatisfied and revengeful feeling?

In the morning Ivan Dmitritch got up from his bed in a state of horror, with cold perspiration on his forehead, completely convinced that he might be arrested any minute. Since his gloomy thoughts of yesterday had haunted him so long, he thought, it must be that there was some truth in them. They could not, indeed, have come into his mind without any grounds whatever.

A policeman walking slowly passed by the windows: that was not for nothing. Here were two men standing still and silent near the house. Why were they silent? And agonizing days and nights followed for Ivan Dmitritch. Everyone who passed by the windows or came into the yard seemed to him a spy or a detective. At midday the chief of the police usually drove down the street with a pair of horses; he was going from his estate near the town to the police department; but Ivan Dmitritch fancied every time that he was driving especially quickly, and that he had a peculiar expression: it was evident that he was in haste to announce that there was a very important criminal in the town. Ivan Dmitritch started at every ring at the bell and knock at the gate, and was agitated whenever he came upon anyone new at his landlady's; when he met police officers and gendarmes he smiled and began whistling so as to seem unconcerned. He could not sleep for whole nights in succession expecting to be arrested, but he snored loudly and sighed as though in deep sleep, that his landlady might think he was asleep; for if he could not sleep it meant that he was tormented by the stings of conscience—what a piece of evidence! Facts and common sense persuaded him that all these terrors were nonsense and morbidity, that if one looked at the matter more broadly there was nothing really terrible in arrest and imprisonment—so long as the conscience is at ease; but the more sensibly and logically he reasoned, the more acute and agonizing his mental distress became. It might be compared with the story of a hermit who tried to cut a dwelling-place for himself in a virgin forest; the more zealously he worked with his axe, the thicker the forest grew. In the end

Ivan Dmitritch, seeing it was useless, gave up reasoning altogether, and abandoned himself entirely to despair and terror.

He began to avoid people and to seek solitude. His official work had been distasteful to him before: now it became unbearable to him. He was afraid they would somehow get him into trouble, would put a bribe in his pocket unnoticed and then denounce him, or that he would accidentally make a mistake in official papers that would appear to be fraudulent, or would lose other people's money. It is strange that his imagination had never at other times been so agile and inventive as now, when every day he thought of thousands of different reasons for being seriously anxious over his freedom and honour; but, on the other hand, his interest in the outer world, in books in particular, grew sensibly fainter, and his memory began to fail him.

In the spring when the snow melted there were found in the ravine near the cemetery two half-decomposed corpses—the bodies of an old woman and a boy bearing the traces of death by violence. Nothing was talked of but these bodies and their unknown murderers. That people might not think he had been guilty of the crime, Ivan Dmitritch walked about the streets, smiling, and when he met acquaintances he turned pale, flushed, and began declaring that there was no greater crime than the murder of the weak and defenceless. But this duplicity soon exhausted him, and after some reflection he decided that in his position the best thing to do was to hide in his landlady's cellar. He sat in the cellar all day and then all night, then another day, was fearfully cold, and waiting till dusk, stole secretly like a thief back to his room. He stood in the middle of the room till daybreak, listening without stirring. Very early in the morning, before sunrise, some workmen came into the house. Ivan Dmitritch knew perfectly well that they had come to mend the stove in the kitchen, but terror told him that they were police officers disguised as workmen. He slipped stealthily out of the flat, and, overcome by terror, ran along the street without his cap and coat. Dogs raced after him barking, a peasant shouted somewhere behind him, the wind whistled in his ears, and it seemed to Ivan Dmitritch that the force and violence of the whole world was massed together behind his back and was chasing after him.

He was stopped and brought home, and his landlady sent for a doctor. Doctor Andrey Yefimitch, of whom we shall have more to say hereafter, prescribed cold compresses on his head and laurel drops, shook his head, and went away, telling the landlady he should not come again, as one should not interfere with people who are going out of their minds. As he had not the means to live at home and be nursed, Ivan Dmitritch was soon sent to the hospital, and was there put into the ward for venereal patients. He could not sleep at night, was full of whims and fancies, and disturbed the patients, and was soon afterwards, by Andrey Yefimitch's orders, transferred to Ward No. 6.

Within a year Ivan Dmitritch was completely forgotten in the town, and his books, heaped up by his landlady in a sledge in the shed, were pulled to pieces by boys.

IV

Ivan Dmitritch's neighbour on the left hand is, as I have said already, the Jew Moiseika; his neighbour on the right hand is a peasant so rolling in fat that he is almost spherical, with a blankly stupid face, utterly devoid of thought. This is a motionless, gluttonous, unclean animal who has long ago lost all powers of thought or feeling.   An acrid, stifling stench always comes from him.

Nikita, who has to clean up after him, beats him terribly with all his might, not sparing his fists; and what is dreadful is not his being beaten—that one can get used to—but the fact that this stupefied creature does not respond to the blows with a sound or a movement, nor by a look in the eyes, but only sways a little like a heavy barrel.

The fifth and last inhabitant of Ward No. 6 is a man of the artisan class who has once been a sorter in the post office, a thinnish, fair little man with a good-natured but rather sly face.   To judge from the clear, cheerful look in his calm and intelligent eyes, he has some pleasant idea in his mind, and has some very important and agreeable secret.   He has under his pillow and under his mattress something that he never shows anyone, not from fear of its being taken from him and stolen, but from modesty. Sometimes he goes to the window, and turning his back to his companions, puts something on his breast, and bending his head, looks at it; if you go up to him at such a moment, he is overcome with confusion and snatches something off his breast. But it is not difficult to guess his secret.

" Congratulate me," he often says to Ivan Dmitritch; " I have been presented with the Stanislav order of the second degree with the star. The second degree with the star is only given to foreigners, but for some reason they want to make an exception for me," he says with a smile, shrugging his shoulders in perplexity. " That I must confess I did not expect."

" I don't understand anything about that," Ivan Dmitritch replies morosely.

" But do you know what I shall attain to sooner or later?" the former sorter persists, screwing up his eyes slily. " I shall certainly get the Swedish ' Polar Star.' That's an order it is worth working for, a white cross with a black ribbon. It's very beautiful."

Probably in no other place is life so monotonous as in this ward. In the morning the patients, except the paralytic and the fat peasant, wash in the entry at a big tub and wipe themselves with the skirts of their dressing-gowns; after that they drink tea out of tin mugs which Nikita brings them out of the main building. Everyone is allowed one mugful. At midday they have soup made out of sour cabbage and boiled grain, in the evening their supper consists of grain left from dinner. In the intervals they lie down, sleep, look out of window, and walk from one corner to the other. And so every day. Even the former sorter always talks of the same orders.

Fresh faces are rarely seen in Ward No. 6. The doctor has not taken in any new mental cases for a long time, and the people who are fond of visiting lunatic asylums are few in this world. Once every two months Semyon Lazaritch, the barber, appears in the ward. How he cuts the patients' hair, and how Nikita helps him to do it, and what a trepidation the lunatics are always thrown into by the arrival of the drunken, smiling barber, we will not describe.

No one even looks into the ward except the barber. The patients are condemned to see day after day no one but Nikita.

A rather strange rumour has, however, been circulating in the hospital of late.

It is rumoured that the doctor has begun to visit Ward No. 6.

V

A strange rumour!

Dr. Andrey Yefimitch Ragin is a strange man in his way. They say that when he was young he was very religious, and prepared himself for a clerical career, and that when he had finished his studies at the high school in 1863 he intended to enter a theological academy, but that his father, a surgeon and doctor of medicine, jeered at him and declared point-blank that he would disown him if he became a priest. How far this is true I don't know, but Andrey Yefimitch himself has more than once confessed that he has never had a natural bent for medicine or science in general.

However that may have been, when he finished his studies in the medical faculty he did not enter the priesthood. He showed no special devoutness, and was no more like a priest at the beginning of his medical career than he is now.

His exterior is heavy, coarse like a peasant's, his face, his beard, his flat hair, and his coarse, clumsy figure, suggest an overfed, intemperate, and harsh innkeeper on the highroad. His face is surly-looking and covered with blue veins, his eyes are little and his nose is red. With his height and broad shoulders he has huge hands and feet; one would think that a blow from his fist would knock the life out of anyone, but his step is soft, and his walk is cautious and insinuating; when he meets anyone in a narrow passage he is always the first to stop and make way, and to say, not in a bass, as one would expect, but in a high, soft tenor: " I beg your pardon! " He has a little swelling on his neck which prevents him from wearing stiff starched collars, and so he always goes about in soft linen or cotton shirts. Altogether he does not dress like a doctor. He wears the same suit for ten years, and the new clothes, which he usually buys at a Jewish shop, look as shabby and crumpled on him as his old ones; he sees patients and dines and pays visits all in the same coat; but this is not due to niggardliness, but to complete carelessness about his appearance.

When Andrey Yefimitch came to the town to take up his duties the " institution founded to the glory of God " was in a terrible condition. One could hardly breathe for the stench in the wards, in the passages, and in the courtyards of the hospital. The hospital servants, the nurses, and their children slept in the wards together with the patients. They complained that there was no living for beetles, bugs, and mice. The surgical wards were never free from erysipelas. There were only two scalpels and not one thermometer in the whole hospital; potatoes were kept in the baths. The superintendent, the housekeeper, and the medical assistant robbed the patients, and of the old doctor, Andrey Yefimitch's predecessor, people declared that he secretly sold the hospital alcohol, and that he kept a regular harem consisting of nurses and female patients. These disorderly proceedings were perfectly well known in the town, and were even exaggerated, but people took them calmly; some justified them on the ground that there were only peasants and working men in the hospital, who could not be dissatisfied, since they were much worse off at home than in the hospital—they couldn't be fed on woodcocks! Others said in excuse that the town alone, without help from the Zemstvo, was not equal to maintaining a good hospital; thank God for having one at all, even a poor one. And the newly formed Zemstvo did not open infirmaries either in the town or the neighbourhood, relying on the fact that the town already had its hospital.

After looking over the hospital Andrey Yefimitch came to the conclusion that it was an immoral institution and extremely prejudicial to the health of the townspeople. In his opinion the most sensible thing that could be done was to let out the patients and close the hospital. But he reflected that his will alone was not enough to do this, and that it would be useless; if physical and moral impurity were driven out of one place, they would only move to another; one must wait for it to wither away of itself. Besides, if people open a hospital and put up with having it, it must be because they need it; superstition and all the nastiness and abominations of daily life were necessary, since in process of time they worked out to something sensible, just as manure turns into black earth. There was nothing on earth so good that it had not something nasty about its first origin.

When Andrey Yefimitch undertook his duties he was apparently not greatly concerned about the irregularities at the hospital. He only asked the attendants and nurses not to sleep in the wards, and had two cupboards of instruments put up; the superintendent, the housekeeper, the medical assistant, and the erysipelas remained unchanged.

Andrey Yefimitch loved intelligence and honesty intensely, but he had no strength of will nor belief in his right to organize an intelligent and honest life about him. He was absolutely unable to give orders, to forbid things, and to insist. It seemed as though he had taken a vow never to raise his voice and never to make use of the imperative. It was difficult for him to say " Fetch " or " Bring "; when he wanted his meals he would cough hesitatingly and say to the cook: " How about tea? . . ." or " How about dinner? . . ." To dismiss the superintendent or to tell him to leave off stealing, or to abolish the unnecessary parasitic post altogether, was absolutely beyond his powers. When Andrey Yefimitch was deceived or flattered, or accounts he knew to be cooked were brought him to sign, he would turn as red as a crab and feel guilty, but yet he would sign the accounts. When

the patients complained to him of being hungry or of
the roughness of the nurses, he would be confused
and mutter guiltily: " Very well, very well, I will
go into it later. . . .   Most likely there is some
misunderstanding. . . ."

At first Andrey Yefimitch worked very zealously.
He saw patients every day from morning till dinner-
time, performed operations, and even attended con-
finements. The ladies said of him that he was atten-
tive and clever at diagnosing diseases, especially
those of women and children. But in process of time
the work unmistakably wearied him by its monotony
and obvious uselessness. To-day one sees thirty
patients, and to-morrow they have increased to
thirty-five, the next day forty, and so on from day
to day, from year to year, while the mortality in the
town did not decrease and the patients did not leave
off coming. To be any real help to forty patients
between morning and dinner was not physically possible, so it could but lead to deception. If twelve
thousand patients were seen in a year it meant, if
one looked at it simply, that twelve thousand men
were deceived. To put those who were seriously ill
into wards, and to treat them according to the principles of science, was impossible, too, because though
there were principles there was no science ; if he were
to put aside philosophy and pedantically follow the
rules as other doctors did, the things above all necessary were cleanliness and ventilation instead of
dirt, wholesome nourishment instead of broth made
of stinking, sour cabbage, and good assistants instead
of thieves ; and, indeed, why hinder people dying if
death is the normal and legitimate end of everyone?

What is gained if some shopkeeper or clerk lives an extra five or ten years? If the aim of medicine is by drugs to alleviate suffering, the question forces itself on one: why alleviate it? In the first place, they say that suffering leads man to perfection; and in the second, if mankind really learns to alleviate its sufferings with pills and drops, it will completely abandon religion and philosophy, in which it has hitherto found not merely protection from all sorts of trouble, but even happiness. Pushkin suffered terrible agonies before his death, poor Heine lay paralyzed for several years; why, then, should not some Andrey Yefimitch or Matryona Savishna be ill, since their lives had nothing of importance in them, and would have been entirely empty and like the life of an amœba except for suffering?

Oppressed by such reflections, Andrey Yefimitch relaxed his efforts and gave up visiting the hospital every day.

VI

His life was passed like this. As a rule he got up at eight o'clock in the morning, dressed, and drank his tea. Then he sat down in his study to read, or went to the hospital. At the hospital the out-patients were sitting in the dark, narrow little corridor waiting to be seen by the doctor. The nurses and the attendants, tramping with their boots over the brick floors, ran by them; gaunt-looking patients in dressing-gowns passed; dead bodies and vessels full of filth were carried by; the children were crying, and there was a cold draught. Andrey Yefimitch

knew that such surroundings were torture to feverish, consumptive, and impressionable patients; but
what could be done? In the consulting-room he was
met by his assistant, Sergey Sergeyitch—a fat little
man with a plump, well-washed shaven face, with
soft, smooth manners, wearing a new loosely cut
suit, and looking more like a senator than a medical
assistant. He had an immense practice in the town,
wore a white tie, and considered himself more pro-
ficient than the doctor, who had no practice. In the
corner of the consulting-room there stood a huge
ikon in a shrine with a heavy lamp in front of it, and
near it a candle-stand with a white cover on it. On
the walls hung portraits of bishops, a view of the
Svyatogorsky Monastery, and wreaths of dried cornflowers. Sergey Sergeyitch was religious, and liked
solemnity and decorum. The ikon had been put up
at his expense; at his instructions some one of the
patients read the hymns of praise in the consulting-
room on Sundays, and after the reading Sergey
Sergeyitch himself went through the wards with a
censer and burned incense.

There were a great many patients, but the time
was short, and so the work was confined to the asking of a few brief questions and the administration
of some drugs, such as castor-oil or volatile oint-
ment. Andrey Yefimitch would sit with his cheek
resting in his hand, lost in thought and asking questions mechanically. Sergey Sergeyitch sat down too,
rubbing his hands, and from time to time putting in
his word.

"We suffer pain and poverty," he would say,

" because we do not pray to the merciful God as we should. Yes !"

Andrey Yefimitch never performed any operations when he was seeing patients; he had long ago given up doing so, and the sight of blood upset him. When he had to open a child's mouth in order to look at its throat, and the child cried and tried to defend itself with its little hands, the noise in his ears made his head go round and brought tears into his eyes. He would make haste to prescribe a drug, and motion to the woman to take the child away.

He was soon wearied by the timidity of the patients and their incoherence, by the proximity of the pious Sergey Sergeyitch, by the portraits on the walls, and by his own questions which he had asked over and over again for twenty years. And he would go away after seeing five or six patients. The rest would be seen by his assistant in his absence.

With the agreeable thought that, thank God, he had no private practice now, and that no one would interrupt him, Andrey Yefimitch sat down to the table immediately on reaching home and took up a book. He read a great deal and always with enjoyment. Half his salary went on buying books, and of the six rooms that made up his abode three were heaped up with books and old magazines. He liked best of all works on history and philosophy; the only medical publication to which he subscribed was *The Doctor,* of which he always read the last pages first. He would always go on reading for several hours without a break and without being weary. He did not read as rapidly and impulsively as Ivan Dmitritch had done in the past, but slowly and with concentration, often pausing over a passage which he liked or did not find intelligible. Near the books there always stood a decanter of vodka, and a salted cucumber or a pickled apple lay beside it, not on a plate, but on the baize table-cloth. Every half-hour he would pour himself out a glass of vodka and drink it without taking his eyes off the book. Then without looking at it he would feel for the cucumber and bite off a bit.

At three o'clock he would go cautiously to the kitchen door, cough, and say: "Daryushka, what about dinner? . . ."

After his dinner—a rather poor and untidily served one—Andrey Yefimitch would walk up and down his rooms with his arms folded, thinking. The clock would strike four, then five, and still he would be walking up and down thinking. Occasionally the kitchen door would creak, and the red and sleepy face of Daryushka would appear.

"Andrey Yefimitch, isn't it time for you to have your beer?" she would ask anxiously.

"No, it is not time yet . . ." he would answer. "I'll wait a little. . . . I'll wait a little. . . ."

Towards the evening the postmaster, Mihail Averyanitch, the only man in the town whose society did not bore Andrey Yefimitch, would come in. Mihail Averyanitch had once been a very rich land-owner, and had served in the cavalry, but had come to ruin, and was forced by poverty to take a job in the post office late in life. He had a hale and hearty appearance, luxuriant grey whiskers, the manners of a well-bred man, and a loud, pleasant voice. He was good-natured and emotional, but hot-tempered.

When anyone in the post office made a protest, expressed disagreement, or even began to argue, Mihail Averyanitch would turn crimson, shake all over, and shout in a voice of thunder, " Hold your tongue! " so that the post office had long enjoyed the reputation of an institution which it was terrible to visit. Mihail Averyanitch liked and respected Andrey Yefimitch for his culture and the loftiness of his soul; he treated the other inhabitants of the town superciliously, as though they were his subordinates.

" Here I am," he would say, going in to Andrey Yefimitch. " Good-evening, my dear fellow! I'll be bound, you are getting sick of me, aren't you? "

" On the contrary, I am delighted," said the doctor. " I am always glad to see you."

The friends would sit down on the sofa in the study and for some time would smoke in silence.

" Daryushka, what about the beer? " Andrey Yefimitch would say.

They would drink their first bottle still in silence, the doctor brooding and Mihail Averyanitch with a gay and animated face, like a man who has something very interesting to tell. The doctor was always the one to begin the conversation.

" What a pity," he would say quietly and slowly, not looking his friend in the face (he never looked anyone in the face)—" what a great pity it is that there are no people in our town who are capable of carrying on intelligent and interesting conversation, or care to do so. It is an immense privation for us. Even the educated class do not rise above vulgarity; the level of their development, I assure you, is not a bit higher than that of the lower orders."

"Perfectly true. I agree."

"You know, of course," the doctor went on quietly and deliberately, "that everything in this world is insignificant and uninteresting except the higher spiritual manifestations of the human mind. Intellect draws a sharp line between the animals and man, suggests the divinity of the latter, and to some extent even takes the place of the immortality which does not exist. Consequently the intellect is the only possible source of enjoyment. We see and hear of no trace of intellect about us, so we are deprived of enjoyment. We have books, it is true, but that is not at all the same as living talk and converse. If you will allow me to make a not quite apt comparison: books are the printed score, while talk is the singing."

"Perfectly true."

A silence would follow. Daryushka would come out of the kitchen and with an expression of blank dejection would stand in the doorway to listen, with her face propped on her fist.

"Eh!" Mihail Averyanitch would sigh. "To expect intelligence of this generation!"

And he would describe how wholesome, entertaining, and interesting life had been in the past. How intelligent the educated class in Russia used to be, and what lofty ideas it had of honour and friendship; how they used to lend money without an IOU, and it was thought a disgrace not to give a helping hand to a comrade in need; and what campaigns, what adventures, what skirmishes, what comrades, what women! And the Caucasus, what a marvellous country! The wife of a battalion commander, a queer woman, used to put on an officer's uniform and drive off into the mountains in the evening, alone, without a guide. It was said that she had a love affair with some princeling in the native village.

"Queen of Heaven, Holy Mother . . ." Daryushka would sigh.

"And how we drank! And how we ate! And what desperate liberals we were!"

Andrey Yefimitch would listen without hearing; he was musing as he sipped his beer.

"I often dream of intellectual people and conversation with them," he said suddenly, interrupting Mihail Averyanitch. "My father gave me an excellent education, but under the influence of the ideas of the sixties made me become a doctor. I believe if I had not obeyed him then, by now I should have been in the very centre of the intellectual movement. Most likely I should have become a member of some university. Of course, intellect, too, is transient and not eternal, but you know why I cherish a partiality for it. Life is a vexatious trap; when a thinking man reaches maturity and attains to full consciousness he cannot help feeling that he is in a trap from which there is no escape. Indeed, he is summoned without his choice by fortuitous circumstances from non-existence into life . . . what for? He tries to find out the meaning and object of his existence; he is told nothing, or he is told absurdities; he knocks and it is not opened to him; death comes to him— also without his choice. And so, just as in prison men held together by common misfortune feel more at ease when they are together, so one does not notice the trap in life when people with a bent for analysis and generalization meet together and pass their time in the interchange of proud and free ideas. In that sense the intellect is the source of an enjoyment nothing can replace."

" Perfectly true."

Not looking his friend in the face, Andrey Yefimitch would go on, quietly and with pauses, talking about intellectual people and conversation with them, and Mihail Averyanitch would listen attentively and agree: " Perfectly true."

" And you do not believe in the immortality of the soul?" he would ask suddenly.

" No, honoured Mihail Averyanitch; I do not believe it, and have no grounds for believing it."

" I must own I doubt it too. And yet I have a feeling as though I should never die. Oh, I think to myself: ' Old fogey, it is time you were dead!' But there is a little voice in my soul says: ' Don't believe it; you won't die.' "

Soon after nine o'clock Mihail Averyanitch would go away. As he put on his fur coat in the entry he would say with a sigh:

" What a wilderness fate has carried us to, though, really! What's most vexatious of all is to have to die here. Ech! . . ."

VII

After seeing his friend out Andrey Yefimitch would sit down at the table and begin reading again. The stillness of the evening, and afterwards of the night, was not broken by a single sound, and it

seemed as though time were standing still and brooding with the doctor over the book, and as though
there were nothing in existence but the books and the
lamp with the green shade. The doctor's coarse
peasant-like face was gradually lighted up by a smile
of delight and enthusiasm over the progress of the
human intellect. Oh, why is not man immortal? he
thought. What is the good of the brain centres and
convolutions, what is the good of sight, speech, self-
consciousness, genius, if it is all destined to depart
into the soil, and in the end to grow cold together
with the earth's crust, and then for millions of years
to fly with the earth round the sun with no meaning
and no object? To do that there was no need at all
to draw man with his lofty, almost godlike intellect
out of non-existence, and then, as though in mockery,
to turn him into clay. The transmutation of substances! But what cowardice to comfort oneself
with that cheap substitute for immortality! The
unconscious processes that take place in nature are
lower even than the stupidity of man, since in stupidity there is, anyway, consciousness and will, while
in those processes there is absolutely nothing. Only
the coward who has more fear of death than dignity
can comfort himself with the fact that his body will
in time live again in the grass, in the stones, in the
toad. To find one's immortality in the transmutation of substances is as strange as to prophesy a
brilliant future for the case after a precious violin
has been broken and become useless.

When the clock struck, Andrey Yefimitch would
sink back into his chair and close his eyes to think
a little. And under the influence of the fine ideas

of which he had been reading he would, unawares, recall his past and his present. The past was hateful—better not to think of it. And it was the same in the present as in the past. He knew that at the very time when his thoughts were floating together with the cooling earth round the sun, in the main building beside his abode people were suffering in sickness and physical impurity: someone perhaps could not sleep and was making war upon the insects, someone was being infected by erysipelas, or moaning over too tight a bandage; perhaps the patients were playing cards with the nurses and drinking vodka. According to the yearly return, twelve thousand people had been deceived; the whole hospital rested as it had done twenty years ago on thieving, filth, scandals, gossip, on gross quackery, and, as before, it was an immoral institution extremely injurious to the health of the inhabitants. He knew that Nikita knocked the patients about behind the barred windows of Ward No. 6, and that Moiseika went about the town every day begging alms.

On the other hand, he knew very well that a magical change had taken place in medicine during the last twenty-five years. When he was studying at the university he had fancied that medicine would soon be overtaken by the fate of alchemy and metaphysics; but now when he was reading at night the science of medicine touched him and excited his wonder, and even enthusiasm. What unexpected brilliance, what a revolution! Thanks to the antiseptic system operations were performed such as the great Pirogov had considered impossible even *in spe*. Ordinary Zemstvo doctors were venturing to perform the resection of the kneecap; of abdominal operations only one per cent. was fatal; while stone was considered such a trifle that they did not even write about it. A radical cure for syphilis had been discovered. And the theory of heredity, hypnotism, the discoveries of Pasteur and of Koch, hygiene based on statistics, and the work of our Zemstvo doctors!

Psychiatry with its modern classification of mental diseases, methods of diagnosis, and treatment, was a perfect Elborus in comparison with what had been in the past. They no longer poured cold water on the heads of lunatics nor put strait-waistcoats upon them; they treated them with humanity, and even, so it was stated in the papers, got up balls and entertainments for them. Andrey Yefimitch knew that with modern tastes and views such an abomination as Ward No. 6 was possible only a hundred and fifty miles from a railway in a little town where the mayor and all the town council were half-illiterate tradesmen who looked upon the doctor as an oracle who must be believed without any criticism even if he had poured molten lead into their mouths; in any other place the public and the newspapers would long ago have torn this little Bastille to pieces.

"But, after all, what of it?" Andrey Yefimitch would ask himself, opening his eyes. "There is the antiseptic system, there is Koch, there is Pasteur, but the essential reality is not altered a bit; ill-health and mortality are still the same. They get up balls and entertainments for the mad, but still they don't let them go free; so it's all nonsense and vanity, and there is no difference in reality between the best

Vienna clinic and my hospital." But depression and
a feeling akin to envy prevented him from feeling
indifferent; it must have been owing to exhaustion.
His heavy head sank on to the book, he put his hands
under his face to make it softer, and thought: " I
serve in a pernicious institution and receive a salary
from people whom I am deceiving. I am not honest,
but then, I of myself am nothing, I am only part of
an inevitable social evil: all local officials are pernicious and receive their salary for doing nothing.
. . . And so for my dishonesty it is not I who am
to blame, but the times. . . . If I had been
born two hundred years later I should have been
different. . . ."

When it struck three he would put out his lamp
and go into his bedroom; he was not sleepy.

VIII

Two years before, the Zemstvo in a liberal mood
had decided to allow three hundred roubles a year
to pay for additional medical service in the town till
the Zemstvo hospital should be opened, and the district doctor, Yevgeny Fyodoritch Hobotov, was invited to the town to assist Andrey Yefimitch. He
was a very young man—not yet thirty—tall and
dark, with broad cheek-bones and little eyes; his
forefathers had probably come from one of the many
alien races of Russia. He arrived in the town without a farthing, with a small portmanteau, and a plain
young woman whom he called his cook. This woman
had a baby at the breast. Yevgeny Fyodoritch used
to go about in a cap with a peak, and in high

boots, and in the winter wore a sheepskin. He made great friends with Sergey Sergeyitch, the medical assistant, and with the treasurer, but held aloof from the other officials, and for some reason called them aristocrats. He had only one book in his lodgings, " The Latest Prescriptions of the Vienna Clinic for 1881." When he went to a patient he always took this book with him. He played billiards in the evening at the club: he did not like cards. He was very fond of using in conversation such expressions as " endless bobbery," " canting soft soap," " shut up with your finicking. . . ."

He visited the hospital twice a week, made the round of the wards, and saw out-patients. The complete absence of antiseptic treatment and the cupping roused his indignation, but he did not introduce any new system, being afraid of offending Andrey Yefimitch. He regarded his colleague as a sly old rascal, suspected him of being a man of large means, and secretly envied him. He would have been very glad to have his post.

IX

On a spring evening towards the end of March, when there was no snow left on the ground and the starlings were singing in the hospital garden, the doctor went out to see his friend the postmaster as far as the gate. At that very moment the Jew Moiseika, returning with his booty, came into the yard. He had no cap on, and his bare feet were thrust into goloshes; in his hand he had a little bag of coppers.

" Give me a kopeck ! " he said to the doctor, smiling, and shivering with cold. Andrey Yefimitch, who could never refuse anyone anything, gave him a ten-kopeck piece.

" How bad that is ! " he thought, looking at the Jew's bare feet with their thin red ankles. " Why, it's wet."

And stirred by a feeling akin both to pity and disgust, he went into the lodge behind the Jew, looking now at his bald head, now at his ankles. As the doctor went in, Nikita jumped up from his heap of litter and stood at attention.

" Good-day, Nikita," Andrey Yefimitch said mildly. " That Jew should be provided with boots or something, he will catch cold."

" Certainly, your honour. I'll inform the superintendent."

" Please do; ask him in my name. Tell him that I asked."

The door into the ward was open. Ivan Dmitritch, lying propped on his elbow on the bed, listened in alarm to the unfamiliar voice, and suddenly recognized the doctor. He trembled all over with anger, jumped up, and with a red and wrathful face, with his eyes starting out of his head, ran out into the middle of the road.

" The doctor has come ! " he shouted, and broke into a laugh. " At last ! Gentlemen, I congratulate you. The doctor is honouring us with a visit ! Cursed reptile ! " he shrieked, and stamped in a frenzy such as had never been seen in the ward before. " Kill the reptile ! No, killing's too good. Drown him in the midden-pit ! "

Andrey Yefimitch, hearing this, looked into the ward from the entry and asked gently: "What for?"

"What for?" shouted Ivan Dmitritch, going up to him with a menacing air and convulsively wrapping himself in his dressing-gown. "What for? Thief!" he said with a look of repulsion, moving his lips as though he would spit at him. "Quack! hangman!"

"Calm yourself," said Andrey Yefimitch, smiling guiltily. "I assure you I have never stolen anything; and as to the rest, most likely you greatly exaggerate. I see you are angry with me. Calm yourself, I beg, if you can, and tell me coolly what are you angry for?"

"What are you keeping me here for?"

"Because you are ill."

"Yes, I am ill. But you know dozens, hundreds of madmen are walking about in freedom because your ignorance is incapable of distinguishing them from the sane. Why am I and these poor wretches to be shut up here like scapegoats for all the rest? You, your assistant, the superintendent, and all your hospital rabble, are immeasurably inferior to every one of us morally; why then are we shut up and you not? Where's the logic of it?"

"Morality and logic don't come in, it all depends on chance. If anyone is shut up he has to stay, and if anyone is not shut up he can walk about, that's all. There is neither morality nor logic in my being a doctor and your being a mental patient, there is nothing but idle chance."

"That twaddle I don't understand . . ." Ivan

Dmitritch brought out in a hollow voice, and he sat down on his bed.

Moiseika, whom Nikita did not venture to search in the presence of the doctor, laid out on his bed pieces of bread, bits of paper, and little bones, and, still shivering with cold, began rapidly in a singsong voice saying something in Yiddish. He most likely imagined that he had opened a shop.

"Let me out," said Ivan Dmitritch, and his voice quivered.

"I cannot."

"But why, why?"

"Because it is not in my power. Think, what use will it be to you if I do let you out? Go. The townspeople or the police will detain you or bring you back."

"Yes, yes, that's true," said Ivan Dmitritch, and he rubbed his forehead. "It's awful! But what am I to do, what?"

Andrey Yefimitch liked Ivan Dmitritch's voice and his intelligent young face with its grimaces. He longed to be kind to the young man and soothe him; he sat down on the bed beside him, thought, and said:

"You ask me what to do. The very best thing in your position would be to run away. But, unhappily, that is useless. You would be taken up. When society protects itself from the criminal, mentally deranged, or otherwise inconvenient people, it is invincible. There is only one thing left for you: to resign yourself to the thought that your presence here is inevitable."

"It is no use to anyone."

" So long as prisons and madhouses exist someone must be shut up in them. If not you, I. If not I, some third person. Wait till in the distant future prisons and madhouses no longer exist, and there will be neither bars on the windows nor hospital gowns. Of course, that time will come sooner or later."

Ivan Dmitritch smiled ironically.

" You are jesting," he said, screwing up his eyes. " Such gentlemen as you and your assistant Nikita have nothing to do with the future, but you may be sure, sir, better days will come! I may express myself cheaply, you may laugh, but the dawn of a new life is at hand; truth and justice will triumph, and—our turn will come! I shall not live to see it, I shall perish, but some people's great-grandsons will see it. I greet them with all my heart and rejoice, rejoice with them! Onward! God be your help, friends! "

With shining eyes Ivan Dmitritch got up, and stretching his hands towards the window, went on with emotion in his voice:

" From behind these bars I bless you! Hurrah for truth and justice! I rejoice! "

" I see no particular reason to rejoice," said Andrey Yefimitch, who thought Ivan Dmitritch's movement theatrical, though he was delighted by it. " Prisons and madhouses there will not be, and truth, as you have just expressed it, will triumph; but the reality of things, you know, will not change, the laws of nature will still remain the same. People will suffer pain, grow old, and die just as they do now. However magnificent a dawn lighted up your life, you would yet in the end be nailed up in a coffin and thrown into a hole."

" And immortality? "

" Oh, come, now! "

" You don't believe in it, but I do. Somebody in Dostoevsky or Voltaire said that if there had not been a God men would have invented him. And I firmly believe that if there is no immortality the great intellect of man will sooner or later invent it."

" Well said," observed Andrey Yefimitch, smiling with pleasure; " it's a good thing you have faith. With such a belief one may live happily even shut up within walls. You have studied somewhere, I presume? "

" Yes, I have been at the university, but did not complete my studies."

" You are a reflecting and a thoughtful man. In any surroundings you can find tranquillity in yourself. Free and deep thinking which strives for the comprehension of life, and complete contempt for the foolish bustle of the world—those are two blessings beyond any that man has ever known. And you can possess them even though you lived behind threefold bars. Diogenes lived in a tub, yet he was happier than all the kings of the earth."

" Your Diogenes was a blockhead," said Ivan Dmitritch morosely. " Why do you talk to me about Diogenes and some foolish comprehension of life? " he cried, growing suddenly angry and leaping up. " I love life; I love it passionately. I have the mania of persecution, a continual agonizing terror; but I have moments when I am overwhelmed by the thirst for life, and then I am afraid of going mad. I want dreadfully to live, dreadfully!"

He walked up and down the ward in agitation, and said, dropping his voice:

"When I dream I am haunted by phantoms. People come to me, I hear voices and music, and I fancy I am walking through woods or by the seashore, and I long so passionately for movement, for interests. . . . Come, tell me, what news is there?" asked Ivan Dmitritch; "what's happening?"

"Do you wish to know about the town or in general?"

"Well, tell me first about the town, and then in general."

"Well, in the town it is appallingly dull. . . . There's no one to say a word to, no one to listen to. There are no new people. A young doctor called Hobotov has come here recently."

"He had come in my time. Well, he is a low cad, isn't he?"

"Yes, he is a man of no culture. It's strange, you know. . . . Judging by every sign, there is no intellectual stagnation in our capital cities; there is a movement—so there must be real people there too; but for some reason they always send us such men as I would rather not see. It's an unlucky town!"

"Yes, it is an unlucky town," sighed Ivan Dmitritch, and he laughed. "And how are things in general? What are they writing in the papers and reviews?"

It was by now dark in the ward. The doctor got up, and, standing, began to describe what was being written abroad and in Russia, and the tendency of thought that could be noticed now. Ivan Dmitritch listened attentively and put questions, but suddenly, as though recalling something terrible, clutched at his head and lay down on the bed with his back to the doctor.

"What's the matter?" asked Andrey Yefimitch.

"You will not hear another word from me," said Ivan Dmitritch rudely. "Leave me alone."

"Why so?"

"I tell you, leave me alone. Why the devil do you persist?"

Andrey Yefimitch shrugged his shoulders, heaved a sigh, and went out. As he crossed the entry he said: "You might clear up here, Nikita . . . there's an awfully stuffy smell."

"Certainly, your honour."

"What an agreeable young man!" thought Andrey Yefimitch, going back to his flat. "In all the years I have been living here I do believe he is the first I have met with whom one can talk. He is capable of reasoning and is interested in just the right things."

While he was reading, and afterwards, while he was going to bed, he kept thinking about Ivan Dmitritch, and when he woke next morning he remembered that he had the day before made the acquaintance of an intelligent and interesting man, and determined to visit him again as soon as possible.

X

Ivan Dmitritch was lying in the same position as on the previous day, with his head clutched in both hands and his legs drawn up. His face was not visible.

"Good-day, my friend," said Andrey Yefimitch. "You are not asleep, are you?"

"In the first place, I am not your friend," Ivan Dmitritch articulated into the pillow; "and in the second, your efforts are useless; you will not get one word out of me."

"Strange," muttered Andrey Yefimitch in confusion. "Yesterday we talked peacefully, but suddenly for some reason you took offence and broke off all at once. . . . Probably I expressed myself awkwardly, or perhaps gave utterance to some idea which did not fit in with your convictions. . . ."

"Yes, a likely idea!" said Ivan Dmitritch, sitting up and looking at the doctor with irony and uneasiness. His eyes were red. "You can go and spy and probe somewhere else, it's no use your doing it here. I knew yesterday what you had come for."

"A strange fancy," laughed the doctor. "So you suppose me to be a spy?"

"Yes, I do. . . . A spy or a doctor who has been charged to test me—it's all the same——"

"Oh, excuse me, what a queer fellow you are really!"

The doctor sat down on the stool near the bed and shook his head reproachfully.

"But let us suppose you are right," he said, "let us suppose that I am treacherously trying to trap you into saying something so as to betray you to the police. You would be arrested and then tried. But would you be any worse off being tried and in prison than you are here? If you are banished to a settlement, or even sent to penal servitude, would it be worse than being shut up in this ward? I imagine it would be no worse. . . . What, then, are you afraid of?"

These words evidently had an effect on Ivan Dmitritch. He sat down quietly.

It was between four and five in the afternoon—the time when Andrey Yefimitch usually walked up and down his rooms, and Daryushka asked whether it was not time for his beer. It was a still, bright day.

"I came out for a walk after dinner, and here I have come, as you see," said the doctor. "It is quite spring."

"What month is it? March?" asked Ivan Dmitritch.

"Yes, the end of March."

"Is it very muddy?"

"No, not very. There are already paths in the garden."

"It would be nice now to drive in an open carriage somewhere into the country," said Ivan Dmitritch, rubbing his red eyes as though he were just awake, "then to come home to a warm, snug study, and . . . and to have a decent doctor to cure one's headache. . . . It's so long since I have lived like a human being. It's disgusting here! Insufferably disgusting!"

After his excitement of the previous day he was exhausted and listless, and spoke unwillingly. His fingers twitched, and from his face it could be seen that he had a splitting headache.

"There is no real difference between a warm,

snug study and this ward," said Andrey Yefimitch. " A man's peace and contentment do not lie outside a man, but in himself."

" What do you mean? "

" The ordinary man looks for good and evil in external things—that is, in carriages, in studies— but a thinking man looks for it in himself."

" You should go and preach that philosophy in Greece, where it's warm and fragrant with the scent of pomegranates, but here it is not suited to the climate. With whom was it I was talking of Diogenes? Was it with you? "

" Yes, with me yesterday."

" Diogenes did not need a study or a warm habita- tion; it's hot there without. You can lie in your tub and eat oranges and olives. But bring him to Rus- sia to live: he'd be begging to be let indoors in May, let alone December. He'd be doubled up with the cold."

" No. One can be insensible to cold as to every other pain. Marcus Aurelius says: ' A pain is a vivid idea of pain; make an effort of will to change that idea, dismiss it, cease to complain, and the pain will disappear.' That is true. The wise man, or simply the reflecting, thoughtful man, is distinguished precisely by his contempt for suffering; he is always contented and surprised at nothing."

" Then I am an idiot, since I suffer and am dis- contented and surprised at the baseness of man- kind."

" You are wrong in that; if you will reflect more on the subject you will understand how insignificant is all that external world that agitates us. One must strive for the comprehension of life, and in that is true happiness."

"Comprehension . . ." repeated Ivan Dmitritch frowning. "External, internal. . . . Excuse me, but I don't understand it. I only know," he said, getting up and looking angrily at the doctor—" I only know that God has created me of warm blood and nerves, yes, indeed! If organic tissue is capable of life it must react to every stimulus. And I do! To pain I respond with tears and outcries, to baseness with indignation, to filth with loathing. To my mind, that is just what is called life. The lower the organism, the less sensitive it is, and the more feebly it reacts to stimulus; and the higher it is, the more responsively and vigorously it reacts to reality. How is it you don't know that? A doctor, and not know such trifles! To despise suffering, to be always contented, and to be surprised at nothing, one must reach this condition "—and Ivan Dmitritch pointed to the peasant who was a mass of fat—" or to harden oneself by suffering to such a point that one loses all sensibility to it—that is, in other words, to cease to live. You must excuse me, I am not a sage or a philosopher," Ivan Dmitritch continued with irritation, " and I don't understand anything about it. I am not capable of reasoning."

" On the contrary, your reasoning is excellent."

" The Stoics, whom you are parodying, were remarkable people, but their doctrine crystallized two thousand years ago and has not advanced, and will not advance, an inch forward, since it is not practical or living. It had a success only with the minority which spends its life in savouring all sorts of theories and ruminating over them; the majority did not understand it. A doctrine which advocates indifference to wealth and to the comforts of life, and a contempt for suffering and death, is quite unintelligible to the vast majority of men, since that majority has never known wealth or the comforts of life; and to despise suffering would mean to it despising life itself, since the whole existence of man is made up of the sensations of hunger, cold, injury, loss, and a Hamlet-like dread of death. The whole of life lies in these sensations; one may be oppressed by it, one may hate it, but one cannot despise it. Yes, so, I repeat, the doctrine of the Stoics can never have a future; from the beginning of time up to to-day you see continually increasing the struggle, the sensibility to pain, the capacity of responding to stimulus."

Ivan Dmitritch suddenly lost the thread of his thoughts, stopped, and rubbed his forehead with vexation.

" I meant to say something important, but I have lost it," he said. " What was I saying? Oh, yes! This is what I mean: one of the Stoics sold himself into slavery to redeem his neighbour, so, you see, even a Stoic did react to stimulus, since, for such a generous act as the destruction of oneself for the sake of one's neighbour, he must have had a soul capable of pity and indignation. Here in prison I have forgotten everything I have learned, or else I could have recalled something else. Take Christ, for instance: Christ responded to reality by weeping, smiling, being sorrowful and moved to wrath, even overcome by misery. He did not go to meet

His sufferings with a smile, He did not despise death, but prayed in the Garden of Gethsemane that this cup might pass Him by."

Ivan Dmitritch laughed and sat down.

" Granted that a man's peace and contentment lie not outside but in himself," he said, " granted that one must despise suffering and not be surprised at anything, yet on what ground do you preach the theory? Are you a sage? A philosopher? "

" No, I am not a philosopher, but everyone ought to preach it because it is reasonable."

" No, I want to know how it is that you consider yourself competent to judge of ' comprehension,' contempt for suffering, and so on. Have you ever suffered? Have you any idea of suffering? Allow me to ask you, were you ever thrashed in your childhood? "

" No, my parents had an aversion for corporal punishment."

" My father used to flog me cruelly; my father was a harsh, sickly Government clerk with a long nose and a yellow neck. But let us talk of you. No one has laid a finger on you all your life, no one has scared you nor beaten you; you are as strong as a bull. You grew up under your father's wing and studied at his expense, and then you dropped at once into a sinecure. For more than twenty years you have lived rent free with heating, lighting, and service all provided, and had the right to work how you pleased and as much as you pleased, even to do nothing. You were naturally a flabby, lazy man, and so you have tried to arrange your life so that nothing should disturb you or make you

move. You have handed over your work to the
assistant and the rest of the rabble while you sit
in peace and warmth, save money, read, amuse yourself with reflections, with all sorts of lofty nonsense,
and " (Ivan Dmitritch looked at the doctor's red
nose) " with boozing; in fact, you have seen nothing
of life, you know absolutely nothing of it, and are
only theoretically acquainted with reality; you
despise suffering and are surprised at nothing for a
very simple reason: vanity of vanities, the external
and the internal, contempt for life, for suffering
and for death, comprehension, true happiness—
that's the philosophy that suits the Russian sluggard
best. You see a peasant beating his wife, for instance. Why interfere? Let him beat her, they
will both die sooner or later, anyway; and, besides,
he who beats injures by his blows, not the person he
is beating, but himself. To get drunk is stupid and
unseemly, but if you drink you die, and if you don't
drink you die. A peasant woman comes with toothache . . . well, what of it? Pain is the idea of
pain, and besides ' there is no living in this world
without illness; we shall all die, and so, go away,
woman, don't hinder me from thinking and drinking
vodka.' A young man asks advice, what he is to
do, how he is to live; anyone else would think before
answering, but you have got the answer ready: strive
for ' comprehension ' or for true happiness. And
what is that fantastic ' true happiness '? There's
no answer, of course. We are kept here behind
barred windows, tortured, left to rot; but that is
very good and reasonable, because there is no difference at all between this ward and a warm, snug study.

A convenient philosophy. You can do nothing, and your conscience is clear, and you feel you are wise. . . . No, sir, it is not philosophy, it's not thinking, it's not breadth of vision, but laziness, fakirism, drowsy stupefaction. Yes," cried Ivan Dmitritch, getting angry again, " you despise suffering, but I'll be bound if you pinch your finger in the door you will howl at the top of your voice."

" And perhaps I shouldn't howl," said Andrey Yefimitch, with a gentle smile.

" Oh, I dare say! Well, if you had a stroke of paralysis, or supposing some fool or bully took advantage of his position and rank to insult you in public, and if you knew he could do it with impunity, then you would understand what it means to put people off with comprehension and true happiness."

" That's original," said Andrey Yefimitch, laughing with pleasure and rubbing his hands. "I am agreebly struck by your inclination for drawing generalizations, and the sketch of my character you have just drawn is simply brilliant. I must confess that talking to you gives me great pleasure. Well, I've listened to you, and now you must graciously listen to me."

XI

The conversation went on for about an hour longer, and apparently made a deep impression an Andrey Yefimitch. He began going to the ward every day. He went there in the mornings and after dinner, and often the dusk of evening found

him in conversation with Ivan Dmitritch. At first
Ivan Dmitritch held aloof from him, suspected him
of evil designs, and openly expressed his hostility.
But afterwards he got used to him, and his abrupt
manner changed to one of condescending irony.

Soon it was all over the hospital that the doctor,
Andrey Yefimitch, had taken to visiting Ward No.
6. No one—neither Sergey Sergeyitch, nor Nikita,
nor the nurses—could conceive why he went there,
why he stayed there for hours together, what he
was talking about, and why he did not write prescriptions. His actions seemed strange. Often Mihail
Averyanitch did not find him at home, which had
never happened in the past, and Daryushka was
greatly perturbed, for the doctor drank his beer now
at no definite time, and sometimes was even late for
dinner.

One day—it was at the end of June—Dr.
Hobotov went to see Andrey Yefimitch about something. Not finding him at home, he proceeded to
look for him in the yard; there he was told that
the old doctor had gone to see the mental patients.
Going into the lodge and stopping in the entry,
Hobotov heard the following conversation:

"We shall never agree, and you will not succeed
in converting me to your faith," Ivan Dmitritch was
saying irritably; "you are utterly ignorant of reality,
and you have never known suffering, but have only
like a leech fed beside the sufferings of others, while
I have been in continual suffering from the day of my
birth till to-day. For that reason, I tell you frankly,
I consider myself superior to you and more com-

petent in every respect. It's not for you to teach me."

"I have absolutely no ambition to convert you to my faith," said Andrey Yefimitch gently, and with regret that the other refused to understand him. "And that is not what matters, my friend; what matters is not that you have suffered and I have not. Joy and suffering are passing; let us leave them, never mind them. What matters is that you and I think; we see in each other people who are capable of thinking and reasoning, and that is a common bond between us however different our views. If you knew, my friend, how sick I am of the universal senselessness, ineptitude, stupidity, and with what delight I always talk with you! You are an intelligent man, and I enjoy your company."

Hobotov opened the door an inch and glanced into the ward; Ivan Dmitritch in his night-cap and the doctor Andrey Yefimitch were sitting side by side on the bed. The madman was grimacing, twitching, and convulsively wrapping himself in his gown, while the doctor sat motionless with bowed Lead, and his face was red and look helpless and sorrowful. Hobotov shrugged his shoulders, grinned, and glanced at Nikita. Nikita shrugged his shoulders too.

Next day Hobotov went to the lodge, accompanied by the assistant. Both stood in the entry and listened.

"I fancy our old man has gone clean off his chump!" said Hobotov as he came out of the lodge.

"Lord have mercy upon us sinners!" sighed the

decorous Sergey Sergeyitch, scrupulously avoiding the puddles that he might not muddy his polished boots. "I must own, honoured Yevgeny Fyodoritch, I have been expecting it for a long time."

XII

After this Andrey Yefimitch began to notice a mysterious air in all around him. The attendants, the nurses, and the patients looked at him inquisitively when they met him, and then whispered together. The superintendent's little daughter Masha, whom he liked to meet in the hospital garden, for some reason ran away from him now when he went up with a smile to stroke her on the head. The postmaster no longer said, "Perfectly true," as he listened to him, but in unaccountable confusion muttered, "Yes, yes, yes . . ." and looked at him with a grieved and thoughtful expression; for some reason he took to advising his friend to give up vodka and beer, but as a man of delicate feeling he did not say this directly, but hinted it, telling him first about the commanding officer of his battalion, an excellent man, and then about the priest of the regiment, a capital fellow, both of whom drank and fell ill, but on giving up drinking completely regained their health. On two or three occasions Andrey Yefimitch was visited by his colleague Hobotov, who also advised him to give up spirituous liquors, and for no apparent reason recommended him to take bromide.

In August Andrey Yefimitch got a letter from the mayor of the town asking him to come on very important business. On arriving at the town hall at the time fixed, Andrey Yefimitch found there the military commander, the superintendent of the district school, a member of the town council, Hobotov, and a plump, fair gentleman who was introduced to him as a doctor. This doctor, with a Polish surname difficult to pronounce, lived at a pedigree stud-farm twenty miles away, and was now on a visit to the town.

" There's something that concerns you," said the member of the town council, addressing Andrey Yefimitch after they had all greeted one another and sat down to the table. " Here Yevgeny Fyodoritch says that there is not room for the dispensary in the main building, and that it ought to be transferred to one of the lodges. That's of no consequence—of course it can be transferred, but the point is that the lodge wants doing up."

" Yes, it would have to be done up," said Andrey Yefimitch after a moment's thought. " If the corner lodge, for instance, were fitted up as a dispensary, I imagine it would cost at least five hundred roubles. An unproductive expenditure! "

Everyone was silent for a space.

" I had the honour of submitting to you ten years ago," Andrey Yefimitch went on in a low voice, " that the hospital in its present form is a luxury for the town beyond its means. It was built in the forties, but things were different then. The town spends too much on unnecessary buildings and superfluous staff. I believe with a different system two model hospitals might be maintained for the same money."

" Well, let us have a different system, then!"
the member of the town council said briskly.

" I have already had the honour of submitting to
you that the medical department should be transferred to the supervision of the Zemstvo."

" Yes, transfer the money to the Zemstvo and
they will steal it," laughed the fair-haired doctor.

" That's what it always comes to," the member
of the council assented, and he also laughed.

Andrey Yefimitch looked with apathetic, lustreless
eyes at the fair-haired doctor and said: " One
should be just."

Again there was silence. Tea was brought in.
The military commander, for some reason much
embarrassed, touched Andrey Yefimitch's hand
across the table and said: "You have quite forgotten us, doctor. But of course you are a hermit:
you don't play cards and don't like women. You
would be dull with fellows like us."

They all began saying how boring it was for a
decent person to live in such a town. No theatre,
no music, and at the last dance at the club there
had been about twenty ladies and only two gentlemen. The young men did not dance, but spent all
the time crowding round the refreshment bar or
playing cards.

Not looking at anyone and speaking slowly in a
low voice, Andrey Yefimitch began saying what
a pity, what a terrible pity it was that the townspeople should waste their vital energy, their hearts,
and their minds on cards and gossip, and should
have neither the power nor the inclination to spend
their time in interesting conversation and reading,

and should refuse to take advantage of the enjoyments of the mind. The mind alone was interesting and worthy of attention, all the rest was low and petty. Hobotov listened to his colleague attentively and suddenly asked:

"Andrey Yefimitch, what day of the month is it?"

Having received an answer, the fair-haired doctor and he, in the tone of examiners conscious of their lack of skill, began asking Andrey Yefimitch what was the day of the week, how many days there were in the year, and whether it was true that there was a remarkable prophet living in Ward No. 6.

In response to the last question Andrey Yefimitch turned rather red and said: "Yes, he is mentally deranged, but he is an interesting young man."

They asked him no other questions.

When he was putting on his overcoat in the entry, the military commander laid a hand on his shoulder and said with a sigh:

"It's time for us old fellows to rest!"

As he came out of the hall, Andrey Yefimitch understood that it had been a committee appointed to enquire into his mental condition. He recalled the questions that had been asked him, flushed crimson, and for some reason, for the first time in his life, felt bitterly grieved for medical science.

"My God . . ." he thought, remembering how these doctors had just examined him; "why, they have only lately been hearing lectures on mental pathology; they had passed an examination—what's the explanation of this crass ignorance? They have not a conception of mental pathology!"

And for the first time in his life he felt insulted and moved to anger.

In the evening of the same day Mihail Averyanitch came to see him. The postmaster went up to him without waiting to greet him, took him by both hands, and said in an agitated voice:

" My dear fellow, my dear friend, show me that you believe in my genuine affection and look on me as your friend! " And preventing Andrey Yefimitch from speaking, he went on, growing excited: " I love you for your culture and nobility of soul. Listen to me, my dear fellow. The rules of their profession compel the doctors to conceal the truth from you, but I blurt out the plain truth like a soldier. You are not well! Excuse me, my dear fellow, but it is the truth; everyone about you has been noticing it for a long time. Dr. Yevgeny Fyodoritch has just told me that it is essential for you to rest and distract your mind for the sake of your health. Perfectly true! Excellent! In a day or two I am taking a holiday and am going away for a sniff of a different atmosphere. Show that you are a friend to me, let us go together! Let us go for a jaunt as in the good old days."

" I feel perfectly well," said Andrey Yefimitch after a moment's thought. " I can't go away. Allow me to show you my friendship in some other way."

To go off with no object, without his books, without his Daryushka, without his beer, to break abruptly through the routine of life, established for twenty years—the idea for the first minute struck him as wild and fantastic, but he remembered the conversation at the Zemstvo committee and the depressing feelings with which he had returned home, and the thought of a brief absence from the town in which stupid people looked on him as a madman was pleasant to him.

"And where precisely do you intend to go?" he asked.

"To Moscow, to Petersburg, to Warsaw. . . . I spent the five happiest years of my life in Warsaw. What a marvellous town! Let us go, my dear fellow!"

XIII

A week later it was suggested to Andrey Yefimitch that he should have a rest—that is, send in his resignation—a suggestion he received with indifference, and a week later still, Mihail Averyanitch and he were sitting in a posting carriage driving to the nearest railway station. The days were cool and bright, with a blue sky and a transparent distance. They were two days driving the hundred and fifty miles to the railway station, and stayed two nights on the way. When at the posting station the glasses given them for their tea had not been properly washed, or the drivers were slow in harnessing the horses, Mihail Averyanitch would turn crimson, and quivering all over would shout:

"Hold your tongue! Don't argue!"

And in the carriage he talked without ceasing for a moment, describing his campaigns in the Caucasus and in Poland. What adventures he had had, what meetings! He talked loudly and opened his eyes so wide with wonder that he might well be thought to be lying. Moreover, as he talked he

breathed in Andrey Yefimitch's face and laughed
into his ear. This bothered the doctor and prevented him from thinking or concentrating his mind.

In the train they travelled, from motives of
economy, third-class in a non-smoking compartment.
Half the passengers were decent people. Mihail
Averyanitch soon made friends with everyone, and
moving from one seat to another, kept saying loudly
that they ought not to travel by these appalling lines.
It was a regular swindle! A very different thing
riding on a good horse: one could do over seventy
miles a day and feel fresh and well after it. And
our bad harvests were due to the draining of the
Pinsk marshes; altogether, the way things were done
was dreadful. He got excited, talked loudly, and
would not let others speak. This endless chatter
to the accompaniment of loud laughter and expres-
sive gestures wearied Andrey Yefimitch.

" Which of us is the madman? " he thought with
vexation. " I, who try not to disturb my fellow-
passengers in any way, or this egoist who thinks
that he is cleverer and more interesting than anyone
here, and so will leave no one in peace? "

In Moscow Mihail Averyanitch put on a military
coat without epaulettes and trousers with red braid
on them. He wore a military cap and overcoat in
the street, and soldiers saluted him. It seemed to
Andrey Yefimitch, now, that his companion was a
man who had flung away all that was good and
kept only what was bad of all the characteristics of
a country gentleman that he had once possessed.
He liked to be waited on even when it was quite
unnecessary. The matches would be lying before

him on the table, and he would see them and shout to the waiter to give him the matches; he did not hesitate to appear before a maidservant in nothing but his underclothes; he used the familiar mode of address to all footmen indiscriminately, even old men, and when he was angry called them fools and blockheads. This, Andrey Yefimitch thought, was like a gentleman, but disgusting.

First of all Mihail Averyanitch led his friend to the Iversky Madonna. He prayed fervently, shedding tears and bowing down to the earth, and when he had finished, heaved a deep sigh and said:

" Even though one does not believe it makes one somehow easier when one prays a little. Kiss the ikon, my dear fellow."

Andrey Yefimitch was embarrassed and he kissed the image, while Mihail Averyanitch pursed up his lips and prayed in a whisper, and again tears came into his eyes. Then they went to the Kremlin and looked there at the Tsar-cannon and the Tsar-bell, and even touched them with their fingers, admired the view over the river, visited St. Saviour's and the Rumyantsev museum.

They dined at Tyestov's. Mihail Averyanitch looked a long time at the menu, stroking his whiskers, and said in the tone of a gourmand accustomed to dine in restaurants:

" We shall see what you give us to eat to-day, angel ! "

XIV

The doctor walked about, looked at things, ate and drank, but he had all the while one feeling: annoyance with Mihail Averyanitch. He longed to have a rest from his friend, to get away from him, to hide himself, while the friend thought it his duty not to let the doctor move a step away from him, and to provide him with as many distractions as possible. When there was nothing to look at he entertained him with conversation. For two days Andrey Yefimitch endured it, but on the third he announced to his friend that he was ill and wanted to stay at home for the whole day; his friend replied that in that case he would stay too—that really he needed rest, for he was run off his legs already. Andrey Yefimitch lay on the sofa, with his face to the back, and clenching his teeth, listened to his friend, who assured him with heat that sooner or later France would certainly thrash Germany, that there were a great many scoundrels in Moscow, and that it was impossible to judge of a horse's quality by its outward appearance. The doctor began to have a buzzing in his ears and palpitations of the heart, but out of delicacy could not bring himself to beg his friend to go away or hold his tongue. Fortunately Mihail Averyanitch grew weary of sitting in the hotel room, and after dinner he went out for a walk.

As soon as he was alone Andrey Yefimitch abandoned himself to a feeling of relief. How pleasant to lie motionless on the sofa and to know that one is alone in the room! Real happiness is impossible without solitude. The fallen angel betrayed God probably because he longed for solitude, of which the angels know nothing. Andrey Yefimitch wanted to think about what he had seen and heard during the last few days, but he could not get Mihail Averyanitch out of his head.

"Why, he has taken a holiday and come with me out of friendship, out of generosity," thought the doctor with vexation; "nothing could be worse than this friendly supervision. I suppose he is good-natured and generous and a lively fellow, but he is a bore. An insufferable bore. In the same way there are people who never say anything but what is clever and good, yet one feels that they are dull-witted people."

For the following days Andrey Yefimitch declared himself ill and would not leave the hotel room; he lay with his face to the back of the sofa, and suffered agonies of weariness when his friend entertained him with conversation, or rested when his friend was absent. He was vexed with himself for having come, and with his friend, who grew every day more talkative and more free-and-easy; he could not succeed in attuning his thoughts to a serious and lofty level.

"This is what I get from the real life Ivan Dmitritch talked about," he thought, angry at his own pettiness. "It's of no consequence, though. . . . I shall go home, and everything will go on as before. . . ."

It was the same thing in Petersburg too; for whole days together he did not leave the hotel room, but lay on the sofa and only got up to drink beer.

Mihail Averyanitch was all haste to get to Warsaw.

"My dear man, what should I go there for?"

said Andrey Yefimitch in an imploring voice. " You go alone and let me get home ! I entreat you ! "

" On no account," protested Mihail Averyanitch. " It's a marvellous town."

Andrey Yefimitch had not the strength of will to insist on his own way, and much against his inclination went to Warsaw. There he did not leave the hotel room, but lay on the sofa, furious with himself, with his friend, and with the waiters, who obstinately refused to understand Russian; while Mihail Averyanitch, healthy, hearty, and full of spirits as usual, went about the town from morning to night, looking for his old acquaintances. Several times he did not return home at night. After one night spent in some unknown haunt he returned home early in the morning, in a violently excited condition, with a red face and tousled hair. For a long time he walked up and down the rooms muttering something to himself, then stopped and said:

" Honour before everything."

After walking up and down a little longer he clutched his head in both hands and pronounced in a tragic voice: " Yes, honour before everything ! Accursed be the moment when the idea first entered my head to visit this Babylon ! My dear friend," he added, addressing the doctor, " you may despise me, I have played and lost; lend me five hundred roubles ! "

Andrey Yefimitch counted out five hundred roubles and gave them to his friend without a word. The latter, still crimson with shame and anger, incoherently articulated some useless vow, put on his cap, and went out. Returning two hours later he flopped into an easy-chair, heaved a loud sigh, and said:

" My honour is saved. Let us go, my friend; I do not care to remain another hour in this accursed town. Scoundrels! Austrian spies! "

By the time the friends were back in their own town it was November, and deep snow was lying in the streets. Dr. Hobotov had Andrey Yefimitch's post; he was still living in his old lodgings, waiting for Andrey Yefimitch to arrive and clear out of the hospital apartments. The plain woman whom he called his cook was already established in one of the lodges.

Fresh scandals about the hospital were going the round of the town. It was said that the plain woman had quarrelled with the superintendent, and that the latter had crawled on his knees before her begging forgiveness. On the very first day he arrived Andrey Yefimitch had to look out for lodgings.

" My friend," the postmaster said to him timidly, " excuse an indiscreet question: what means have you at your disposal? "

Andrey Yefimitch, without a word, counted out his money and said: " Eighty-six roubles."

" I don't mean that," Mihail Averyanitch brought out in confusion, misunderstanding him; " I mean, what have you to live on? "

" I tell you, eighty-six roubles . . . I have nothing else."

Mihail Averyanitch looked upon the doctor as an honourable man, yet he suspected that he had accumulated a fortune of at least twenty thousand. Now learning that Andrey Yefimitch was a beggar, that he had nothing to live on he was for some reason suddenly moved to tears and embraced his friend.

XV

Andrey Yefimitch now lodged in a little house with three windows. There were only three rooms besides the kitchen in the little house. The doctor lived in two of them which looked into the street, while Daryushka and the landlady with her three children lived in the third room and the kitchen. Sometimes the landlady's lover, a drunken peasant who was rowdy and reduced the children and Daryushka to terror, would come for the night. When he arrived and established himself in the kitchen and demanded vodka, they all felt very uncomfortable, and the doctor would be moved by pity to take the crying children into his room and let them lie on his floor, and this gave him great satisfaction.

He got up as before at eight o'clock, and after his morning tea sat down to read his old books and magazines: he had no money for new ones. Either because the books were old, or perhaps because of the change in his surroundings, reading exhausted him, and did not grip his attention as before. That he might not spend his time in idleness he made a detailed catalogue of his books and gummed little labels on their backs, and this mechanical, tedious work seemed to him more interesting than reading. The monotonous, tedious work lulled his thoughts to sleep in some unaccountable way, and the time passed quickly while he thought of nothing. Even sitting in the kitchen, peeling potatoes with Daryushka or picking over the buckwheat grain, seemed to him interesting. On Saturdays and Sundays he went to church. Standing near the wall and half closing his eyes, he listened to the singing and thought of his father, of his mother, of the university, of the religions of the world; he felt calm and melancholy, and as he went out of the church afterwards he regretted that the service was so soon over. He went twice to the hospital to talk to Ivan Dmitritch. But on both occasions Ivan Dmitritch was unusually excited and ill-humoured; he bade the doctor leave him in peace, as he had long been sick of empty chatter, and declared, to make up for all his sufferings, he asked from the damned scoundrels only one favour—solitary confinement. Surely they would not refuse him even that? On both occasions when Andrey Yefimitch was taking leave of him and wishing him good-night, he answered rudely and said:

" Go to hell! "

And Andrey Yefimitch did not know now whether to go to him for the third time or not. He longed to go.

In old days Andrey Yefimitch used to walk about his rooms and think in the interval after dinner, but now from dinner-time till evening tea he lay on the sofa with his face to the back and gave himself up to trivial thoughts which he could not struggle against. He was mortified that after more than twenty years of service he had been given neither a pension nor any assistance. It is true that he had not done his work honestly, but, then, all who are in the Service get a pension without distinction whether they are honest or not. Contemporary justice lies precisely in the bestowal of grades, orders, and pensions, not for moral qualities or capacities, but for service whatever it may have been like. Why was he alone to be an exception? He had no money at all. He was ashamed to pass by the shop and look at the woman who owned it. He owed thirty-two roubles for beer already. There was money owing to the landlady also. Daryushka sold old clothes and books on the sly, and told lies to the landlady, saying that the doctor was just going to receive a large sum of money.

He was angry with himself for having wasted on travelling the thousand roubles he had saved up. How useful that thousand roubles would have been now! He was vexed that people would not leave him in peace. Hobotov thought it his duty to look in on his sick colleague from time to time. Everything about him was revolting to Andrey Yefimitch —his well-fed face and vulgar, condescending tone, and his use of the word " colleague," and his high top-boots; the most revolting thing was that he thought it was his duty to treat Andrey Yefimitch, and thought that he really was treating him. On every visit he brought a bottle of bromide and rhubarb pills.

Mihail Averyanitch, too, thought it his duty to visit his friend and entertain him. Every time he went in to Andrey Yefimitch with an affectation of ease, laughed constrainedly, and began assuring him that he was looking very well to-day, and that, thank

God, he was on the highroad to recovery, and from this it might be concluded that he looked on his friend's condition as hopeless. He had not yet repaid his Warsaw debt, and was overwhelmed by shame; he was constrained, and so tried to laugh louder and talk more amusingly. His anecdotes and descriptions seemed endless now, and were an agony both to Andrey Yefimitch and himself.

In his presence Andrey Yefimitch usually lay on the sofa with his face to the wall, and listened with his teeth clenched; his soul was oppressed with rankling disgust, and after every visit from his friend he felt as though this disgust had risen higher, and was mounting into his throat.

To stifle petty thoughts he made haste to reflect that he himself, and Hobotov, and Mihail Averyanitch, would all sooner or later perish without leaving any trace on the world. If one imagined some spirit flying by the earthly globe in space in a million years he would see nothing but clay and bare rocks. Everything—culture and the moral law—would pass away and not even a burdock would grow out of them. Of what consequence was shame in the presence of a shopkeeper, of what consequence was the insignificant Hobotov or the wearisome friendship of Mihail Averyanitch? It was all trivial and nonsensical.

But such reflections did not help him now. Scarcely had he imagined the earthly globe in a million years, when Hobotov in his high top-boots or Mihail Averyanitch with his forced laugh would appear from behind a bare rock, and he even heard the shamefaced whisper: "The Warsaw debt. . . .

I will repay it in a day or two, my dear fellow, with-out fail. . . ."

XVI

One day Mihail Averyanitch came after dinner when Andrey Yefimitch was lying on the sofa. It so happened that Hobotov arrived at the same time with his bromide. Andrey Yefimitch got up heavily and sat down, leaning both arms on the sofa.

"You have a much better colour to-day than you had yesterday, my dear man," began Mihail Averya-nitch. "Yes, you look jolly. Upon my soul, you do!"

"It's high time you were well, colleague," said Hobotov, yawning. "I'll be bound, you are sick of this bobbery."

"And we shall recover," said Mihail Averya-nitch cheerfully. "We shall live another hundred years! To be sure!"

"Not a hundred years, but another twenty," Hobotov said reassuringly. "It's all right, all right, colleague; don't lose heart. . . . Don't go piling it on!"

"We'll show what we can do," laughed Mihail Averyanitch, and he slapped his friend on the knee. "We'll show them yet! Next summer, please God, we shall be off to the Caucasus, and we will ride all over it on horseback—trot, trot, trot! And when we are back from the Caucasus I shouldn't wonder if we will all dance at the wedding." Mihail Averya-nitch gave a sly wink. "We'll marry you, my dear boy, we'll marry you. . . ."

Andrey Yefimitch felt suddenly that the rising disgust had mounted to his throat, his heart began beating violently.

"That's vulgar," he said, getting up quickly and walking away to the window. "Don't you understand that you are talking vulgar nonsense?"

He meant to go on softly and politely, but against his will he suddenly clenched his fists and raised them above his head.

"Leave me alone," he shouted in a voice unlike his own, flushing crimson and shaking all over. "Go away, both of you!"

Mihail Averyanitch and Hobotov got up and stared at him first with amazement and then with alarm.

"Go away, both!" Andrey Yefimitch went on shouting. "Stupid people! Foolish people! I don't want either your friendship or your medicines, stupid man! Vulgar! Nasty!"

Hobotov and Mihail Averyanitch, looking at each other in bewilderment, staggered to the door and went out. Andrey Yefimitch snatched up the bottle of bromide and flung it after them; the bottle broke with a crash on the door-frame.

"Go to the devil!" he shouted in a tearful voice, running out into the passage. "To the devil!"

When his guests were gone Andrey Yefimitch lay down on the sofa, trembling as though in a fever, and went on for a long while repeating: "Stupid people! Foolish people!"

When he was calmer, what occurred to him first of all was the thought that poor Mihail Averyanitch must be feeling fearfully ashamed and depressed now, and that it was all dreadful. Nothing like this had ever happened to him before. Where was his intelligence and his tact? Where was his comprehension of things and his philosophical indifference?

The doctor could not sleep all night for shame and vexation with himself, and at ten o'clock next morning he went to the post office and apologized to the postmaster.

"We won't think again of what has happened," Mihail Averyanitch, greatly touched, said with a sigh, warmly pressing his hand. "Let bygones be bygones. Lyubavkin," he suddenly shouted so loud that all the postmen and other persons present started, "hand a chair; and you wait," he shouted to a peasant woman who was stretching out a registered letter to him through the grating. "Don't you see that I am busy? We will not remember the past," he went on, affectionately addressing Andrey Yefimitch; "sit down, I beg you, my dear fellow."

For a minute he stroked his knees in silence, and then said:

"I have never had a thought of taking offence. Illness is no joke, I understand. Your attack frightened the doctor and me yesterday, and we had a long talk about you afterwards. My dear friend, why won't you treat your illness seriously? You can't go on like this. . . . Excuse me speaking openly as a friend," whispered Mihail Averyanitch. "You live in the most unfavourable surroundings, in a crowd, in uncleanliness, no one to look after you, no money for proper treatment. . . . My dear friend, the doctor and I implore you with all our hearts, listen to our advice: go into the hospital! There you will have wholesome food and attendance and treatment. Though, between ourselves, Yevgeny Fyodoritch is *mauvais ton,* yet he does understand his work, you can fully rely upon him. He has promised me he will look after you."

Andrey Yefimitch was touched by the postmaster's genuine sympathy and the tears which suddenly glittered on his cheeks.

"My honoured friend, don't believe it!" he whispered, laying his hand on his heart; "don't believe them. It's all a sham. My illness is only that in twenty years I have only found one intelligent man in the whole town, and he is mad. I am not ill at all, it's simply that I have got into an enchanted circle which there is no getting out of. I don't care; I am ready for anything."

"Go into the hospital, my dear fellow."

"I don't care if it were into the pit."

"Give me your word, my dear man, that you will obey Yevgeny Fyodoritch in everything."

"Certainly I will give you my word. But I repeat, my honoured friend, I have got into an enchanted circle. Now everything, even the genuine sympathy of my friends, leads to the same thing—to my ruin. I am going to my ruin, and I have the manliness to recognize it."

"My dear fellow, you will recover."

"What's the use of saying that?" said Andrey Yefimitch, with irritation. "There are few men who at the end of their lives do not experience what I am experiencing now. When you are told that you have something such as diseased kidneys or enlarged heart, and you begin being treated for it, or are told you are mad or a criminal—that is, in fact, when people suddenly turn their attention to you—you may be sure you have got into an enchanted circle from which you will not escape. You will try to escape and make things worse. You had better give in, for no human efforts can save you. So it seems to me."

Meanwhile the public was crowding at the grating. That he might not be in their way, Andrey Yefimitch got up and began to take leave. Mihail Averyanitch made him promise on his honour once more, and escorted him to the outer door.

Towards evening on the same day Hobotov, in his sheepskin and his high top-boots, suddenly made his appearance, and said to Andrey Yefimitch in a tone as though nothing had happened the day before:

"I have come on business, colleague. I have come to ask you whether you would not join me in a consultation. Eh?"

Thinking that Hobotov wanted to distract his mind with an outing, or perhaps really to enable him to earn something, Andrey Yefimitch put on his coat and hat, and went out with him into the street. He was glad of the opportunity to smooth over his fault of the previous day and to be reconciled, and in his heart thanked Hobotov, who did not even allude to yesterday's scene and was evidently sparing him. One would never have expected such delicacy from this uncultured man.

"Where is your invalid?" asked Andrey Yefimitch.

"In the hospital. . . . I have long wanted to show him to you. A very interesting case."

They went into the hospital yard, and going round the main building, turned towards the lodge where the mental cases were kept, and all this, for some reason, in silence. When they went into the lodge Nikita as usual jumped up and stood at attention.

"One of the patients here has a lung complication," Hobotov said in an undertone, going into the ward with Andrey Yefimitch. "You wait here, I'll be back directly. I am going for a stethoscope."

And he went away.

XVII

It was getting dusk. Ivan Dmitritch was lying on his bed with his face thrust into his pillow; the paralytic was sitting motionless, crying quietly and moving his lips. The fat peasant and the former sorter were asleep. It was quiet.

Andrey Yefimitch sat down on Ivan Dmitritch's bed and waited. But half an hour passed, and instead of Hobotov, Nikita came into the ward with a dressing-gown, some underlinen, and a pair of slippers in a heap on his arm.

"Please change your things, your honour," he said softly. "Here is your bed; come this way," he added, pointing to an empty bedstead which had obviously been recently brought into the ward. "It's all right; please God, you will recover."

Andrey Yefimitch understood it all. Without

saying a word he crossed to the bed to which Nikita
pointed and sat down; seeing that Nikita was standing waiting, he undressed entirely and he felt
ashamed. Then he put on the hospital clothes; the
drawers were very short, the shirt was long, and
the dressing-gown smelt of smoked fish.

" Please God, you will recover," repeated Nikita,
and he gathered up Andrey Yefimitch's clothes into
his arms, went out, and shut the door after him.

" No matter . . ." thought Andrey Yefimitch,
wrapping himself in his dressing-gown in a shamefaced way and feeling that he looked like a convict
in his new costume. " It's no matter. . . . It does
not matter whether it's a dress-coat or a uniform
or this dressing-gown. . . ."

But how about his watch? And the notebook
that was in the side-pocket? And his cigarettes?
Where had Nikita taken his clothes? Now perhaps
to the day of his death he would not put on trousers,
a waistcoat, and high boots. It was all somehow
strange and even incomprehensible at first. Andrey
Yefimitch was even now convinced that there was
no difference between his landlady's house and Ward
No. 6, that everything in this world was nonsense
and vanity of vanities. And yet his hands were
trembling, his feet were cold, and he was filled with
dread at the thought that soon Ivan Dmitritch would
get up and see that he was in a dressing-gown. He
got up and walked across the room and sat down
again.

Here he had been sitting already half an hour, an
hour, and he was miserably sick of it: was it really
possible to live here a day, a week, and even years

like these people? Why, he had been sitting here, had walked about and sat down again; he could get up and look out of window and walk from corner to corner again, and then what? Sit so all the time, like a post, and think? No, that was scarcely possible.

Andrey Yefimitch lay down, but at once got up, wiped the cold sweat from his brow with his sleeve, and felt that his whole face smelt of smoked fish. He walked about again.

" It's some misunderstanding . . ." he said, turning out the palms of his hands in perplexity. " It must be cleared up. There is a misunderstanding. . . ."

Meanwhile Ivan Dmitritch woke up; he sat up and propped his cheeks on his fists. He spat. Then he glanced lazily at the doctor, and apparently for the first minute did not understand; but soon his sleepy face grew malicious and mocking.

" Aha! so they have put you in here, too, old fellow? " he said in a voice husky from sleepiness, screwing up one eye. " Very glad to see you. You sucked the blood of others, and now they will suck yours. Excellent! "

" It's a misunderstanding . . ." Andrey Yefimitch brought out, frightened by Ivan Dmitritch's words; he shrugged his shoulders and repeated: " It's some misunderstanding. . . ."

Ivan Dmitritch spat again and lay down.

" Cursed life," he grumbled, " and what's bitter and insulting, this life will not end in compensation for our sufferings, it will not end with apotheosis as it would in an opera, but with death; peasants will come and drag one's dead body by the arms and the legs to the cellar. Ugh! Well, it does not matter. . . . We shall have our good time in the other world. . . . I shall come here as a ghost from the other world and frighten these reptiles. I'll turn their hair grey."

Moiseika returned, and, seeing the doctor, held out his hand.

"Give me one little kopeck," he said.

XVIII

Andrey Yefimitch walked away to the window and looked out into the open country. It was getting dark, and on the horizon to the right a cold crimson moon was mounting upwards. Not far from the hospital fence, not much more than two hundred yards away, stood a tall white house shut in by a stone wall. This was the prison.

"So this is real life," thought Andrey Yefimitch, and he felt frightened.

The moon and the prison, and the nails on the fence, and the far-away flames at the bone-charring factory were all terrible. Behind him there was the sound of a sigh. Andrey Yefimitch looked round and saw a man with glittering stars and orders on his breast, who was smiling and slily winking. And this, too, seemed terrible.

Andrey Yefimitch assured himself that there was nothing special about the moon or the prison, that even sane persons wear orders, and that everything in time will decay and turn to earth, but he was suddenly overcome with despair; he clutched at the grating with both hands and shook it with all his might. The strong grating did not yield.

Then that it might not be so dreadful he went to Ivan Dmitritch's bed and sat down.

" I have lost heart, my dear fellow," he muttered, trembling and wiping away the cold sweat, " I have lost heart."

"You should be philosophical," said Ivan Dmitritch ironically.

" My God, my God. . . . Yes, yes. . . . You were pleased to say once that there was no philosophy in Russia, but that all people, even the paltriest, talk philosophy. But you know the philosophizing of the paltriest does not harm anyone," said Andrey Yefimitch in a tone as if he wanted to cry and complain. " Why, then, that malignant laugh, my friend, and how can these paltry creatures help philosophizing if they are not satisfied? For an intelligent, educated man, made in God's image, proud and loving freedom, to have no alternative but to be a doctor in a filthy, stupid, wretched little town, and to spend his whole life among bottles, leeches, mustard plasters! Quackery, narrowness, vulgarity! Oh, my God! "

" You are talking nonsense. If you don't like being a doctor you should have gone in for being a statesman."

" I could not, I could not do anything. We are weak, my dear friend. . . . I used to be indifferent. I reasoned boldly and soundly, but at the first coarse touch of life upon me I have lost heart. . . . Prostration. . . . We are weak, we are poor creatures . . . and you, too, my dear friend, you are intelligent, generous, you drew in good impulses with your mother's milk, but you had hardly entered upon life when you were exhausted and fell ill. . . . Weak, weak!"

Andrey Yefimitch was all the while at the approach of evening tormented by another persistent sensation besides terror and the feeling of resentment. At last he realized that he was longing for a smoke and for beer.

"I am going out, my friend," he said. "I will tell them to bring a light; I can't put up with this. . . . I am not equal to it. . . ."

Andrey Yefimitch went to the door and opened it, but at once Nikita jumped up and barred his way.

"Where are you going? You can't, you can't!" he said. "It's bedtime."

"But I'm only going out for a minute to walk about the yard," said Andrey Yefimitch.

"You can't, you can't; it's forbidden. You know that yourself."

"But what difference will it make to anyone if I do go out?" asked Andrey Yefimitch, shrugging his shoulders. "I don't understand. Nikita, I must go out!" he said in a trembling voice. "I must."

"Don't be disorderly, it's not right," Nikita said peremptorily.

"This is beyond everything," Ivan Dmitritch cried suddenly, and he jumped up. "What right has he not to let you out? How dare they keep us here? I believe it is clearly laid down in the law that no one can be deprived of freedom without trial! It's an outrage! It's tyranny!"

"Of course it's tyranny," said Andrey Yefimitch,

encouraged by Ivan Dmitritch's outburst. " I must
go out, I want to. He has no right! Open, I tell
you."

" Do you hear, you dull-witted brute ?" cried Ivan
Dmitritch, and he banged on the door with his fist.
" Open the door, or I will break it open!
Torturer! "

" Open the door," cried Andrey Yefimitch, trembling all over; " I insist! "

" Talk away! " Nikita answered through the
door, " talk away. . . ."

" Anyhow, go and call Yevgeny Fyodoritch! Say
that I beg him to come for a minute! "

" His honour will come of himself to-morrow."

" They will never let us out," Ivan Dmitritch was
going on meanwhile. " They will leave us to rot
here! Oh, Lord, can there really be no hell in the
next world, and will these wretches be forgiven?
Where is justice? Open the door, you wretch! I
am choking! " he cried in a hoarse voice, and flung
himself upon the door. " I'll dash out my brains,
murderers! "

Nikita opened the door quickly, and roughly with
both his hands and his knee shoved Andrey Yefimitch back, then swung his arm and punched him
in the face with his fist. It seemed to Andrey
Yefimitch as though a huge salt wave enveloped him
from his head downwards and dragged him to the
bed; there really was a salt taste in his mouth: most
likely the blood was running from his teeth. He
waved his arms as though he were trying to swim out
and clutched at a bedstead, and at the same moment
felt Nikita hit him twice on the back.

Ivan Dmitritch gave a loud scream. He must have been beaten too.

Then all was still, the faint moonlight came through the grating, and a shadow like a net lay on the floor. It was terrible. Andrey Yefimitch lay and held his breath: he was expecting with horror to be struck again. He felt as though some-one had taken a sickle, thrust it into him, and turned it round several times in his breast and bowels. He bit the pillow from pain and clenched his teeth, and all at once through the chaos in his brain there flashed the terrible unbearable thought that these people, who seemed now like black shadows in the moonlight, had to endure such pain day by day for years. How could it have happened that for more than twenty years he had not known it and had re-fused to know it? He knew nothing of pain, had no conception of it, so he was not to blame, but his conscience, as inexorable and as rough as Nikita, made him turn cold from the crown of his head to his heels. He leaped up, tried to cry out with all his might, and to run in haste to kill Nikita, and then Hobotov, the superintendent and the assistant, and then himself; but no sound came from his chest, and his legs would not obey him. Gasping for breath, he tore at the dressing-gown and the shirt on his breast, rent them, and fell senseless on the bed.

XIX

Next morning his head ached, there was a droning in his ears and a feeling of utter weakness all over.

He was not ashamed at recalling his weakness the day before. He had been cowardly, had even been afraid of the moon, had openly expressed thoughts and feelings such as he had not expected in himself before; for instance, the thought that the paltry people who philosophized were really dissatisfied. But now nothing mattered to him.

He ate nothing, he drank nothing. He lay motionless and silent.

"It is all the same to me," he thought when they asked him questions. "I am not going to answer. . . . It's all the same to me."

After dinner Mihail Averyanitch brought him a quarter of a pound of tea and a pound of fruit pastilles. Daryushka came too and stood for a whole hour by the bed with an expression of dull grief on her face. Dr. Hobotov visited him. He brought a bottle of bromide and told Nikita to fumigate the ward with something.

Towards evening Andrey Yefimitch died of an apoplectic stroke. At first he had a violent shivering fit and a feeling of sickness; something revolting as it seemed, penetrating through his whole body, even to his finger-tips, strained from his stomach to his head and flooded his eyes and ears. There was a greenness before his eyes. Andrey Yefimitch understood that his end had come, and remembered that Ivan Dmitritch, Mihail Averyanitch, and millions of people believed in immortality. And what if it really existed? But he did not want immortality, and he thought of it only for one instant. A herd of deer, extraordinarily beautiful and graceful, of which he had been reading the day before, ran by him; then a peasant woman stretched out her hand to him with a registered letter. . . . Mihail Averyanitch said something, then it all vanished, and Andrey Yefimitch sank into oblivion for ever.

The hospital porters came, took him by his arms and his legs, and carried him away to the chapel.

There he lay on the table, with open eyes, and the moon shed its light upon him at night. In the morning Sergey Sergeyitch came, prayed piously before the crucifix, and closed his former chief's eyes.

Next day Andrey Yefimitch was buried. Mihail Averyanitch and Daryushka were the only people at the funeral.

1892

THE PETCHENYEG

THE PETCHENYEG

IVAN ABRAMITCH ZHMUHIN, a retired Cossack officer, who had once served in the Caucasus, but now lived on his own farm, and who had once been young, strong, and vigorous, but now was old, dried up, and bent, with shaggy eyebrows and a greenish-grey moustache, was returning from the town to his farm one hot summer's day. In the town he had confessed and received absolution, and had made his will at the notary's (a fortnight before he had had a slight stroke), and now all the while he was in the railway carriage he was haunted by melancholy, serious thoughts of approaching death, of the vanity of vanities, of the transitoriness of all things earthly. At the station of Provalye—there is such a one on the Donetz line—a fair-haired, plump, middle-aged gentleman with a shabby portfolio stepped into the carriage and sat down opposite. They got into conversation.

"Yes," said Ivan Abramitch, looking pensively out of window, "it is never too late to marry. I myself married when I was forty-eight; I was told it was late, but it has turned out that it was not late or early, but simply that it would have been better not to marry at all. Everyone is soon tired of his wife, but not everyone tells the truth, because, you know, people are ashamed of an unhappy home life and conceal it. It's 'Manya this' and 'Manya that' with many a man by his wife's side, but if he had his way he'd put that Manya in a sack and drop her in the water. It's dull with one's wife, it's mere foolishness. And it's no better with one's children, I make bold to assure you. I have two of them, the rascals. There's nowhere for them to be taught out here in the steppe; I haven't the money to send them to school in Novo Tcherkask, and they live here like young wolves. Next thing they will be murdering someone on the highroad."

The fair-haired gentleman listened attentively, answered questions briefly in a low voice, and was apparently a gentleman of gentle and modest disposition. He mentioned that he was a lawyer, and that he was going to the village Dyuevka on business.

"Why, merciful heavens, that is six miles from me!" said Zhmuhin in a tone of voice as though someone were disputing with him. "But excuse me, you won't find horses at the station now. To my mind, the very best thing you can do, you know, is to come straight to me, stay the night, you know, and in the morning drive over with my horses."

The lawyer thought a moment and accepted the invitation.

When they reached the station the sun was already low over the steppe. They said nothing all the way from the station to the farm: the jolting prevented conversation. The trap bounded up and down, squeaked, and seemed to be sobbing, and the lawyer, who was sitting very uncomfortably, stared before him, miserably hoping to see the farm. After they had driven five or six miles there came into view in the distance a low-pitched house and a yard en-

closed by a fence made of dark, flat stones standing on end; the roof was green, the stucco was
peeling off, and the windows were little narrow slits
like screwed-up eyes. The farm stood in the full
sunshine, and there was no sign either of water or
trees anywhere round. Among the neighbouring
landowners and the peasants it was known as the
Petchenyegs' farm. Many years before, a land surveyor, who was passing through the neighbourhood
and put up at the farm, spent the whole night talking
to Ivan Abramitch, was not favourably impressed,
and as he was driving away in the morning said to
him grimly:

" You are a Petchenyeg,* my good sir!"

From this came the nickname, the Petchenyegs'
farm, which stuck to the place even more when
Zhmuhin's boys grew up and began to make raids
on the orchards and kitchen-gardens. Ivan Abramitch was called " You Know," as he usually talked
a very great deal and frequently made use of that
expression.

In the yard near a barn Zhmuhin's sons were
standing, one a young man of nineteen, the other
a younger lad, both barefoot and bareheaded. Just
at the moment when the trap drove into the yard
the younger one flung high up a hen which, cackling,
described an arc in the air; the elder shot at it with
a gun and the hen fell dead on the earth.

" Those are my boys learning to shoot birds flying," said Zhmuhin.

* The Petchenyegs were a tribe of wild Mongolian nomads
who made frequent inroads upon the Russians in the tenth and
eleventh centuries.—*Translator's Note.*

In the entry the travellers were met by a little thin woman with a pale face, still young and beautiful; from her dress she might have been taken for a servant.

"And this, allow me to introduce her," said Zhmuhin, "is the mother of my young cubs. Come, Lyubov Osipovna," he said, addressing her, "you must be spry, mother, and get something for our guest. Let us have supper. Look sharp!"

The house consisted of two parts: in one was the parlour and beside it old Zhmuhin's bedroom, both stuffy rooms with low ceilings and multitudes of flies and wasps, and in the other was the kitchen in which the cooking and washing was done and the labourers had their meals; here geese and turkey-hens were sitting on their eggs under the benches, and here were the beds of Lyubov Osipovna and her two sons. The furniture in the parlour was unpainted and evidently roughly made by a carpenter; guns, game-bags, and whips were hanging on the walls, and all this old rubbish was covered with the rust of years and looked grey with dust. There was not one picture; in the corner was a dingy board which had at one time been an ikon.

A young Little Russian woman laid the table and handed ham, then beetroot soup. The visitor refused vodka and ate only bread and cucumbers.

"How about ham?" asked Zhmuhin.

"Thank you, I don't eat it," answered the visitor, "I don't eat meat at all."

"Why is that?"

"I am a vegetarian. Killing animals is against my principles."

Zhmuhin thought a minute and then said slowly with a sigh:

"Yes . . . to be sure. . . . I saw a man who did not eat meat in town, too. It's a new religion they've got now. Well, it's good. We can't go on always shooting and slaughtering, you know; we must give it up some day and leave even the beasts in peace. It's a sin to kill, it's a sin, there is no denying it. Sometimes one kills a hare and wounds him in the leg, and he cries like a child. . . . So it must hurt him!"

"Of course it hurts him; animals suffer just like human beings."

"That's true," Zhmuhin assented. "I understand that very well," he went on, musing, "only there is this one thing I don't understand: suppose, you know, everyone gave up eating meat, what would become of the domestic animals—fowls and geese, for instance?"

"Fowls and geese would live in freedom like wild birds."

"Now I understand. To be sure, crows and jackdaws get on all right without us. Yes. . . . Fowls and geese and hares and sheep, all will live in freedom, rejoicing, you know, and praising God; and they will not fear us, peace and concord will come. Only there is one thing, you know, I can't understand," Zhmuhin went on, glancing at the ham. "How will it be with the pigs? What is to be done with them?"

"They will be like all the rest—that is, they will live in freedom."

"Ah! Yes. But allow me to say, if they were

not slaughtered they would multiply, you know, and then good-bye to the kitchen-gardens and the meadows. Why, a pig, if you let it free and don't look after it, will ruin everything in a day. A pig is a pig, and it is not for nothing it is called a pig. . . ."

They finished supper. Zhmuhin got up from the table and for a long while walked up and down the room, talking and talking. . . . He was fond of talking of something important or serious and was fond of meditating, and in his old age he had a longing to reach some haven, to be reassured, that he might not be so frightened of dying. He had a longing for meekness, spiritual calm, and confidence in himself, such as this guest of theirs had, who had satisfied his hunger on cucumbers and bread, and believed that doing so made him more perfect; he was sitting on a chest, plump and healthy, keeping silent and patiently enduring his boredom, and in the dusk when one glanced at him from the entry he looked like a big round stone which one could not move from its place. If a man has something to lay hold of in life he is all right.

Zhmuhin went through the entry to the porch, and then he could be heard sighing and saying reflectively to himself: " Yes. . . . To be sure. . . ." By now it was dark, and here and there stars could be seen in the sky. They had not yet lighted up indoors. Someone came into the parlour as noiselessly as a shadow and stood still near the door. It was Lyubov Osipovna, Zhmuhin's wife.

" Are you from the town? " she asked timidly, not looking at her visitor.

" Yes, I live in the town."

" Perhaps you are something in the learned way, sir; be so kind as to advise us. We ought to send in a petition."

" To whom? " asked the visitor.

" We have two sons, kind gentleman, and they ought to have been sent to school long ago, but we never see anyone and have no one to advise us. And I know nothing. For if they are not taught they will have to serve in the army as common Cossacks. It's not right, sir! They can't read and write, they are worse than peasants, and Ivan Abramitch himself can't stand them and won't let them indoors. But they are not to blame. The younger one, at any rate, ought to be sent to school, it is such a pity! " she said slowly, and there was a quiver in her voice; and it seemed incredible that a woman so small and so youthful could have grown-up children. " Oh, it's such a pity! "

" You don't know anything about it, mother, and it is not your affair," said Zhmuhin, appearing in the doorway. " Don't pester our guest with your wild talk. Go away, mother! "

Lyubov Osipovna went out, and in the entry repeated once more in a thin little voice: " Oh, it's such a pity! "

A bed was made up for the visitor on the sofa in the parlour, and that it might not be dark for him they lighted the lamp before the ikon. Zhmuhin went to bed in his own room. And as he lay there he thought of his soul, of his age, of his recent stroke which had so frightened him and made him think of death. He was fond of philosophizing when he was in quietness by himself, and then he fancied that he was a very earnest, deep thinker, and that nothing in this world interested him but serious questions. And now he kept thinking and he longed to pitch upon some one significant thought unlike others, which would be a guide to him in life, and he wanted to think out principles of some sort for himself so as to make his life as deep and earnest as he imagined that he felt himself to be. It would be a good thing for an old man like him to abstain altogether from meat, from superfluities of all sorts. The time when men give up killing each other and animals would come sooner or later, it could not but be so, and he imagined that time to himself and clearly pictured himself living in peace with all the animals, and suddenly he thought again of the pigs, and everything was in a tangle in his brain.

" It's a queer business, Lord have mercy upon us," he muttered, sighing heavily. " Are you asleep? " he asked.

" No."

Zhmuhin got out of bed and stopped in the doorway with nothing but his shirt on, displaying to his guest his sinewy legs, that looked as dry as sticks.

" Nowadays, you know," he began, " all sorts of telegraphs, telephones, and marvels of all kinds, in fact, have come in, but people are no better than they were. They say that in our day, thirty or forty years ago, men were coarse and cruel; but isn't it just the same now? We certainly did not stand on ceremony in our day. I remember in the

Caucasus when we were stationed by a little river
with nothing to do for four whole months—I was
an under-officer at that time—something queer
happened, quite in the style of a novel. Just on the
banks of that river, you know, where our division
was encamped, a wretched prince whom we had
killed not long before was buried. And at night,
you know, the princess used to come to his grave
and weep. She would wail and wail, and moan and
moan, and make us so depressed we couldn't sleep,
and that's the fact. We couldn't sleep one night,
we couldn't sleep a second; well, we got sick of it.
And from a common-sense point of view you really
can't go without your sleep for the devil knows what
(excuse the expression). We took that princess and
gave her a good thrashing, and she gave up coming.
There's an instance for you. Nowadays, of course,
there is not the same class of people, and they are
not given to thrashing and they live in cleaner style,
and there is more learning, but, you know, the soul
is just the same: there is no change. Now, look
here, there's a landowner living here among us; he
has mines, you know; all sorts of tramps without
passports who don't know where to go work for
him. On Saturdays he has to settle up with the
workmen, but he doesn't care to pay them, you know,
he grudges the money. So he's got hold of a foreman who is a tramp too, though he does wear a hat.
'Don't you pay them anything,' he says, 'not a
kopeck; they'll beat you, and let them beat you,'
says he, 'but you put up with it, and I'll pay you
ten roubles every Saturday for it.' So on the Saturday evening the workmen come to settle up in the

usual way; the foreman says to them: ' Nothing! '
Well, word for word, as the master said, they begin
swearing and using their fists. . . . They beat him
and they kick him . . . you know, they are a set of
men brutalized by hunger—they beat him till he is
senseless, and then they go each on his way. The
master gives orders for cold water to be poured on
the foreman, then flings ten roubles in his face. And
he takes it and is pleased too, for indeed he'd be
ready to be hanged for three roubles, let alone ten.
Yes . . . and on Monday a new gang of workmen
arrive; they work, for they have nowhere to go.
. . . On Saturday it is the same story over again."

The visitor turned over on the other side with his
face to the back of the sofa and muttered something.

"And here's another instance," Zhmuhin went
on. "We had the Siberian plague here, you know
—the cattle die off like flies, I can tell you—and the
veterinary surgeons came here, and strict orders
were given that the dead cattle were to be buried
at a distance deep in the earth, that lime was to be
thrown over them, and so on, you know, on scientific
principles. My horse died too. I buried it with
every precaution, and threw over three hundred-
weight of lime over it. And what do you think?
My fine fellows—my precious sons, I mean—dug it
up, skinned it, and sold the hide for three roubles;
there's an instance for you. So people have grown
no better, and however you feed a wolf he will always look towards the forest; there it is. It gives
one something to think about, eh? How do you
look at it? "

On one side a flash of lightning gleamed through

a chink in the window-blinds. There was the stifling feeling of a storm coming, the gnats were biting, and Zhmuhin, as he lay in his bedroom meditating, sighed and groaned and said to himself: " Yes, to be sure——" and there was no possibility of getting to sleep. Somewhere far, far away there was a growl of thunder.

" Are you asleep? "

" No," answered the visitor.

Zhmuhin got up, and thudding with his heels walked through the parlour and the entry to the kitchen to get a drink of water.

" The worst thing in the world, you know, is stupidity," he said a little later, coming back with a dipper. " My Lyubov Osipovna is on her knees saying her prayers. She prays every night, you know, and bows down to the ground, first that her children may be sent to school; she is afraid her boys will go into the army as simple Cossacks, and that they will be whacked across their backs with sabres. But for teaching one must have money, and where is one to get it? You may break the floor beating your head against it, but if you haven't got it you haven't. And the other reason she prays is because, you know, every woman imagines there is no one in the world as unhappy as she is. I am a plain-spoken man, and I don't want to conceal anything from you. She comes of a poor family, a village priest's daughter. I married her when she was seventeen, and they accepted my offer chiefly because they hadn't enough to eat; it was nothing but poverty and misery, while I have anyway land, you see—a farm—and after all I am an officer; it was a step up for her to marry me, you know. On the very first day when she was married she cried, and she has been crying ever since, all these twenty years; she has got a watery eye. And she's always sitting and thinking, and what do you suppose she is thinking about? What can a woman think about? Why, nothing. I must own I don't consider a woman a human being."

The visitor got up abruptly and sat on the bed.

"Excuse me, I feel stifled," he said; "I will go outside."

Zhmuhin, still talking about women, drew the bolt in the entry and they both went out. A full moon was floating in the sky just over the yard, and in the moonlight the house and barn looked whiter than by day; and on the grass brilliant streaks of moonlight, white too, stretched between the black shadows. Far away on the right could be seen the steppe, above it the stars were softly glowing—and it was all mysterious, infinitely far away, as though one were gazing into a deep abyss; while on the left heavy storm-clouds, black as soot, were piling up one upon another above the steppe; their edges were lighted up by the moon, and it looked as though there were mountains there with white snow on their peaks, dark forests, the sea. There was a flash of lightning, a faint rumble of thunder, and it seemed as though a battle were being fought in the mountains. . . .

Quite close to the house a little night-owl screeched monotonously:

"Asleep! asleep!"

" What time is it now? " asked the visitor.

" Just after one."

" How long it is still to dawn! "

They went back to the house and lay down again. It was time to sleep, and one can usually sleep so splendidly before rain; but the old man had a hankering after serious, weighty thoughts; he wanted not simply to think but to meditate, and he meditated how good it would be, as death was near at hand, for the sake of his soul to give up the idleness which so imperceptibly swallowed up day after day, year after year, leaving no trace; to think out for himself some great exploit—for instance, to walk on foot far, far away, or to give up meat like this young man. And again he pictured to himself the time when animals would not be killed, pictured it clearly and distinctly as though he were living through that time himself; but suddenly it was all in a tangle again in his head and all was muddled.

The thunderstorm had passed over, but from the edges of the storm-clouds came rain softly pattering on the roof. Zhmuhin got up, stretching and groaning with old age, and looked into the parlour. Noticing that his visitor was not asleep, he said:

" When we were in the Caucasus, you know, there was a colonel there who was a vegetarian, too; he didn't eat meat, never went shooting, and would not let his servants catch fish. Of course, I understand that every animal ought to live in freedom and enjoy its life; only I don't understand how a pig can go about where it likes without being looked after. . . ."

The visitor got up and sat down. His pale, haggard face expressed weariness and vexation; it was evident that he was exhausted, and only his gentleness and the delicacy of his soul prevented him from expressing his vexation in words.

"It's getting light," he said mildly. "Please have the horse brought round for me."

"Why so? Wait a little and the rain will be over."

"No, I entreat you," said the visitor in horror, with a supplicating voice; "it is essential for me to go at once."

And he began hurriedly dressing.

By the time the horse was harnessed the sun was rising. It had just left off raining, the clouds were racing swiftly by, and the patches of blue were growing bigger and bigger in the sky. The first rays of the sun were timidly reflected below in the big puddles. The visitor walked through the entry with his portfolio to get into the trap, and at that moment Zhmuhin's wife, pale, and it seemed paler than the day before, with tear-stained eyes, looked at him intently without blinking, with the naïve expression of a little girl, and it was evident from her dejected face that she was envying him his freedom—oh, with what joy she would have gone away from there!—and she wanted to say something to him, most likely to ask advice about her children. And what a pitiable figure she was! This was not a wife, not the head of a house, not even a servant, but more like a dependent, a poor relation not wanted by anyone, a nonentity. . . . Her husband, fussing about, talking unceasingly, was seeing his visitor off, continually running in front of him, while she huddled up to the wall with a timid, guilty air, waiting for a convenient minute to speak.

" Please come again another time," the old man kept repeating incessantly; " what we have we are glad to offer, you know."

The visitor hurriedly got into the trap, evidently with relief, as though he were afraid every minute that they would detain him. The trap lurched about as it had the day before, squeaked, and furiously rattled the pail that was tied on at the back. He glanced round at Zhmuhin with a peculiar expression; it looked as though he wanted to call him a Petchenyeg, as the surveyor had once done, or some such name, but his gentleness got the upper hand. He controlled himself and said nothing. But in the gateway he suddenly could not restrain himself; he got up and shouted loudly and angrily: " You have bored me to death."

And he disappeared through the gate.

Near the barn Zhmuhin's sons were standing; the elder held a gun, while the younger had in his hands a grey cockerel with a bright red comb. The younger flung up the cockerel with all his might; the bird flew upwards higher than the house and turned over in the air like a pigeon. The elder boy fired and the cockerel fell like a stone.

The old man, overcome with confusion, not knowing how to explain the visitor's strange, unexpected shout, went slowly back into the house. And sitting down at the table he spent a long while meditating on the intellectual tendencies of the day, on the universal immorality, on the telegraph, on the telephone, on velocipedes, on how unnecessary it all was; little by little he regained his composure, then slowly had a meal, drank five glasses of tea, and lay down for a nap.

1897

A DEAD BODY

A DEAD BODY

A STILL August night. A mist is rising slowly from the fields and casting an opaque veil over everything within eyesight. Lighted up by the moon, the mist gives the impression at one moment of a calm, boundless sea, at the next of an immense white wall. The air is damp and chilly. Morning is still far off. A step from the bye-road which runs along the edge of the forest a little fire is gleaming. A dead body, covered from head to foot with new white linen, is lying under a young oak-tree. A wooden ikon is lying on its breast. Beside the corpse almost on the road sits the "watch"—two peasants performing one of the most disagreeable and uninviting of peasants' duties. One, a tall young fellow with a scarcely perceptible moustache and thick black eyebrows, in a tattered sheepskin and bark shoes, is sitting on the wet grass, his feet stuck out straight in front of him, and is trying to while away the time with work. He bends his long neck, and breathing loudly through his nose, makes a spoon out of a big crooked bit of wood; the other—a little scraggy, pock-marked peasant with an aged face, a scanty moustache, and a little goat's beard—sits with his hands dangling loose on his knees, and without moving gazes listlessly at the light. A small camp-fire is lazily burning down between them, throwing a red glow on their faces. There is perfect stillness. The only sounds are the scrape of the knife on the wood and the crackling of damp sticks in the fire.

" Don't you go to sleep, Syoma . . ." says the young man.

" I . . . I am not asleep . . ." stammers the goat-beard.

" That's all right. . . . It would be dreadful to sit here alone, one would be frightened. You might tell me something, Syoma."

" I . . . I can't. . . ."

" You are a queer fellow, Syomushka! Other people will laugh and tell a story and sing a song, but you—there is no making you out. You sit like a scarecrow in the garden and roll your eyes at the fire. You can't say anything properly . . . when you speak you seem frightened. I dare say you are fifty, but you have less sense than a child. . . . Aren't you sorry that you are a simpleton?"

" I am sorry," the goat-beard answers gloomily.

" And we are sorry to see your foolishness, you may be sure. You are a good-natured, sober peasant, and the only trouble is that you have no sense in your head. You should have picked up some sense for yourself if the Lord has afflicted you and given you no understanding. You must make an effort, Syoma. . . . You should listen hard when anything good's being said, note it well, and keep thinking and thinking. . . . If there is any word you don't understand, you should make an effort and think over in your head in what meaning the word is used. Do you see? Make an effort! If you don't gain some sense for yourself you'll be a simpleton and of no account at all to your dying day."

All at once a long drawn-out, moaning sound is heard in the forest. Something rustles in the leaves as though torn from the very top of the tree and falls to the ground. All this is faintly repeated by the echo. The young man shudders and looks enquiringly at his companion.

"It's an owl at the little birds," says Syoma, gloomily.

"Why, Syoma, it's time for the birds to fly to the warm countries!"

"To be sure, it is time."

"It is chilly at dawn now. It is co-old. The crane is a chilly creature, it is tender. Such cold is death to it. I am not a crane, but I am frozen. . . . Put some more wood on!"

Syoma gets up and disappears in the dark undergrowth. While he is busy among the bushes, breaking dry twigs, his companion puts his hand over his eyes and starts at every sound. Syoma brings an armful of wood and lays it on the fire. The flame irresolutely licks the black twigs with its little tongues, then suddenly, as though at the word of command, catches them and throws a crimson light on the faces, the road, the white linen with its prominences where the hands and feet of the corpse raise it, the ikon. The "watch" is silent. The young man bends his neck still lower and sets to work with still more nervous haste. The goat-beard sits motionless as before and keeps his eyes fixed on the fire. . . .

"Ye that love not Zion . . . shall be put to shame by the Lord." A falsetto voice is suddenly heard singing in the stillness of the night, then slow footsteps are audible, and the dark figure of a man in a short monkish cassock and a broad-brimmed hat, with a wallet on his shoulders, comes into sight on the road in the crimson firelight.

"Thy will be done, O Lord! Holy Mother!" the figure says in a husky falsetto. "I saw the fire in the outer darkness and my soul leapt for joy. . . . At first I thought it was men grazing a drove of horses, then I thought it can't be that, since no horses were to be seen. 'Aren't they thieves,' I wondered, 'aren't they robbers lying in wait for a rich Lazarus? Aren't they the gypsy people offering sacrifices to idols? And my soul leapt for joy. 'Go, Feodosy, servant of God,' I said to myself, 'and win a martyr's crown!' And I flew to the fire like a light-winged moth. Now I stand before you, and from your outer aspect I judge of your souls: you are not thieves and you are not heathens. Peace be to you!"

"Good-evening."

"Good orthodox people, do you know how to reach the Makuhinsky Brickyards from here?"

"It's close here. You go straight along the road; when you have gone a mile and a half there will be Ananova, our village. From the village, father, you turn to the right by the river-bank, and so you will get to the brickyards. It's two miles from Ananova."

"God give you health. And why are you sitting here?"

"We are sitting here watching. You see, there is a dead body. . . ."

"What? what body? Holy Mother!"

The pilgrim sees the white linen with the ikon on it, and starts so violently that his legs give a little skip. This unexpected sight has an overpowering effect upon him. He huddles together and stands as though rooted to the spot, with wide-open mouth and staring eyes. For three minutes he is silent as though he could not believe his eyes, then begins muttering:

"O Lord! Holy Mother! I was going along not meddling with anyone, and all at once such an affliction."

"What may you be?" enquires the young man. "Of the clergy?"

"No . . . no. . . . I go from one monastery to another. . . . Do you know Mi . . . Mihail Polikarpitch, the foreman of the brickyard? Well, I am his nephew. . . . Thy will be done, O Lord! Why are you here?"

"We are watching . . . we are told to."

"Yes, yes . . ." mutters the man in the cassock, passing his hand over his eyes. "And where did the deceased come from?"

"He was a stranger."

"Such is life! But I'll . . . er . . . be getting on, brothers. . . . I feel flustered. I am more afraid of the dead than of anything, my dear souls! And only fancy! while this man was alive he wasn't noticed, while now when he is dead and given over to corruption we tremble before him as before some famous general or a bishop. . . . Such is life; was he murdered, or what?"

"The Lord knows! Maybe he was murdered, or maybe he died of himself."

"Yes, yes. . . . Who knows, brothers? Maybe his soul is now tasting the joys of Paradise."

"His soul is still hovering here, near his body," says the young man. "It does not depart from the body for three days."

"H'm, yes! . . . How chilly the nights are now! It sets one's teeth chattering. . . . So then I am to go straight on and on? . . ."

"Till you get to the village, and then you turn to the right by the river-bank."

"By the river-bank. . . . To be sure. . . . Why am I standing still? I must go on. Farewell, brothers."

The man in the cassock takes five steps along the road and stops.

"I've forgotten to put a kopeck for the burying," he says. "Good orthodox friends, can I give the money?"

"You ought to know best, you go the round of the monasteries. If he died a natural death it would go for the good of his soul; if it's a suicide it's a sin."

"That's true. . . . And maybe it really was a suicide! So I had better keep my money. Oh, sins, sins! Give me a thousand roubles and I would not consent to sit here. . . . Farewell, brothers."

The cassock slowly moves away and stops again.

"I can't make up my mind what I am to do," he mutters. "To stay here by the fire and wait till daybreak. . . . I am frightened; to go on is dreadful, too. The dead man will haunt me all the way in the darkness. . . . The Lord has chastised me indeed! Over three hundred miles I have come on foot and nothing happened, and now I am near home and there's trouble. I can't go on. . . ."

" It is dreadful, that is true."

" I am not afraid of wolves, of thieves, or of darkness, but I am afraid of the dead. I am afraid of them, and that is all about it. Good orthodox brothers, I entreat you on my knees, see me to the village."

" We've been told not to go away from the body."

"No one will see, brothers. Upon my soul, no one will see! The Lord will reward you a hundred-fold! Old man, come with me, I beg! Old man! Why are you silent? "

" He is a bit simple," says the young man.

" You come with me, friend; I will give you five kopecks."

" For five kopecks I might," says the young man, scratching his head, " but I was told not to. If Syoma here, our simpleton, will stay alone, I will take you. Syoma, will you stay here alone? "

" I'll stay," the simpleton consents.

" Well, that's all right, then. Come along! "

The young man gets up, and goes with the cassock. A minute later the sound of their steps and their talk dies away. Syoma shuts his eyes and gently dozes. The fire begins to grow dim, and a big black shadow falls on the dead body.

1885

A HAPPY ENDING

A HAPPY ENDING

LYUBOV GRIGORYEVNA, a substantial, buxom lady of forty who undertook matchmaking and many other matters of which it is usual to speak only in whispers, had come to see Stytchkin, the head guard, on a day when he was off duty. Stytchkin, somewhat embarrassed, but, as always, grave, practical, and severe, was walking up and down the room, smoking a cigar and saying:

"Very pleased to make your acquaintance. Semyon Ivanovitch recommended you on the ground that you may be able to assist me in a delicate and very important matter affecting the happiness of my life. I have, Lyubov Grigoryevna, reached the age of fifty-two; that is a period of life at which very many have already grown-up children. My position is a secure one. Though my fortune is not large, yet I am in a position to support a beloved being and children at my side. I may tell you between ourselves that apart from my salary I have also money in the bank which my manner of living has enabled me to save. I am a practical and sober man, I lead a sensible and consistent life, so that I may hold myself up as an example to many. But one thing I lack—a domestic hearth of my own and a partner in life, and I live like a wandering Magyar, moving from place to place without any satisfaction. I have no one with whom to take counsel, and when

I am ill no one to give me water, and so on. Apart from that, Lyubov Grigoryevna, a married man has always more weight in society than a bachelor. . . . I am a man of the educated class, with money, but if you look at me from a point of view, what am I? A man with no kith and kin, no better than some Polish priest. And therefore I should be very desirous to be united in the bonds of Hymen—that is, to enter into matrimony with some worthy person."

" An excellent thing," said the matchmaker, with a sigh.

" I am a solitary man and in this town I know no one. Where can I go, and to whom can I apply, since all the people here are strangers to me? That is why Semyon Ivanovitch advised me to address myself to a person who is a specialist in this line, and makes the arrangement of the happiness of others her profession. And therefore I most earnestly beg you, Lyubov Grigoryevna, to assist me in ordering my future. You know all the marriageable young ladies in the town, and it is easy for you to accommodate me."

" I can. . . ."

" A glass of wine, I beg you. . . ."

With an habitual gesture the matchmaker raised her glass to her mouth and tossed it off without winking.

" I can," she repeated. " And what sort of bride would you like, Nikolay Nikolayitch? "

" Should I like? The bride fate sends me."

" Well, of course it depends on your fate, but everyone has his own taste, you know. One likes dark ladies, the other prefers fair ones."

" You see, Lyubov Grigoryevna," said Stytchkin, sighing sedately, " I am a practical man and a man of character; for me beauty and external appearance generally take a secondary place, for, as you know yourself, beauty is neither bowl nor platter, and a pretty wife involves a great deal of anxiety. The way I look at it is, what matters most in a woman is not what is external, but what lies within—that is, that she should have soul and all the qualities. A glass of wine, I beg. . . . Of course, it would be very agreeable that one's wife should be rather plump, but for mutual happiness it is not of great consequence; what matters is the mind. Properly speaking, a woman does not need mind either, for if she has brains she will have too high an opinion of herself, and take all sorts of ideas into her head. One cannot do without education nowadays, of course, but education is of different kinds. It would be pleasing for one's wife to know French and German, to speak various languages, very pleasing; but what's the use of that if she can't sew on one's buttons, perhaps? I am a man of the educated class; I am just as much at home, I may say, with Prince Kanitelin as I am with you here now. But my habits are simple, and I want a girl who is not too much a fine lady. Above all, she must have respect for me and feel that I have made her happiness."

"To be sure."

"Well, now as regards the essential. . . . I do not want a wealthy bride; I would never condescend to anything so low as to marry for money. I desire not to be kept by my wife, but to keep her, and that she may be sensible of it.   But I do not want a poor girl either.   Though I am a man of means, and am marrying not from mercenary motives, but from love, yet I cannot take a poor girl, for, as you know yourself, prices have gone up so, and there will be children."

" One might find one with a dowry," said the matchmaker.

" A glass of wine, I beg. . . ."

There was a pause of five minutes.

The matchmaker heaved a sigh, took a sidelong glance at the guard, and asked:

"Well, now, my good sir . . . do you want anything in the bachelor line?   I have some fine bargains.   One is a French girl and one is a Greek. Well worth the money."

The guard thought a moment and said:

" No, I thank you.   In view of your favourable disposition, allow me to enquire now how much you ask for your exertions in regard to a bride? "

" I don't ask much.   Give me twenty-five roubles and the stuff for a dress, as is usual, and I will say thank you . . . but for the dowry, that's a different account."

Stytchkin folded his arms over his chest and fell to pondering in silence.   After some thought he heaved a sigh and said:

" That's dear. . . ."

" It's not at all dear, Nikolay Nikolayitch!   In old days when there were lots of weddings one did do it cheaper, but nowadays what are our earnings? If you make fifty roubles in a month that is not a fast, you may be thankful. It's not on weddings we make our money, my good sir."

Stytchkin looked at the matchmaker in amazement and shrugged his shoulders.

" H'm! . . . Do you call fifty roubles little? " he asked.

" Of course it is little! In old days we sometimes made more than a hundred."

" H'm! I should never have thought it was possible to earn such a sum by these jobs. Fifty roubles! It is not every man that earns as much! Pray drink your wine. . . ."

The matchmaker drained her glass without winking. Stytchkin looked her over from head to foot in silence, then said:

" Fifty roubles. . . . Why, that is six hundred roubles a year. . . . Please take some more. . . . With such dividends, you know, Lyubov Grigoryevna, you would have no difficulty in making a match for yourself. . . ."

" For myself," laughed the matchmaker, " I am an old woman."

" Not at all. . . . You have such a figure, and your face is plump and fair, and all the rest of it."

The matchmaker was embarrassed. Stytchkin was also embarrassed and sat down beside her.

" You are still very attractive," said he; " if you met with a practical, steady, careful husband, with his salary and your earnings you might even attract him very much, and you'd get on very well together. . . ."

" Goodness knows what you are saying, Nikolay Nikolayitch."

" Well, I meant no harm. . . ."

A silence followed. Stytchkin began loudly blowing his nose, while the matchmaker turned crimson, and looking bashfully at him, asked:

" And how much do you get, Nikolay Nikolayitch?"

" I?   Seventy-five roubles, besides tips. . . . Apart from that we make something out of candles and hares."

" You go hunting, then? "

" No.   Passengers who travel without tickets are called hares with us."

Another minute passed in silence. Stytchkin got up and walked about the room in excitement.

" I don't want a young wife," said he. " I am a middle-aged man, and I want someone who . . . as it might be like you . . . staid and settled . . . and a figure something like yours. . . ."

" Goodness knows what you are saying . . ." giggled the matchmaker, hiding her crimson face in her kerchief.

" There is no need to be long thinking about it. You are after my own heart, and you suit me in your qualities. I am a practical, sober man, and if you like me . . . what could be better? Allow me to make you a proposal! "

The matchmaker dropped a tear, laughed, and, in token of her consent, clinked glasses with Stytchkin.

" Well," said the happy railway guard, " now allow me to explain to you the behaviour and manner of life I desire from you. . . . I am a strict, respectable, practical man. I take a gentlemanly view of everything. And I desire that my wife should be strict also, and should understand that to her I am a benefactor and the foremost person in the world."

He sat down, and, heaving a deep sigh, began expounding to his bride-elect his views on domestic life and a wife's duties.

1887

THE LOOKING-GLASS

THE LOOKING-GLASS

New Year's Eve. Nellie, the daughter of a land-owner and general, a young and pretty girl, dreaming day and night of being married, was sitting in her room, gazing with exhausted, half-closed eyes into the looking-glass. She was pale, tense, and as motionless as the looking-glass.

The non-existent but apparent vista of a long, narrow corridor with endless rows of candles, the reflection of her face, her hands, of the frame—all this was already clouded in mist and merged into a boundless grey sea. The sea was undulating, gleaming and now and then flaring crimson. . . .

Looking at Nellie's motionless eyes and parted lips, one could hardly say whether she was asleep or awake, but nevertheless she was seeing. At first she saw only the smile and soft, charming expression of someone's eyes, then against the shifting grey background there gradually appeared the outlines of a head, a face, eyebrows, beard. It was he, the destined one, the object of long dreams and hopes. The destined one was for Nellie everything, the significance of life, personal happiness, career, fate. Outside him, as on the grey background of the looking-glass, all was dark, empty, meaningless. And so it was not strange that, seeing before her a handsome, gently smiling face, she was conscious of bliss, of an unutterably sweet dream that could not

151

be expressed in speech or on paper. Then she heard his voice, saw herself living under the same roof with him, her life merged into his. Months and years flew by against the grey background. And Nellie saw her future distinctly in all its details.

Picture followed picture against the grey background. Now Nellie saw herself one winter night knocking at the door of Stepan Lukitch, the district doctor. The old dog hoarsely and lazily barked behind the gate. The doctor's windows were in darkness. All was silence.

"For God's sake, for God's sake!" whispered Nellie.

But at last the garden gate creaked and Nellie saw the doctor's cook.

"Is the doctor at home?"

"His honour's asleep," whispered the cook into her sleeve, as though afraid of waking her master. "He's only just got home from his fever patients, and gave orders he was not to be waked."

But Nellie scarcely heard the cook. Thrusting her aside, she rushed headlong into the doctor's house. Running through some dark and stuffy rooms, upsetting two or three chairs, she at last reached the doctor's bedroom. Stepan Lukitch was lying on his bed, dressed, but without his coat, and with pouting lips was breathing into his open hand. A little night-light glimmered faintly beside him. Without uttering a word Nellie sat down and began to cry. She wept bitterly, shaking all over.

"My husband is ill!" she sobbed out. Stepan Lukitch was silent. He slowly sat up, propped his head on his hand, and looked at his visitor with fixed, sleepy eyes. " My husband is ill ! " Nellie continued, restraining her sobs. " For mercy's sake come quickly. Make haste. . . . Make haste ! "

" Eh ? " growled the doctor, blowing into his hand.

" Come ! Come this very minute ! Or . . . it's terrible to think ! For mercy's sake ! "

And pale, exhausted Nellie, gasping and swallowing her tears, began describing to the doctor her husband's illness, her unutterable terror. Her sufferings would have touched the heart of a stone, but the doctor looked at her, blew into his open hand, and—not a movement.

" I'll come to-morrow ! " he muttered.

" That's impossible ! " cried Nellie. " I know my husband has typhus ! At once . . . this very minute you are needed ! "

" I . . . er . . . have only just come in," muttered the doctor. " For the last three days I've been away, seeing typhus patients, and I'm exhausted and ill myself. . . . I simply can't ! Absolutely ! I've caught it myself ! There ! "

And the doctor thrust before her eyes a clinical thermometer.

" My temperature is nearly forty. . . . I absolutely can't. I can scarcely sit up. Excuse me. I'll lie down. . . ."

The doctor lay down.

" But I implore you, doctor," Nellie moaned in despair. " I beseech you ! Help me, for mercy's sake ! Make a great effort and come ! I will repay you, doctor ! "

" Oh, dear! . . . Why, I have told you already. Ah ! "

Nellie leapt up and walked nervously up and down the bedroom. She longed to explain to the doctor, to bring him to reason. . . . She thought if only he knew how dear her husband was to her and how unhappy she was, he would forget his exhaustion and his illness. But how could she be eloquent enough ?

" Go to the Zemstvo doctor," she heard Stepan Lukitch's voice.

" That's impossible ! He lives more than twenty miles from here, and time is precious. And the horses can't stand it. It is thirty miles from us to you, and as much from here to the Zemstvo doctor. No, it's impossible ! Come along, Stepan Lukitch. I ask of you an heroic deed. Come, perform that heroic deed ! Have pity on us ! "

" It's beyond everything. . . . I'm in a fever . . . my head's in a whirl . . . and she won't understand ! Leave me alone ! "

" But you are in duty bound to come ! You cannot refuse to come ! It's egoism ! A man is bound to sacrifice his life for his neighbour, and you . . . you refuse to come ! I will summon you before the Court."

Nellie felt that she was uttering a false and undeserved insult, but for her husband's sake she was capable of forgetting logic, tact, sympathy for others. . . . In reply to her threats, the doctor greedily gulped a glass of cold water. Nellie fell to entreating and imploring like the very lowest beggar. . . . At last the doctor gave way. He slowly got up, puffing and panting, looking for his coat.

"Here it is!" cried Nellie, helping him. "Let me put it on to you. Come along! I will repay you. . . . All my life I shall be grateful to you. . . ."

But what agony! After putting on his coat the doctor lay down again. Nellie got him up and dragged him to the hall. Then there was an agonizing to-do over his goloshes, his overcoat. . . . His cap was lost. . . . But at last Nellie was in the carriage with the doctor. Now they had only to drive thirty miles and her husband would have a doctor's help. The earth was wrapped in darkness. One could not see one's hand before one's face. . . . A cold winter wind was blowing. There were frozen lumps under their wheels. The coachman was continually stopping and wondering which road to take.

Nellie and the doctor sat silent all the way. It was fearfully jolting, but they felt neither the cold nor the jolts.

"Get on, get on!" Nellie implored the driver.

At five in the morning the exhausted horses drove into the yard. Nellie saw the familiar gates, the well with the crane, the long row of stables and barns. At last she was at home.

"Wait a moment, I will be back directly," she said to Stepan Lukitch, making him sit down on the sofa in the dining-room. "Sit still and wait a little, and I'll see how he is going on."

On her return from her husband, Nellie found the doctor lying down. He was lying on the sofa and muttering.

" Doctor, please ! . . . doctor ! "

" Eh ? Ask Domna ! " muttered Stepan Lukitch.

" What ? "

" They said at the meeting . . . Vlassov said
. . . Who ? . . . what ? "

And to her horror Nellie saw that the doctor was
as delirious as her husband. What was to be done ?

" I must go for the Zemstvo doctor," she decided.

Then again there followed darkness, a cutting
cold wind, lumps of frozen earth. She was suffering in body and in soul, and delusive nature has
no arts, no deceptions to compensate these sufferings. . . .

Then she saw against the grey background how
her husband every spring was in straits for money
to pay the interest for the mortgage to the bank.
He could not sleep, she could not sleep, and both
racked their brains till their heads ached, thinking
how to avoid being visited by the clerk of the Court.

She saw her children : the everlasting apprehen-
sion of colds, scarlet fever, diphtheria, bad marks at
school, separation. Out of a brood of five or six
one was sure to die.

The grey background was not untouched by death.
That might well be. A husband and wife cannot
die simultaneously. Whatever happened one must
bury the other. And Nellie saw her husband dying.
This terrible event presented itself to her in every
detail. She saw the coffin, the candles, the deacon,
and even the footmarks in the hall made by the
undertaker.

" Why is it, what is it for ? " she asked, looking
blankly at her husband's face.

And all the previous life with her husband seemed to her a stupid prelude to this.

Something fell from Nellie's hand and knocked on the floor. She started, jumped up, and opened her eyes wide. One looking-glass she saw lying at her feet. The other was standing as before on the table.

She looked into the looking-glass and saw a pale, tear-stained face. There was no grey background now.

"I must have fallen asleep," she thought with a sigh of relief.

1885

OLD AGE

OLD AGE

UZELKOV, an architect with the rank of civil councillor, arrived in his native town, to which he had been invited to restore the church in the cemetery. He had been born in the town, had been at school, had grown up and married in it. But when he got out of the train he scarcely recognized it. Everything was changed. . . . Eighteen years ago when he had moved to Petersburg the street-boys used to catch marmots, for instance, on the spot where now the station was standing; now when one drove into the chief street, a hotel of four storeys stood facing one; in old days there was an ugly grey fence just there; but nothing—neither fences nor houses—had changed as much as the people. From his enquiries of the hotel waiter Uzelkov learned that more than half of the people he remembered were dead, reduced to poverty, forgotten.

" And do you remember Uzelkov? " he asked the old waiter about himself. " Uzelkov the architect who divorced his wife? He used to have a house in Svirebeyevsky Street . . . you must remember."

" I don't remember, sir."

" How is it you don't remember? The case made a lot of noise, even the cabmen all knew about it. Think, now! Shapkin the attorney managed my divorce for me, the rascal . . . the notorious cardsharper, the fellow who got a thrashing at the club. . . .

" Ivan Nikolaitch ? "

" Yes, yes. . . . Well, is he alive ? Is he dead ? "

" Alive, sir, thank God. He is a notary now and has an office. He is very well off. He has two houses in Kirpitchny Street. . . . His daughter was married the other day. . . ."

Uzelkov paced up and down the room, thought a bit, and in his boredom made up his mind to go and see Shapkin at his office. When he walked out of the hotel and sauntered slowly towards Kirpitchny Street it was midday. He found Shapkin at his office and scarcely recognized him. From the once well-made, adroit attorney with a mobile, insolent, and always drunken face Shapkin had changed into a modest, grey-headed, decrepit old man.

" You don't recognize me, you have forgotten me," began Uzelkov. " I am your old client, Uzelkov."

" Uzelkov, what Uzelkov? Ah ! " Shapkin remembered, recognized, and was struck all of a heap. There followed a shower of exclamations, questions, recollections.

" This is a surprise ! This is unexpected ! " cackled Shapkin. " What can I offer you? Do you care for champagne? Perhaps you would like oysters? My dear fellow, I have had so much from you in my time that I can't offer you anything equal to the occasion. . . ."

" Please don't put yourself out . . ." said Uzelkov. " I have no time to spare. I must go at once to the cemetery and examine the church; I have undertaken the restoration of it."

" That's capital ! We'll have a snack and a drink

and drive together. I have capital horses. I'll take
you there and introduce you to the church-warden;
I will arrange it all. . . . But why is it, my angel,
you seem to be afraid of me and hold me at arm's
length? Sit a little nearer! There is no need for
you to be afraid of me nowadays. He-he! . . . At
one time, it is true, I was a cunning blade, a dog of
a fellow . . . no one dared approach me; but now
I am stiller than water and humbler than the grass.
I have grown old, I am a family man, I have children. It's time I was dead."

The friends had lunch, had a drink, and with
a pair of horses drove out of the town to the
cemetery.

"Yes, those were times!" Shapkin recalled as he
sat in the sledge. "When you remember them you
simply can't believe in them. Do you remember how
you divorced your wife? It's nearly twenty years
ago, and I dare say you have forgotten it all; but
I remember it as though I'd divorced you yesterday.
Good Lord, what a lot of worry I had over it! I
was a sharp fellow, tricky and cunning, a desperate
character. . . . Sometimes I was burning to tackle
some ticklish business, especially if the fee were a
good one, as, for instance, in your case. What did
you pay me then? Five or six thousand! That was
worth taking trouble for, wasn't it? You went off
to Petersburg and left the whole thing in my hands
to do the best I could, and, though Sofya Mihailovna, your wife, came only of a merchant family,
she was proud and dignified. To bribe her to take
the guilt on herself was difficult, awfully difficult!
I would go to negotiate with her, and as soon as she

saw me she called to her maid: 'Masha, didn't I tell you not to admit that scoundrel?' Well, I tried one thing and another. . . . I wrote her letters and contrived to meet her accidentally—it was no use! I had to act through a third person. I had a lot of trouble with her for a long time, and she only gave in when you agreed to give her ten thousand. . . . She couldn't resist ten thousand, she couldn't hold out. . . . She cried, she spat in my face, but she consented, she took the guilt on herself!"

"I thought it was fifteen thousand she had from me, not ten," said Uzelkov.

"Yes, yes . . . fifteen—I made a mistake," said Shapkin in confusion. "It's all over and done with, though, it's no use concealing it. I gave her ten and the other five I collared for myself. I deceived you both. . . . It's all over and done with, it's no use to be ashamed. And indeed, judge for yourself, Boris Petrovitch, weren't you the very person for me to get money out of? . . . You were a wealthy man and had everything you wanted. . . . Your marriage was an idle whim, and so was your divorce. You were making a lot of money. . . . I remember you made a scoop of twenty thousand over one contract. Whom should I have fleeced if not you? And I must own I envied you. If you grabbed anything they took off their caps to you, while they would thrash me for a rouble and slap me in the face at the club. . . . But there, why recall it? It is high time to forget it."

"Tell me, please, how did Sofya Mihailovna get on afterwards?"

"With her ten thousand? Very badly. God

knows what it was—she lost her head, perhaps, or maybe her pride and her conscience tormented her at having sold her honour, or perhaps she loved you; but, do you know, she took to drink. . . . As soon as she got her money she was off driving about with officers. It was drunkenness, dissipation, debauchery. . . . When she went to a restaurant with officers she was not content with port or anything light, she must have strong brandy, fiery stuff to stupefy her."

"Yes, she was eccentric. . . . I had a lot to put up with from her . . . sometimes she would take offence at something and begin being hysterical. . . . And what happened afterwards?"

"One week passed and then another. . . . I was sitting at home, writing something. All at once the door opened and she walked in . . . drunk. 'Take back your cursed money,' she said, and flung a roll of notes in my face. . . . So she could not keep it up. I picked up the notes and counted them. It was five hundred short of the ten thousand, so she had only managed to get through five hundred."

"Where did you put the money?"

"It's all ancient history . . . there's no reason to conceal it now. . . . In my pocket, of course. Why do you look at me like that? Wait a bit for what will come later. . . . It's a regular novel, a pathological study. A couple of months later I was going home one night in a nasty drunken condition. . . . I lighted a candle, and lo and behold! Sofya Mihailovna was sitting on my sofa, and she was drunk, too, and in a frantic state—as wild as though she had run out of Bedlam. 'Give

me back my money,' she said, ' I have changed my
mind; if I must go to ruin I won't do it by halves,
I'll have my fling! Be quick, you scoundrel, give me
my money!' A disgraceful scene!"

"And you . . . gave it her?"

"I gave her, I remember, ten roubles."

"Oh! How could you?" cried Uzelkov, frowning. "If you couldn't or wouldn't have given it
her, you might have written to me. . . . And I
didn't know! I didn't know!"

"My dear fellow, what use would it have been for
me to write, considering that she wrote to you herself
when she was lying in the hospital afterwards?"

"Yes, but I was so taken up then with my second
marriage. I was in such a whirl that I had no
thoughts to spare for letters. . . . But you were
an outsider, you had no antipathy for Sofya . . .
why didn't you give her a helping hand? . . ."

"You can't judge by the standards of to-day,
Boris Petrovitch; that's how we look at it now, but
at the time we thought very differently. . . . Now
maybe I'd give her a thousand roubles, but then even
that ten-rouble note I did not give her for nothing.
It was a bad business! . . . We must forget it.
. . . But here we are. . . ."

The sledge stopped at the cemetery gates. Uzelkov and Shapkin got out of the sledge, went in at
the gate, and walked up a long, broad avenue. The
bare cherry-trees and acacias, the grey crosses and
tombstones, were silvered with hoar-frost, every
little grain of snow reflected the bright, sunny day.
There was the smell there always is in cemeteries,
the smell of incense and freshly dug earth. . . .

" Our cemetery is a pretty one," said Uzelkov,
" quite a garden ! "

" Yes, but it is a pity thieves steal the tombstones.
. . . And over there, beyond that iron monument
on the right, Sofya Mihailovna is buried. Would
you like to see ? "

The friends turned to the right and walked
through the deep snow to the iron monument.

" Here it is," said Shapkin, pointing to a little
slab of white marble. " A lieutenant put the stone
on her grave."

Uzelkov slowly took off his cap and exposed his
bald head to the sun. Shapkin, looking at him, took
off his cap too, and another bald patch gleamed in
the sunlight. There was the stillness of the tomb
all around as though the air, too, were dead. The
friends looked at the grave, pondered, and said
nothing.

" She sleeps in peace," said Shapkin, breaking the
silence. " It's nothing to her now that she took the
blame on herself and drank brandy. You must
own, Boris Petrovitch . . ."

" Own what ?" Uzelkov asked gloomily.

" Why. . . . However hateful the past, it was
better than this."

And Shapkin pointed to his grey head.

" I used not to think of the hour of death. . . .
I fancied I could have given death points and won
the game if we had had an encounter; but now. . . .
But what's the good of talking ! "

Uzelkov was overcome with melancholy. He
suddenly had a passionate longing to weep, as once
he had longed for love, and he felt those tears would

have tasted sweet and refreshing. A moisture came into his eyes and there was a lump in his throat, but . . . Shapkin was standing beside him and Uzelkov was ashamed to show weakness before a witness. He turned back abruptly and went into the church.

Only two hours later, after talking to the church-warden and looking over the church, he seized a moment when Shapkin was in conversation with the priest and hastened away to weep. . . . He stole up to the grave secretly, furtively, looking round him every minute. The little white slab looked at him pensively, mournfully, and innocently as though a little girl lay under it instead of a dissolute, divorced wife.

" To weep, to weep! " thought Uzelkov.

But the moment for tears had been missed; though the old man blinked his eyes, though he worked up his feelings, the tears did not flow nor the lump come in his throat. After standing for ten minutes, with a gesture of despair, Uzelkov went to look for Shapkin.

1885

DARKNESS

DARKNESS

A YOUNG peasant, with white eyebrows and eye-
lashes and broad cheekbones, in a torn sheepskin
and big black felt overboots, waited till the Zemstvo
doctor had finished seeing his patients and came out
to go home from the hospital; then he went up to
him, diffidently.

" Please, your honour," he said.

" What do you want? "

The young man passed the palm of his hand up
and over his nose, looked at the sky, and then
answered:

" Please, your honour. . . . You've got my
brother Vaska the blacksmith from Varvarino in
the convict ward here, your honour. . . ."

" Yes, what then? "

" I am Vaska's brother, you see. . . . Father
has the two of us: him, Vaska, and me, Kirila; besides us there are three sisters, and Vaska's a married man with a little one. . . . There are a lot of
us and no one to work. . . . In the smithy it's
nearly two years now since the forge has been
heated. I am at the cotton factory, I can't do
smith's work, and how can father work? Let alone
work, he can't eat properly, he can't lift the spoon
to his mouth."

" What do you want from me? "

" Be merciful! Let Vaska go! "

The doctor looked wonderingly at Kirila, and without saying a word walked on. The young peasant ran on in front and flung himself in a heap at his feet.

" Doctor, kind gentleman! " he besought him, blinking and again passing his open hand over his nose. " Show heavenly mercy; let Vaska go home! We shall remember you in our prayers for ever! Your honour, let him go! They are all starving! Mother's wailing day in, day out, Vaska's wife's wailing . . . it's worse than death! I don't care to look upon the light of day. Be merciful; let him go, kind gentleman! "

" Are you stupid or out of your senses? " asked the doctor angrily. " How can I let him go? Why, he is a convict."

Kirila began crying. " Let him go! "

" Tfoo, queer fellow! What right have I? Am I a gaoler or what? They brought him to the hospital for me to treat him, but I have as much right to let him out as I have to put you in prison, silly fellow! "

" But they have shut him up for nothing! He was in prison a year before the trial, and now there is no saying what he is there for. It would have been a different thing if he had murdered someone, let us say, or stolen horses; but as it is, what is it all about? "

" Very likely, but how do I come in? "

" They shut a man up and they don't know themselves what for. He was drunk, your honour, did not know what he was doing, and even hit father on the ear and scratched his own cheek on a branch, and two of our fellows—they wanted some Turkish tobacco, you see—began telling him to go with them and break into the Armenian's shop at night for tobacco. Being drunk, he obeyed them, the fool. They broke the lock, you know, got in, and did no end of mischief; they turned everything upside down, broke the windows, and scattered the flour about. They were drunk, that is all one can say! Well, the constable turned up . . . and with one thing and another they took them off to the magistrate. They have been a whole year in prison, and a week ago, on the Wednesday, they were all three tried in the town. A soldier stood behind them with a gun . . . people were sworn in. Vaska was less to blame than any, but the gentry decided that he was the ringleader. The other two lads were sent to prison, but Vaska to a convict battalion for three years. And what for? One should judge like a Christian!"

"I have nothing to do with it, I tell you again. Go to the authorities."

"I have been already! I've been to the court; I have tried to send in a petition—they wouldn't take a petition; I have been to the police captain, and I have been to the examining magistrate, and everyone says, 'It is not my business!' Whose business is it, then? But there is no one above you here in the hospital; you do what you like, your honour."

"You simpleton," sighed the doctor, " once the jury have found him guilty, not the governor, not even the minister, could do anything, let alone the police captain. It's no good your trying to do anything!"

"And who judged him, then?"

"The gentlemen of the jury. . . ."

"They weren't gentlemen, they were our peasants! Andrey Guryev was one; Aloshka Huk was one."

"Well, I am cold talking to you. . . ."

The doctor waved his hand and walked quickly to his own door. Kirila was on the point of following him, but, seeing the door slam, he stopped.

For ten minutes he stood motionless in the middle of the hospital yard, and without putting on his cap stared at the doctor's house, then he heaved a deep sigh, slowly scratched himself, and walked towards the gate.

"To whom am I to go?" he muttered as he came out on to the road. "One says it is not his business, another says it is not his business. Whose business is it, then? No, till you grease their hands you will get nothing out of them. The doctor says that, but he keeps looking all the while at my fist to see whether I am going to give him a blue note. Well, brother, I'll go, if it has to be to the governor."

Shifting from one foot to the other and continually looking round him in an objectless way, he trudged lazily along the road and was apparently wondering where to go. . . . It was not cold and the snow faintly crunched under his feet. Not more than half a mile in front of him the wretched little district town in which his brother had just been tried lay outstretched on the hill. On the right was the dark prison with its red roof and sentry-boxes at the corners; on the left was the big town copse, now **covered with** hoar-frost. It was still; only an old man, wearing a woman's short jacket and a huge cap, was walking ahead, coughing and shouting to a cow which he was driving to the town.

"Good-day, grandfather," said Kirila, overtaking him.

"Good-day. . . ."

"Are you driving it to the market?"

"No," the old man answered lazily.

"Are you a townsman?"

They got into conversation; Kirila told him what he had come to the hospital for, and what he had been talking about to the doctor.

"The doctor does not know anything about such matters, that is a sure thing," the old man said to him as they were both entering the town; "though he is a gentleman, he is only taught to cure by every means, but to give you real advice, or, let us say, write out a petition for you—that he cannot do. There are special authorities to do that. You have been to the justice of the peace and to the police captain—they are no good for your business either."

"Where am I to go?"

"The permanent member of the rural board is the chief person for peasants' affairs. Go to him, Mr. Sineokov."

"The one who is at Zolotovo?"

"Why, yes, at Zolotovo. He is your chief man. If it is anything that has to do with you peasants even the police captain has no authority against him."

"It's a long way to go, old man. . . . I dare say it's twelve miles and may be more."

"One who needs something will go seventy."

"That is so. . . . Should I send in a petition to him, or what?"

"You will find out there. If you should have a petition the clerk will write you one quick enough. The permanent member has a clerk."

After parting from the old man Kirila stood still in the middle of the square, thought a little, and walked back out of the town. He made up his mind to go to Zolotovo.

Five days later, as the doctor was on his way home after seeing his patients, he caught sight of Kirila again in his yard. This time the young peasant was not alone, but with a gaunt, very pale old man who nodded his head without ceasing, like a pendulum, and mumbled with his lips.

"Your honour, I have come again to ask your gracious mercy," began Kirila. "Here I have come with my father. Be merciful, let Vaska go! The permanent member would not talk to me. He said: 'Go away!'"

"Your honour," the old man hissed in his throat, raising his twitching eyebrows, "be merciful! We are poor people, we cannot repay your honour, but if you graciously please, Kiryushka or Vaska can repay you in work. Let them work."

"We will pay with work," said Kirila, and he raised his hand above his head as though he would take an oath. "Let him go! They are starving, they are crying day and night, your honour!"

The young peasant bent a rapid glance on his father, pulled him by the sleeve, and both of them, as at the word of command, fell at the doctor's feet. The latter waved his hand in despair, and, without looking round, walked quickly in at his door.

1887

THE BEGGAR

THE BEGGAR

"KIND sir, be so good as to notice a poor, hungry man. I have not tasted food for three days. . . . I have not a five-kopeck piece for a night's lodging. . . . I swear by God! For five years I was a village schoolmaster and lost my post through the intrigues of the Zemstvo. I was the victim of false witness. I have been out of a place for a year now."

Skvortsov, a Petersburg lawyer, looked at the speaker's tattered dark blue overcoat, at his muddy, drunken eyes, at the red patches on his cheeks, and it seemed to him that he had seen the man before.

"And now I am offered a post in the Kaluga province," the beggar continued, "but I have not the means for the journey there. Graciously help me! I am ashamed to ask, but . . . I am compelled by circumstances."

Skvortsov looked at his goloshes, of which one was shallow like a shoe, while the other came high up the leg like a boot, and suddenly remembered.

"Listen, the day before yesterday I met you in Sadovoy Street," he said, "and then you told me, not that you were a village schoolmaster, but that you were a student who had been expelled. Do you remember?"

"N-o. No, that cannot be so!" the beggar muttered in confusion. "I am a village schoolmaster, and if you wish it I can show you documents to prove it."

"That's enough lies! You called yourself a student, and even told me what you were expelled for. Do you remember?"

Skvortsov flushed, and with a look of disgust on his face turned away from the ragged figure.

"It's contemptible, sir!" he cried angrily. "It's a swindle! I'll hand you over to the police, damn you! You are poor and hungry, but that does not give you the right to lie so shamelessly!"

The ragged figure took hold of the door-handle and, like a bird in a snare, looked round the hall desperately.

"I . . . I am not lying," he muttered. "I can show documents."

"Who can believe you?" Skvortsov went on, still indignant. "To exploit the sympathy of the public for village schoolmasters and students—it's so low, so mean, so dirty! It's revolting!"

Skvortsov flew into a rage and gave the beggar a merciless scolding. The ragged fellow's insolent lying aroused his disgust and aversion, was an offence against what he, Skvortsov, loved and prized in himself: kindliness, a feeling heart, sympathy for the unhappy. By his lying, by his treacherous assault upon compassion, the individual had, as it were, defiled the charity which he liked to give to the poor with no misgivings in his heart. The beggar at first defended himself, protested with oaths, then he sank into silence and hung his head, overcome with shame.

"Sir!" he said, laying his hand on his heart, "I really was . . . lying! I am not a student and not a village schoolmaster. All that's mere invention! I used to be in the Russian choir, and I was turned out of it for drunkenness. But what can I do? Believe me, in God's name, I can't get on without lying—when I tell the truth no one will give me anything. With the truth one may die of hunger and freeze without a night's lodging! What you say is true, I understand that, but . . . what am I to do?"

"What are you to do? You ask what are you to do?" cried Skvortsov, going close up to him. "Work—that's what you must do! You must work!"

"Work. . . . I know that myself, but where can I get work?"

"Nonsense. You are young, strong, and healthy, and could always find work if you wanted to. But you know you are lazy, pampered, drunken! You reek of vodka like a pothouse! You have become false and corrupt to the marrow of your bones and fit for nothing but begging and lying! If you do graciously condescend to take work, you must have a job in an office, in the Russian choir, or as a billiard-marker, where you will have a salary and have nothing to do! But how would you like to undertake manual labour? I'll be bound, you wouldn't be a house porter or a factory hand! You are too genteel for that!"

"What things you say, really . . ." said the beggar, and he gave a bitter smile. "How can I get manual work? It's rather late for me to be a shopman, for in trade one has to begin from a boy; no one would take me as a house porter, because I am not of that class. . . . And I could not get work in a factory; one must know a trade, and I know nothing."

"Nonsense! You always find some justification! Wouldn't you like to chop wood?"

"I would not refuse to, but the regular wood-choppers are out of work now."

"Oh, all idlers argue like that! As soon as you are offered anything you refuse it. Would you care to chop wood for me?"

"Certainly I will. . . ."

"Very good, we shall see. . . . Excellent. . . . We'll see!" Skvortsov, in nervous haste, and not without malignant pleasure, rubbing his hands, summoned his cook from the kitchen.

"Here, Olga," he said to her, "take this gentleman to the shed and let him chop some wood."

The beggar shrugged his shoulders as though puzzled, and irresolutely followed the cook. It was evident from his demeanour that he had consented to go and chop wood, not because he was hungry and wanted to earn money, but simply from shame and *amour propre,* because he had been taken at his word. It was clear, too, that he was suffering from the effects of vodka, that he was unwell, and felt not the faintest inclination to work.

Skvortsov hurried into the dining-room. There from the window which looked out into the yard he could see the woodshed and everything that happened in the yard. Standing at the window, Skvortsov saw the cook and the beggar come by the back way into the yard and go through the muddy snow to the woodshed. Olga scrutinized her companion angrily, and jerking her elbow unlocked the woodshed and angrily banged the door open.

" Most likely we interrupted the woman drinking her coffee," thought Skvortsov. " What a cross creature she is ! "

Then he saw the pseudo-schoolmaster and pseudo-student seat himself on a block of wood, and, leaning his red cheeks upon his fists, sink into thought. The cook flung an axe at his feet, spat angrily on the ground, and, judging by the expression of her lips, began abusing him. The beggar drew a log of wood towards him irresolutely, set it up between his feet, and diffidently drew the axe across it. The log toppled and fell over. The beggar drew it towards him, breathed on his frozen hands, and again drew the axe along it as cautiously as though he were afraid of its hitting his golosh or chopping off his fingers. The log fell over again.

Skvortsov's wrath had passed off by now, he felt sore and ashamed at the thought that he had forced a pampered, drunken, and perhaps sick man to do hard, rough work in the cold.

" Never mind, let him go on . . ." he thought, going from the dining-room into his study. " I am doing it for his good ! "

An hour later Olga appeared and announced that the wood had been chopped up.

" Here, give him half a rouble," said Skvortsov. " If he likes, let him come and chop wood on the first of every month. . . . There will always be work for him."

On the first of the month the beggar turned up and again earned half a rouble, though he could hardly stand. From that time forward he took to turning up frequently, and work was always found for him: sometimes he would sweep the snow into heaps, or clear up the shed, at another he used to beat the rugs and the mattresses. He always received thirty to forty kopecks for his work, and on one occasion an old pair of trousers was sent out to him.

When he moved, Skvortsov engaged him to assist in packing and moving the furniture. On this occasion the beggar was sober, gloomy, and silent; he scarcely touched the furniture, walked with hanging head behind the furniture vans, and did not even try to appear busy; he merely shivered with the cold, and was overcome with confusion when the men with the vans laughed at his idleness, feebleness, and ragged coat that had once been a gentleman's. After the removal Skvortsov sent for him.

"Well, I see my words have had an effect upon you," he said, giving him a rouble. "This is for your work. I see that you are sober and not disinclined to work. What is your name?"

"Lushkov."

"I can offer you better work, not so rough, Lushkov. Can you write?"

"Yes, sir."

"Then go with this note to-morrow to my colleague and he will give you some copying to do. Work, don't drink, and don't forget what I said to you. Good-bye."

Skvortsov, pleased that he had put a man in the path of rectitude, patted Lushkov genially on the shoulder, and even shook hands with him at parting.

Lushkov took the letter, departed, and from that time forward did not come to the back-yard for work.

Two years passed. One day as Skvortsov was standing at the ticket-office of a theatre, paying for his ticket, he saw beside him a little man with a lambskin collar and a shabby cat's-skin cap. The man timidly asked the clerk for a gallery ticket and paid for it with kopecks.

"Lushkov, is it you?" asked Skvortsov, recognizing in the little man his former woodchopper. "Well, what are you doing? Are you getting on all right?"

"Pretty well. . . . I am in a notary's office now. I earn thirty-five roubles."

"Well, thank God, that's capital. I rejoice for you. I am very, very glad, Lushkov. You know, in a way, you are my godson. It was I who shoved you into the right way. Do you remember what a scolding I gave you, eh? You almost sank through the floor that time. Well, thank you, my dear fellow, for remembering my words."

"Thank you too," said Lushkov. "If I had not come to you that day, maybe I should be calling myself a schoolmaster or a student still. Yes, in your house I was saved, and climbed out of the pit."

"I am very, very glad."

"Thank you for your kind words and deeds. What you said that day was excellent. I am grateful to you and to your cook, God bless that kind, noble-hearted woman. What you said that day was excellent; I am indebted to you as long as I live, of course, but it was your cook, Olga, who really saved me."

" How was that? "

" Why, it was like this. I used to come to you to chop wood and she would begin: ' Ah, you drunkard! You God-forsaken man! And yet death does not take you!' and then she would sit opposite me, lamenting, looking into my face and wailing: ' You unlucky fellow! You have no gladness in this world, and in the next you will burn in hell, poor drunkard! You poor sorrowful creature!' and she always went on in that style, you know. How often she upset herself, and how many tears she shed over me I can't tell you. But what affected me most—she chopped the wood for me! Do you know, sir, I never chopped a single log for you—she did it all! How it was she saved me, how it was I changed, looking at her, and gave up drinking, I can't explain. I only know that what she said and the noble way she behaved brought about a change in my soul, and I shall never forget it. It's time to go up, though, they are just going to ring the bell."

Lushkov bowed and went off to the gallery.

1887

A STORY WITHOUT A TITLE

A STORY WITHOUT A TITLE

In the fifth century, just as now, the sun rose every morning and every evening retired to rest. In the morning, when the first rays kissed the dew, the earth revived, the air was filled with the sounds of rapture and hope; while in the evening the same earth subsided into silence and plunged into gloomy darkness. One day was like another, one night like another. From time to time a storm-cloud raced up and there was the angry rumble of thunder, or a negligent star fell out of the sky, or a pale monk ran to tell the brotherhood that not far from the monastery he had seen a tiger—and that was all, and then each day was like the next.

The monks worked and prayed, and their Father Superior played on the organ, made Latin verses, and wrote music. The wonderful old man possessed an extraordinary gift. He played on the organ with such art that even the oldest monks, whose hearing had grown somewhat dull towards the end of their lives, could not restrain their tears when the sounds of the organ floated from his cell. When he spoke of anything, even of the most ordinary things—for instance of the trees, of the wild beasts, or of the sea—they could not listen to him without a smile or tears, and it seemed that the same chords vibrated in his soul as in the organ. If he were moved to anger or abandoned himself to intense joy, or began speaking of something terrible or grand, then a passionate inspiration took possession of him, tears came into his flashing eyes, his face flushed, and his voice thundered, and as the monks listened to him they felt that their souls were spell-bound by his inspiration; at such marvellous, splendid moments his power over them was boundless, and if he had bidden his elders fling themselves into the sea, they would all, every one of them, have hastened to carry out his wishes.

His music, his voice, his poetry in which he glorified God, the heavens and the earth, were a continual source of joy to the monks. It sometimes happened that through the monotony of their lives they grew weary of the trees, the flowers, the spring, the autumn, their ears were tired of the sound of the sea, and the song of the birds seemed tedious to them, but the talents of their Father Superior were as necessary to them as their daily bread.

Dozens of years passed by, and every day was like every other day, every night was like every other night. Except the birds and the wild beasts, not one soul appeared near the monastery. The nearest human habitation was far away, and to reach it from the monastery, or to reach the monastery from it, meant a journey of over seventy miles across the desert. Only men who despised life, who had renounced it, and who came to the monastery as to the grave, ventured to cross the desert.

What was the amazement of the monks, therefore, when one night there knocked at their gate a man who turned out to be from the town, and the most ordinary sinner who loved life. Before saying his prayers and asking for the Father Superior's blessing, this man asked for wine and food. To the question how he had come from the town into the desert, he answered by a long story of hunting; he had gone out hunting, had drunk too much, and lost his way. To the suggestion that he should enter the monastery and save his soul, he replied with a smile: " I am not a fit companion for you! "

When he had eaten and drunk he looked at the monks who were serving him, shook his head reproachfully, and said:

" You don't do anything, you monks. You are good for nothing but eating and drinking. Is that the way to save one's soul? Only think, while you sit here in peace, eat and drink and dream of beatitude, your neighbours are perishing and going to hell. You should see what is going on in the town! Some are dying of hunger, others, not knowing what to do with their gold, sink into profligacy and perish like flies stuck in honey. There is no faith, no truth in men. Whose task is it to save them? Whose work is it to preach to them? It is not for me, drunk from morning till night as I am. Can a meek spirit, a loving heart, and faith in God have been given you for you to sit here within four walls doing nothing? "

The townsman's drunken words were insolent and unseemly, but they had a strange effect upon the Father Superior. The old man exchanged glances with his monks, turned pale, and said:

" My brothers, he speaks the truth, you know. Indeed, poor people in their weakness and lack of understanding are perishing in vice and infidelity, while we do not move, as though it did not concern us. Why should I not go and remind them of the Christ whom they have forgotten?"

The townsman's words had carried the old man away. The next day he took his staff, said farewell to the brotherhood, and set off for the town. And the monks were left without music, and without his speeches and verses. They spent a month drearily, then a second, but the old man did not come back. At last after three months had passed the familiar tap of his staff was heard. The monks flew to meet him and showered questions upon him, but instead of being delighted to see them he wept bitterly and did not utter a word. The monks noticed that he looked greatly aged and had grown thinner; his face looked exhausted and wore an expression of profound sadness, and when he wept he had the air of a man who has been outraged.

The monks fell to weeping too, and began with sympathy asking him why he was weeping, why his face was so gloomy, but he locked himself in his cell without uttering a word. For seven days he sat in his cell, eating and drinking nothing, weeping and not playing on his organ. To knocking at his door and to the entreaties of the monks to come out and share his grief with them he replied with unbroken silence.

At last he came out. Gathering all the monks around him, with a tear-stained face and with an expression of grief and indignation, he began telling them of what had befallen him during those three months. His voice was calm and his eyes were smiling while he described his journey from the monastery to the town. On the road, he told them, the birds sang to him, the brooks gurgled, and sweet youthful hopes agitated his soul; he marched on and felt like a soldier going to battle and confident of victory; he walked on dreaming, and composed poems and hymns, and reached the end of his journey without noticing it.

But his voice quivered, his eyes flashed, and he was full of wrath when he came to speak of the town and of the men in it. Never in his life had he seen or even dared to imagine what he met with when he went into the town. Only then for the first time in his life, in his old age, he saw and understood how powerful was the devil, how fair was evil and how weak and faint-hearted and worthless were men. By an unhappy chance the first dwelling he entered was the abode of vice. Some fifty men in possession of much money were eating and drinking wine beyond measure. Intoxicated by the wine, they sang songs and boldly uttered terrible, revolting words such as a God-fearing man could not bring himself to pronounce; boundlessly free, self-confident, and happy, they feared neither God nor the devil, nor death, but said and did what they liked, and went whither their lust led them. And the wine, clear as amber, flecked with sparks of gold, must have been irresistibly sweet and fragrant, for each man who drank it smiled blissfully and wanted to drink more. To the smile of man it responded with a smile and sparkled joyfully when they drank it, as though it knew the devilish charm it kept hidden in its sweetness.

The old man, growing more and more incensed

and weeping with wrath, went on to describe what he had seen. On a table in the midst of the revellers, he said, stood a sinful, half-naked woman. It was hard to imagine or to find in nature anything more lovely and fascinating. This reptile, young, long-haired, dark-skinned, with black eyes and full lips, shameless and insolent, showed her snow-white teeth and smiled as though to say: " Look how shameless, how beautiful I am." Silk and brocade fell in lovely folds from her shoulders, but her beauty would not hide itself under her clothes, but eagerly thrust itself through the folds, like the young grass through the ground in spring. The shameless woman drank wine, sang songs, and abandoned herself to anyone who wanted her.

Then the old man, wrathfully brandishing his arms, described the horse-races, the bull-fights, the theatres, the artists' studios where they painted naked women or moulded them of clay. He spoke with inspiration, with sonorous beauty, as though he were playing on unseen chords, while the monks, petrified, greedily drank in his words and gasped with rapture. . . .

After describing all the charms of the devil, the beauty of evil, and the fascinating grace of the dreadful female form, the old man cursed the devil, turned and shut himself up in his cell. . . .

When he came out of his cell in the morning there was not a monk left in the monastery; they had all fled to the town.

1888

IN TROUBLE

IN TROUBLE

PYOTR SEMYONITCH, the bank manager, together with the book-keeper, his assistant, and two members of the board, were taken in the night to prison. The day after the upheaval the merchant Avdeyev, who was one of the committee of auditors, was sitting with his friends in the shop saying:

" So it is God's will, it seems. There is no escaping your fate. Here to-day we are eating caviare and to-morrow, for aught we know, it will be prison, beggary, or maybe death. Anything may happen. Take Pyotr Semyonitch, for instance. . . ."

He spoke, screwing up his drunken eyes, while his friends went on drinking, eating caviare, and listening. Having described the disgrace and helplessness of Pyotr Semyonitch, who only the day before had been powerful and respected by all, Avdeyev went on with a sigh:

" The tears of the mouse come back to the cat. Serve them right, the scoundrels! They could steal, the rooks, so let them answer for it! "

" You'd better look out, Ivan Danilitch, that you don't catch it too! " one of his friends observed.

" What has it to do with me? "

" Why, they were stealing, and what were you auditors thinking about? I'll be bound, you signed the audit."

" It's all very well to talk! " laughed Avdeyev:

" Signed it, indeed! They used to bring the accounts to my shop and I signed them. As though I understood! Give me anything you like, I'll scrawl my name to it. If you were to write that I murdered someone I'd sign my name to it. I haven't time to go into it; besides, I can't see without my spectacles."

After discussing the failure of the bank and the fate of Pyotr Semyonitch, Avdeyev and his friends went to eat pie at the house of a friend whose wife was celebrating her name-day. At the name-day party everyone was discussing the bank failure. Avdeyev was more excited than anyone, and declared that he had long foreseen the crash and knew two years before that things were not quite right at the bank. While they were eating pie he described a dozen illegal operations which had come to his knowledge.

" If you knew, why did you not give information? " asked an officer who was present.

" I wasn't the only one: the whole town knew of it," laughed Avdeyev. " Besides, I haven't the time to hang about the law courts, damn them! "

He had a nap after the pie and then had dinner, then had another nap, then went to the evening service at the church of which he was a warden; after the service he went back to the name-day party and played preference till midnight. Everything seemed satisfactory.

But when Avdeyev hurried home after midnight the cook, who opened the door to him, looked pale, and was trembling so violently that she could not utter a word. His wife, Elizaveta Trofimovna, a

flabby, overfed woman, with her grey hair
hanging loose, was sitting on the sofa in the drawing-room quivering all over, and vacantly rolling
her eyes as though she were drunk. Her elder son,
Vassily, a high-school boy, pale too, and extremely
agitated, was fussing round her with a glass of
water.

"What's the matter?" asked Avdeyev, and
looked angrily sideways at the stove (his family
was constantly being upset by the fumes from it).

"The examining magistrate has just been with
the police," answered Vassily; "they've made a
search."

Avdeyev looked round him. The cupboards, the
chests, the tables—everything bore traces of the
recent search. For a minute Avdeyev stood motionless as though petrified, unable to understand;
then his whole inside quivered and seemed to grow
heavy, his left leg went numb, and, unable to endure
his trembling, he lay down flat on the sofa. He felt
his inside heaving and his rebellious left leg tapping
against the back of the sofa.

In the course of two or three minutes he recalled
the whole of his past, but could not remember any
crime deserving of the attention of the police.

"It's all nonsense," he said, getting up. "They
must have slandered me. To-morrow I must lodge
a complaint of their having dared to do such a
thing."

Next morning after a sleepless night Avdeyev,
as usual, went to his shop. His customers brought
him the news that during the night the public prosecutor had sent the deputy manager and the head-

clerk to prison as well. This news did not disturb Avdeyev. He was convinced that he had been slandered, and that if he were to lodge a complaint to-day the examining magistrate would get into trouble for the search of the night before.

Between nine and ten o'clock he hurried to the town hall to see the secretary, who was the only educated man in the town council.

"Vladimir Stepanitch, what's this new fashion?" he said, bending down to the secretary's ear. "People have been stealing, but how do I come in? What has it to do with me? My dear fellow," he whispered, "there has been a search at my house last night! Upon my word! Have they gone crazy? Why touch me?"

"Because one shouldn't be a sheep," the secretary answered calmly. "Before you sign you ought to look."

"Look at what? But if I were to look at those accounts for a thousand years I could not make head or tail of them! It's all Greek to me! I am no book-keeper. They used to bring them to me and I signed them."

"Excuse me. Apart from that you and your committee are seriously compromised. You borrowed nineteen thousand from the bank, giving no security."

"Lord have mercy upon us!" cried Avdeyev in amazement. "I am not the only one in debt to the bank! The whole town owes it money. I pay the interest and I shall repay the debt. What next! And besides, to tell the honest truth, it wasn't I myself borrowed the money. Pyotr Semyonitch forced it upon me. 'Take it,' he said, 'take it. If you don't take it,' he said, 'it means that you don't trust us and fight shy of us. You take it,' he said, 'and build your father a mill.' So I took it."

"Well, you see, none but children or sheep can reason like that. In any case, *signor,* you need not be anxious. You can't escape trial, of course, but you are sure to be acquitted."

The secretary's indifference and calm tone restored Avdeyev's composure. Going back to his shop and finding friends there, he again began drinking, eating caviare, and airing his views. He almost forgot the police search, and he was only troubled by one circumstance which he could not help noticing: his left leg was strangely numb, and his stomach for some reason refused to do its work.

That evening destiny dealt another overwhelming blow at Avdeyev: at an extraordinary meeting of the town council all members who were on the staff of the bank, Avdeyev among them, were asked to resign, on the ground that they were charged with a criminal offence. In the morning he received a request to give up immediately his duties as church-warden.

After that Avdeyev lost count of the blows dealt him by fate, and strange, unprecedented days flitted rapidly by, one after another, and every day brought some new, unexpected surprise. Among other things, the examining magistrate sent him a summons, and he returned home after the interview, insulted and red in the face.

"He gave me no peace, pestering me to tell him why I had signed. I signed, that's all about it. I didn't do it on purpose. They brought the papers to the shop and I signed them. I am no great hand at reading writing."

Young men with unconcerned faces arrived, sealed up the shop, and made an inventory of all the furniture of the house. Suspecting some intrigue behind this, and, as before, unconscious of any wrongdoing, Avdeyev in his mortification ran from one Government office to another lodging complaints. He spent hours together in waiting-rooms, composed long petitions, shed tears, swore. To his complaints the public prosecutor and the examining magistrate made the indifferent and rational reply: " Come to us when you are summoned: we have not time to attend to you now." While others answered: " It is not our business."

The secretary, an educated man, who, Avdeyev thought, might have helped him, merely shrugged his shoulders and said:

" It's your own fault. You shouldn't have been a sheep."

The old man exerted himself to the utmost, but his left leg was still numb, and his digestion was getting worse and worse. When he was weary of doing nothing and was getting poorer and poorer, he made up his mind to go to his father's mill, or to his brother, and begin dealing in corn. His family went to his father's and he was left alone. The days flitted by, one after another. Without a family, without a shop, and without money, the former churchwarden, an honoured and respected man, spent whole days going the round of his friends' shops, drinking, eating, and listening to advice. In the mornings and in the evenings, to while away the time, he went to church. Looking for hours together at the ikons, he did not pray, but pondered. His conscience was clear, and he ascribed his position to mistake and misunderstanding; to his mind, it was all due to the fact that the officials and the examining magistrates were young men and inexperienced. It seemed to him that if he were to talk it over in detail and open his heart to some elderly judge, everything would go right again. He did not understand his judges, and he fancied they did not understand him.

The days raced by, and at last, after protracted, harassing delays, the day of the trial came. Avdeyev borrowed fifty roubles, and providing himself with spirit to rub on his leg and a decoction of herbs for his digestion, set off for the town where the circuit court was being held.

The trial lasted for ten days. Throughout the trial Avdeyev sat among his companions in misfortune with the stolid composure and dignity befitting a respectable and innocent man who is suffering for no fault of his own: he listened and did not understand a word. He was in an antagonistic mood. He was angry at being detained so long in the court, at being unable to get Lenten food anywhere, at his defending counsel's not understanding him, and, as he thought, saying the wrong thing. He thought that the judges did not understand their business. They took scarcely any notice of Avdeyev, they only addressed him once in three days, and the questions they put to him were of such a character that Avdeyev raised a laugh in the audience each time he answered them. When he tried to speak of the expenses he had incurred, of his losses, and of his meaning to claim his costs from the court, his counsel turned round and made an incomprehensible grimace, the public laughed, and the judge announced sternly that that had nothing to do with the case. The last words that he was allowed to say were not what his counsel had instructed him to say, but something quite different, which raised a laugh again.

During the terrible hour when the jury were consulting in their room he sat angrily in the refreshment bar, not thinking about the jury at all. He did not understand why they were so long deliberating when everything was so clear, and what they wanted of him.

Getting hungry, he asked the waiter to give him some cheap Lenten dish. For forty kopecks they gave him some cold fish and carrots. He ate it and felt at once as though the fish were heaving in a chilly lump in his stomach; it was followed by flatulence, heartburn, and pain.

Afterwards, as he listened to the foreman of the jury reading out the questions point by point, there was a regular revolution taking place in his inside, his whole body was bathed in a cold sweat, his left leg was numb; he did not follow, understood nothing, and suffered unbearably at not being able to sit or lie down while the foreman was reading. At last, when he and his companions were allowed to sit down, the public prosecutor got up and said something unintelligible, and all at once, as though they had sprung out of the earth, some police officers

appeared on the scene with drawn swords and surrounded all the prisoners. Avdeyev was told to get
up and go.

Now he understood that he was found guilty and
in charge of the police, but he was not frightened nor
amazed; such a turmoil was going on in his stomach
that he could not think about his guards.

" So they won't let us go back to the hotel?" he
asked one of his companions. " But I have three
roubles and an untouched quarter of a pound of tea
in my room there."

He spent the night at the police station; all night
he was aware of a loathing for fish, and was thinking
about the three roubles and the quarter of a pound
of tea. Early in the morning, when the sky was
beginning to turn blue, he was told to dress and set
off. Two soldiers with bayonets took him to prison.
Never before had the streets of the town seemed to
him so long and endless. He walked not on the
pavement but in the middle of the road in the
muddy, thawing snow. His inside was still at war
with the fish, his left leg was numb; he had forgotten
his goloshes either in the court or in the police station, and his feet felt frozen.

Five days later all the prisoners were brought
before the court again to hear their sentence.
Avdeyev learnt that he was sentenced to exile in the
province of Tobolsk. And that did not frighten nor
amaze him either. He fancied for some reason that
the trial was not yet over, that there were more
adjournments to come, and that the final decision
had not been reached yet. . . . He went on in the
prison expecting this final decision every day.

Only six months later, when his wife and his son Vassily came to say good-bye to him, and when in the wasted, wretchedly dressed old woman he scarcely recognized his once fat and dignified Eliza-veta Trofimovna, and when he saw his son wearing a short, shabby reefer-jacket and cotton trousers instead of the high-school uniform, he realized that his fate was decided, and that whatever new " deci-sion " there might be, his past would never come back to him. And for the first time since the trial and his imprisonment the angry expression left his face, and he wept bitterly.

1887

FROST

FROST

A " POPULAR " fête with a philanthropic object had
been arranged on the Feast of Epiphany in the provincial town of N———. They had selected a broad
part of the river between the market and the
bishop's palace, fenced it round with a rope, with
fir-trees and with flags, and provided everything
necessary for skating, sledging, and tobogganing.
The festivity was organized on the grandest scale
possible. The notices that were distributed were
of huge size and promised a number of delights:
skating, a military band, a lottery with no blank
tickets, an electric sun, and so on. But the whole
scheme almost came to nothing owing to the hard
frost. From the eve of Epiphany there were
twenty-eight degrees of frost with a strong wind;
it was proposed to put off the fête, and this was
not done only because the public, which for a long
while had been looking forward to the fête impatiently, would not consent to any postponement.

" Only think, what do you expect in winter but
a frost! " said the ladies persuading the governor,
who tried to insist that the fête should be post-
poned. " If anyone is cold he can go and warm
himself."

The trees, the horses, the men's beards were white
with frost; it even seemed that the air itself
crackled, as though unable to endure the cold; but

in spite of that the frozen public were skating. Immediately after the blessing of the waters and precisely at one o'clock the military band began playing.

Between three and four o'clock in the afternoon, when the festivity was at its height, the select society of the place gathered together to warm themselves in the governor's pavilion, which had been put up on the river-bank. The old governor and his wife, the bishop, the president of the local court, the head master of the high school, and many others, were there. The ladies were sitting in armchairs, while the men crowded round the wide glass door, looking at the skating.

"Holy Saints!" said the bishop in surprise; "what flourishes they execute with their legs! Upon my soul, many a singer couldn't do a twirl with his voice as those cut-throats do with their legs. Aie! he'll kill himself!"

"That's Smirnov. . . . That's Gruzdev . . ." said the head master, mentioning the names of the schoolboys who flew by the pavilion.

"Bah! he's all alive-oh!" laughed the governor. "Look, gentlemen, our mayor is coming. . . . He is coming this way. . . . That's a nuisance, he will talk our heads off now."

A little thin old man, wearing a big cap and a fur-lined coat hanging open, came from the opposite bank towards the pavilion, avoiding the skaters. This was the mayor of the town, a merchant, Eremeyev by name, a millionaire and an old inhabitant of N——. Flinging wide his arms and shrugging at the cold, he skipped along, knocking one golosh against the other, evidently in haste to get out of the wind. Half-way he suddenly bent down, stole up to some lady, and plucked at her sleeve from behind. When she looked round he skipped away, and probably delighted at having succeeded in frightening her, went off into a loud, aged laugh.

"Lively old fellow," said the governor. "It's a wonder he's not skating."

As he got near the pavilion the mayor fell into a little tripping trot, waved his hands, and, taking a run, slid along the ice in his huge golosh boots up to the very door.

"Yegor Ivanitch, you ought to get yourself some skates!" the governor greeted him.

"That's just what I am thinking," he answered in a squeaky, somewhat nasal tenor, taking off his cap. "I wish you good health, your Excellency! Your Holiness! Long life to all the other gentlemen and ladies! Here's a frost! Yes, it is a frost, bother it! It's deadly!"

Winking with his red, frozen eyes, Yegor Ivanitch stamped on the floor with his golosh boots and swung his arms together like a frozen cabman.

"Such a damnable frost, worse than any dog!" he went on talking, smiling all over his face. "It's a real affliction!"

"It's healthy," said the governor; "frost strengthens a man and makes him vigorous. . . ."

"Though it may be healthy, it would be better without it at all," said the mayor, wiping his wedge-shaped beard with a red handkerchief. "It would be a good riddance! To my thinking, your Excellency, the Lord sends it us as a punishment—

the frost, I mean.   We sin in the summer and are punished in the winter. . . . Yes! "

Yegor Ivanitch looked round him quickly and flung up his hands.

" Why, where's the needful . . . to warm us up ? " he asked, looking in alarm first at the governor and then at the bishop.   " Your Excellency!   Your Holiness!   I'll be bound, the ladies are frozen too! We must have something, this won't do! "

Everyone began gesticulating and declaring that they had not come to the skating to warm themselves, but the mayor, heeding no one, opened the door and beckoned to someone with his crooked finger.   A workman and a fireman ran up to him.

" Here, run off to Savatin," he muttered, " and tell him to make haste and send here . . . what do you call it? . . . What's it to be?   Tell him to send a dozen glasses . . . a dozen glasses of mulled wine, the very hottest, or punch, perhaps. . . ."

There was laughter in the pavilion.

" A nice thing to treat us to! "

" Never mind, we will drink it," muttered the mayor; " a dozen glasses, then . . . and some Benedictine, perhaps . . . and tell them to warm two bottles of red wine. . . . Oh, and what for the ladies?   Well, you tell them to bring cakes, nuts . . . sweets of some sort, perhaps. . . . There, run along, look sharp! "

The mayor was silent for a minute and then began again abusing the frost, banging his arms across his chest and thumping with his golosh boots.

" No, Yegor Ivanitch," said the governor persuasively, "don't be unfair, the Russian frost has

its charms. I was reading lately that many of the
good qualities of the Russian people are due to the
vast expanse of their land and to the climate, the
cruel struggle for existence . . . that's perfectly
true ! "

"It may be true, your Excellency, but it would
be better without it. The frost did drive out the
French, of course, and one can freeze all sorts of
dishes, and the children can go skating—that's all
true ! For the man who is well fed and well clothed
the frost is only a pleasure, but for the working
man, the beggar, the pilgrim, the crazy wanderer, it's
the greatest evil and misfortune. It's misery, your
Holiness ! In a frost like this poverty is twice as
hard, and the thief is more cunning and evildoers
more violent. There's no gainsaying it ! I am
turned seventy, I've a fur coat now, and at home I
have a stove and rums and punches of all sorts. The
frost means nothing to me now; I take no notice of
it, I don't care to know of it, but how it used to be
in old days, Holy Mother ! It's dreadful to recall
it ! My memory is failing me with years and I have
forgotten everything; my enemies, and my sins and
troubles of all sorts—I forget them all, but the frost
—ough ! How I remember it ! When my mother
died I was left a little devil—this high—a homeless
orphan . . . no kith nor kin, wretched, ragged, little
clothes, hungry, nowhere to sleep—in fact, ' we have
here no abiding city, but seek the one to come.' In
those days I used to lead an old blind woman about
the town for five kopecks a day . . . the frosts
were cruel, wicked. One would go out with the
old woman and begin suffering torments. My

Creator! First of all you would be shivering as in a fever, shrugging and dancing about. Then your ears, your fingers, your feet, would begin aching. They would ache as though someone were squeezing them with pincers. But all that would have been nothing, a trivial matter, of no great consequence. The trouble was when your whole body was chilled. One would walk for three blessed hours in the frost, your Holiness, and lose all human semblance. Your legs are drawn up, there is a weight on your chest, your stomach is pinched; above all, there is a pain in your heart that is worse than anything. Your heart aches beyond all endurance, and there is a wretchedness all over your body as though you were leading Death by the hand instead of an old woman. You are numb all over, turned to stone like a statue; you go on and feel as though it were not you walking, but someone else moving your legs instead of you. When your soul is frozen you don't know what you are doing: you are ready to leave the old woman with no one to guide her, or to pull a hot roll from off a hawker's tray, or to fight with someone. And when you come to your night's lodging into the warmth after the frost, there is not much joy in that either! You lie awake till midnight, crying, and don't know yourself what you are crying for. . . ."

" We must walk about the skating-ground before it gets dark," said the governor's wife, who was bored with listening. " Who's coming with me ? "

The governor's wife went out and the whole company trooped out of the pavilion after her. Only the governor, the bishop, and the mayor remained.

" Queen of Heaven! and what I went through

when I was a shopboy in a fish-shop!" Yegor Ivanitch went on, flinging up his arms so that his fox-
lined coat fell open. "One would go out to the shop
almost before it was light . . . by eight o'clock I
was completely frozen, my face was blue, my fingers
were stiff so that I could not fasten my buttons nor
count the money. One would stand in the cold, turn
numb, and think, 'Lord, I shall have to stand like
this right on till evening!' By dinner-time my
stomach was pinched and my heart was aching. . . .
Yes! And I was not much better afterwards when
I had a shop of my own. The frost was intense and
the shop was like a mouse-trap with draughts blowing in all directions; the coat I had on was, pardon
me, mangy, as thin as paper, threadbare. . . . One
would be chilled through and through, half dazed,
and turn as cruel as the frost oneself: I would pull
one by the ear so that I nearly pulled the ear off; I
would smack another on the back of the head; I'd
glare at a customer like a ruffian, a wild beast, and
be ready to fleece him; and when I got home in the
evening and ought to have gone to bed, I'd be ill-
humoured and set upon my family, throwing it in
their teeth that they were living upon me; I would
make a row and carry on so that half a dozen police-
men couldn't have managed me. The frost makes
one spiteful and drives one to drink."

Yegor Ivanitch clasped his hands and went on:

"And when we were taking fish to Moscow in
the winter, Holy Mother!" And spluttering as
he talked, he began describing the horrors he endured with his shopmen when he was taking fish to
Moscow. . . .

"Yes," sighed the governor, "it is wonderful what a man can endure! You used to take wagon-loads of fish to Moscow, Yegor Ivanitch, while I in my time was at the war. I remember one extraordinary instance. . . ."

And the governor described how, during the last Russo-Turkish War, one frosty night the division in which he was had stood in the snow without moving for thirteen hours in a piercing wind; from fear of being observed the division did not light a fire, nor make a sound or a movement; they were forbidden to smoke. . . .

Reminiscences followed. The governor and the mayor grew lively and good-humoured, and, interrupting each other, began recalling their experiences. And the bishop told them how, when he was serving in Siberia, he had travelled in a sledge drawn by dogs; how one day, being drowsy, in a time of sharp frost he had fallen out of the sledge and been nearly frozen; when the Tunguses turned back and found him he was barely alive. Then, as by common agreement, the old men suddenly sank into silence, sat side by side, and mused.

"Ech!" whispered the mayor; "you'd think it would be time to forget, but when you look at the water-carriers, at the schoolboys, at the convicts in their wretched gowns, it brings it all back! Why, only take those musicians who are playing now. I'll be bound, there is a pain in their hearts; a pinch at their stomachs, and their trumpets are freezing to their lips. . . . They play and think: 'Holy Mother! we have another three hours to sit here in the cold.'"

The old men sank into thought. They thought of that in man which is higher than good birth, higher than rank and wealth and learning, of that which brings the lowest beggar near to God: of the helplessness of man, of his sufferings and his patience. . . .

Meanwhile the air was turning blue . . . the door opened and two waiters from Savatin's walked in, carrying trays and a big muffled teapot. When the glasses had been filled and there was a strong smell of cinnamon and clove in the air, the door opened again, and there came into the pavilion a beardless young policeman whose nose was crimson, and who was covered all over with frost; he went up to the governor, and, saluting, said: " Her Excellency told me to inform you that she has gone home."

Looking at the way the policeman put his stiff, frozen fingers to his cap, looking at his nose, his lustreless eyes, and his hood covered with white frost near the mouth, they all for some reason felt that this policeman's heart must be aching, that his stomach must feel pinched, and his soul numb. . . .

" I say," said the governor hesitatingly, " have a drink of mulled wine! "

" It's all right . . . it's all right! Drink it up! " the mayor urged him, gesticulating; " don't be shy! "

The policeman took the glass in both hands, moved aside, and, trying to drink without making any sound, began discreetly sipping from the glass. He drank and was overwhelmed with embarrassment while the old men looked at him in silence, and they all fancied that the pain was leaving the young policeman's heart, and that his soul was thawing. The governor heaved a sigh.

"It's time we were at home," he said, getting up. "Good-bye! I say," he added, addressing the policeman, "tell the musicians there to . . . leave off playing, and ask Pavel Semyonovitch from me to see they are given . . . beer or vodka."

The governor and the bishop said good-bye to the mayor and went out of the pavilion.

Yegor Ivanitch attacked the mulled wine, and before the policeman had finished his glass succeeded in telling him a great many interesting things. He could not be silent.

1887

A SLANDER

A SLANDER

Sergey Kapitonitch Ahineev, the writing-master, was marrying his daughter Natalya to the teacher of history and geography. The wedding festivities were going off most successfully. In the drawing-room there was singing, playing, and dancing. Waiters hired from the club were flitting distractedly about the rooms, dressed in black swallow-tails and dirty white ties. There was a continual hubbub and din of conversation. Sitting side by side on the sofa, the teacher of mathematics, Tarantulov, the French teacher, Pasdequoi, and the junior assessor of taxes, Mzda, were talking hurriedly and interrupting one another as they described to the guests cases of persons being buried alive, and gave their opinions on spiritualism. None of them believed in spiritualism, but all admitted that there were many things in this world which would always be beyond the mind of man. In the next room the literature master, Dodonsky, was explaining to the visitors the cases in which a sentry has the right to fire on passers-by. The subjects, as you perceive, were alarming, but very agreeable. Persons whose social position precluded them from entering were looking in at the windows from the yard.

Just at midnight the master of the house went into the kitchen to see whether everything was ready for supper. The kitchen from floor to ceiling

was filled with fumes composed of goose, duck, and
many other odours. On two tables the accessories,
the drinks and light refreshments, were set out in
artistic disorder. The cook, Marfa, a red-faced
woman, whose figure was like a barrel with a belt
round it, was bustling about the tables.

"Show me the sturgeon, Marfa," said Ahineev,
rubbing his hands and licking his lips. "What a
perfume, what a miasma! I could eat up the whole
kitchen. Come, show me the sturgeon."

Marfa went up to one of the benches and cautiously lifted a piece of greasy newspaper. Under
the paper on an immense dish there reposed a huge
sturgeon, masked in jelly and decorated with capers,
olives, and carrots. Ahineev gazed at the sturgeon
and gasped. His face beamed, he turned his eyes
up. He bent down and with his lips emitted the
sound of an ungreased wheel. After standing a
moment he snapped his fingers with delight, and
once more smacked his lips.

"Ah-ah! the sound of a passionate kiss. . . .
Who is it you're kissing out there, little Marfa?"
came a voice from the next room, and in the doorway there appeared the cropped head of the assistant usher Vankin. "Who is it? A-a-h! . . .
Delighted to meet you! Sergey Kapitonitch!
You're a fine grandfather, I must say! *Tête-à-tête*
with the fair sex—tette!"

"I'm not kissing," said Ahineev in confusion.
"Who told you so, you fool? I was only . . . I
smacked my lips . . . in reference to . . . as an
indication of . . . pleasure . . . at the sight of the
fish."

" Tell that to the marines! " The intrusive face vanished, wearing a broad grin.

Ahineev flushed.

" Hang it! " he thought, " the beast will go now and talk scandal. He'll disgrace me to all the town, the brute."

Ahineev went timidly into the drawing-room and looked stealthily round for Vankin. Vankin was standing by the piano, and, bending down with a jaunty air, was whispering something to the inspector's sister-in-law, who was laughing.

" Talking about me! " thought Ahineev. " About me, blast him! And she believes it . . . believes it! She laughs! Mercy on us! No, I can't let it pass . . . I can't. I must do something to prevent his being believed. . . . I'll speak to them all, and he'll be shown up for a fool and a gossip."

Ahineev scratched his head, and still overcome with embarrassment, went up to Pasdequoi.

" I've just been in the kitchen to see after the supper," he said to the Frenchman. " I know you are fond of fish, and I've a sturgeon, my dear fellow, beyond everything! A yard and a half long! Ha, ha, ha! And, by the way . . . I was just forgetting. . . . In the kitchen just now, with that sturgeon . . . quite a little story! I went into the kitchen just now and wanted to look at the supper dishes. I looked at the sturgeon and I smacked my lips with relish . . . at the piquancy of it. And at the very moment that fool Vankin came in and said: . . . 'Ha, ha, ha! . . . So you're kissing here!' Kissing Marfa, the cook! What a thing to imagine, silly fool! The woman is a perfect fright, like all the beasts put together, and he talks about kissing! Queer fish!"

"Who's a queer fish?" asked Tarantulov, coming up.

"Why he, over there—Vankin! I went into the kitchen . . ."

And he told the story of Vankin. ". . . He amused me, queer fish! I'd rather kiss a dog than Marfa, if you ask me," added Ahineev. He looked round and saw behind him Mzda.

"We are talking of Vankin," he said. "Queer fish, he is! He went into the kitchen, saw me beside Marfa, and began inventing all sorts of silly stories. 'Why are you kissing?' says he. He must have had a drop too much. 'And I'd rather kiss a turkeycock than Marfa,' I said. 'And I've a wife of my own, you fool,' said I. He did amuse me!"

"Who amused you?" asked the priest who taught Scripture in the school, going up to Ahineev.

"Vankin. I was standing in the kitchen, you know, looking at the sturgeon. . . ."

And so on. Within half an hour or so all the guests knew the incident of the sturgeon and Vankin.

"Let him tell away now!" thought Ahineev, rubbing his hands, "let him! He'll begin telling his story and they'll say to him at once, 'Enough of your nonsense, you fool, we know all about it!'"

And Ahineev was so relieved that in his joy he drank four glasses too many. After escorting the young people to their room he went to bed and slept like an innocent babe, and next day he thought no more of the incident with the sturgeon. But, alas! man proposes, but God disposes. An evil tongue did its evil work, and Ahineev's strategy was of no avail. Just a week later—to be precise, on Wednesday after the third lesson—when Ahineev was standing in the middle of the teachers' room, holding forth on the vicious propensities of a boy called Visekin, the head master went up to him and drew him aside:

"Look here, Sergey Kapitonitch," said the head master, "you must excuse me. . . . It's not my business; but all the same I must make you realize. . . . It's my duty. You see, there are rumours that you are living with that . . . cook. . . . It's nothing to do with me, but . . . Live with her, kiss her . . . as you please, but don't let it be so public, please. I entreat you! Don't forget that you're a schoolmaster."

Ahineev turned cold and faint. He went home like a man stung by a whole swarm of bees, like a man scalded with boiling water. As he walked home, it seemed to him that the whole town was looking at him as though he were smeared with pitch. At home fresh trouble awaited him.

"Why aren't you gobbling up your food as usual?" his wife asked him at dinner. "What are you so pensive about? Brooding over your amours? Pining for your slut of a Marfa? I know all about it, Mahommedan! Kind friends have opened my eyes! O-o-o! . . . you savage!"

And she slapped him in the face. He got up from the table, not feeling the earth under his feet, and without his hat or his coat, made his way to Vankin. He found him at home.

"You scoundrel!" was how he addressed him.

"Why have you covered me with mud before all the town? Why did you set this slander going about me?"

"What slander? What are you talking about?"

"Who was it gossiped of my kissing Marfa? Wasn't it you? Tell me that. Wasn't it you, you brigand?"

Vankin blinked and twitched in every fibre of his battered countenance, raised his eyes to the ikon and articulated, "God blast me! Strike me blind and lay me out, if I said a single word about you! May I be left without house or home, may I be stricken with worse than cholera!"

Vankin's sincerity did not admit of doubt. It was evidently not he who was the author of the slander.

"But who, then, who?" Ahineev wondered, going over all his acquaintances in his mind and beating himself on the breast. "Who, then?"

Who, then? We, too, ask the reader.

1883

MINDS IN FERMENT

MINDS IN FERMENT

(FROM THE ANNALS OF A TOWN)

THE earth was like an oven. The afternoon sun blazed with such energy that even the thermometer hanging in the excise officer's room lost its head: it ran up to 112.5 and stopped there, irresolute. The inhabitants streamed with perspiration like overdriven horses, and were too lazy to mop their faces.

Two of the inhabitants were walking along the market-place in front of the closely shuttered houses. One was Potcheshihin, the local treasury clerk, and the other was Optimov, the agent, for many years a correspondent of the *Son of the Father-land* newspaper. They walked in silence, speechless from the heat. Optimov felt tempted to find fault with the local authorities for the dust and disorder of the market-place, but, aware of the peace-loving disposition and moderate views of his companion, he said nothing.

In the middle of the market-place Potcheshihin suddenly halted and began gazing into the sky.

" What are you looking at? "

" Those starlings that flew up. I wonder where they have settled. Clouds and clouds of them. . . . If one were to go and take a shot at them, and if one were to pick them up . . . and if . . .

They have settled in the Father Prebendary's garden!"

"Oh no! They are not in the Father Prebendary's, they are in the Father Deacon's. If you did have a shot at them from here you wouldn't kill anything. Fine shot won't carry so far; it loses its force. And why should you kill them, anyway? They're birds destructive of the fruit, that's true; still, they're fowls of the air, works of the Lord. The starling sings, you know. . . . And what does it sing, pray? A song of praise. . . . 'All ye fowls of the air, praise ye the Lord.' No. I do believe they have settled in the Father Prebendary's garden."

Three old pilgrim women, wearing bark shoes and carrying wallets, passed noiselessly by the speakers. Looking enquiringly at the gentlemen who were for some unknown reason staring at the Father Prebendary's house, they slackened their pace, and when they were a few yards off stopped, glanced at the friends once more, and then fell to gazing at the house themselves.

"Yes, you were right; they have settled in the Father Prebendary's," said Optimov. "His cherries are ripe now, so they have gone there to peck them."

From the garden gate emerged the Father Prebendary himself, accompanied by the sexton. Seeing the attention directed upon his abode and wondering what people were staring at, he stopped, and he, too, as well as the sexton, began looking upwards to find out.

" The father is going to a service somewhere, I suppose," said Potcheshihin. " The Lord be his succour ! "

Some workmen from Purov's factory, who had been bathing in the river, passed between the friends and the priest. Seeing the latter absorbed in contemplation of the heavens and the pilgrim women, too, standing motionless with their eyes turned upwards, they stood still and stared in the same direction.

A small boy leading a blind beggar and a peasant, carrying a tub of stinking fish to throw into the market-place, did the same.

" There must be something the matter, I should think," said Potcheshihin, " a fire or something. But there's no sign of smoke anywhere. Hey ! Kuzma ! " he shouted to the peasant, " what's the matter ? "

The peasant made some reply, but Potcheshihin and Optimov did not catch it. Sleepy-looking shopmen made their appearance at the doors of all the shops. Some plasterers at work on a warehouse near left their ladders and joined the workmen.

The fireman, who was describing circles with his bare feet, on the watch-tower, halted, and, after looking steadily at them for a few minutes, came down. The watch-tower was left deserted. This seemed suspicious.

" There must be a fire somewhere. Don't shove me ! You damned swine ! "

" Where do you see the fire ? What fire ? Pass on, gentlemen ! I ask you civilly ! "

" It must be a fire indoors ! "

"Asks us civilly and keeps poking with his elbows. Keep your hands to yourself! Though you are a head constable, you have no sort of right to make free with your fists!"

"He's trodden on my corn! Ah! I'll crush you!"

"Crushed? Who's crushed? Lads! a man's been crushed!"

"What's the meaning of this crowd? What do you want?"

"A man's been crushed, please your honour!"

"Where? Pass on! I ask you civilly! I ask you civilly, you blockheads!"

"You may shove a peasant, but you daren't touch a gentleman! Hands off!"

"Did you ever know such people? There's no doing anything with them by fair words, the devils! Sidorov, run for Akim Danilitch! Look sharp! It'll be the worse for you, gentlemen! Akim Danilitch is coming, and he'll give it to you! You here, Parfen? A blind man, and at his age too! Can't see, but he must be like other people and won't do what he's told. Smirnov, put his name down!"

"Yes, sir! And shall I write down the men from Purov's? That man there with the swollen cheek, he's from Purov's works."

"Don't put down the men from Purov's. It's Purov's birthday to-morrow."

The starlings rose in a black cloud from the Father Prebendary's garden, but Potcheshihin and Optimov did not notice them. They stood staring into the air, wondering what could have attracted such a crowd, and what it was looking at.

Akim Danilitch appeared. Still munching and wiping his lips, he cut his way into the crowd, bellowing:

"Firemen, be ready! Disperse! Mr. Optimov, disperse, or it'll be the worse for you! Instead of writing all kinds of things about decent people in the papers, you had better try to behave yourself more conformably! No good ever comes of reading the papers!"

"Kindly refrain from reflections upon literature!" cried Optimov hotly. "I am a literary man, and I will allow no one to make reflections upon literature! though, as is the duty of a citizen, I respect you as a father and benefactor!"

"Firemen, turn the hose on them!"

"There's no water, please your honour!"

"Don't answer me! Go and get some! Look sharp!"

"We've nothing to get it in, your honour. The major has taken the fire-brigade horses to drive his aunt to the station."

"Disperse! Stand back, damnation take you! . . . Is that to your taste? Put him down, the devil!"

"I've lost my pencil, please your honour!"

The crowd grew larger and larger. There is no telling what proportions it might have reached if the new organ just arrived from Moscow had not fortunately begun playing in the tavern close by. Hearing their favourite tune, the crowd gasped and rushed off to the tavern. So nobody ever knew why the crowd had assembled, and Potcheshihin and Optimov had by now forgotten the existence of the starlings who were innocently responsible for the proceedings.

An hour later the town was still and silent again, and only a solitary figure was to be seen—the fireman pacing round and round on the watch-tower.

The same evening Akim Danilitch sat in the grocer's shop drinking *limonade gaseuse* and brandy, and writing:

"In addition to the official report, I venture, your Excellency, to append a few supplementary observations of my own. Father and benefactor! In very truth, but for the prayers of your virtuous spouse in her salubrious villa near our town, there's no knowing what might not have come to pass. What I have been through to-day I can find no words to express. The efficiency of Krushensky and of the major of the fire brigade are beyond all praise! I am proud of such devoted servants of our country! As for me, I did all that a weak man could do, whose only desire is the welfare of his neighbour; and sitting now in the bosom of my family, with tears in my eyes I thank Him Who spared us bloodshed! In absence of evidence, the guilty parties remain in custody, but I propose to release them in a week or so. It was their ignorance that led them astray!"

1884

GONE ASTRAY

GONE ASTRAY

A COUNTRY village wrapped in the darkness of night. One o'clock strikes from the belfry. Two lawyers, called Kozyavkin and Laev, both in the best of spirits and a little unsteady on their legs, come out of the wood and turn towards the cottages.

"Well, thank God, we've arrived," says Kozyavkin, drawing a deep breath. "Tramping four miles from the station in our condition is a feat. I am fearfully done up! And, as ill-luck would have it, not a fly to be seen."

"Petya, my dear fellow. . . . I can't. . . . I feel like dying if I'm not in bed in five minutes."

"In bed! Don't you think it, my boy! First we'll have supper and a glass of red wine, and then you can go to bed. Verotchka and I will wake you up. . . . Ah, my dear fellow, it's a fine thing to be married! You don't understand it, you cold-hearted wretch! I shall be home in a minute, worn out and exhausted. . . . A loving wife will welcome me, give me some tea and something to eat, and repay me for my hard work and my love with such a fond and loving look out of her darling black eyes that I shall forget how tired I am, and forget the burglary and the law courts and the appeal division. . . . It's glorious!"

"Yes—I say, I feel as though my legs were

dropping off, I can scarcely get along. . . . I am frightfully thirsty. . . ."

"Well, here we are at home."

The friends go up to one of the cottages, and stand still under the nearest window.

"It's a jolly cottage," said Kozyavkin. "You will see to-morrow what views we have! There's no light in the windows. Verotchka must have gone to bed, then; she must have got tired of sitting up. She's in bed, and must be worrying at my not having turned up." (He pushes the window with his stick, and it opens.) "Plucky girl! She goes to bed without bolting the window." (He takes off his cape and flings it with his portfolio in at the window.) "I am hot! Let us strike up a serenade and make her laugh!" (He sings.) "The moon floats in the midnight sky. . . . Faintly stir the tender breezes. . . . Faintly rustle in the tree-tops. . . . Sing, sing, Alyosha! Verotchka, shall we sing you Schubert's Serenade?" (He sings.)

His performance is cut short by a sudden fit of coughing. "Tphoo! Verotchka, tell Aksinya to unlock the gate for us!" (A pause.) "Verotchka! don't be lazy, get up, darling!" (He stands on a stone and looks in at the window.) "Verotchka, my dumpling; Verotchka, my poppet . . . my little angel, my wife beyond compare, get up and tell Aksinya to unlock the gate for us! You are not asleep, you know. Little wife, we are really so done up and exhausted that we're not in the mood for jokes. We've trudged all the way from the station! Don't you hear? Ah, hang it all!" (He makes an effort to climb up to the window and falls

down.) " You know this isn't a nice trick to play
on a visitor! I see you are just as great a schoolgirl as ever, Vera, you are always up to mischief! "

" Perhaps Vera Stepanovna is asleep," says Laev.

" She isn't asleep! I bet she wants me to make
an outcry and wake up the whole neighbourhood.
I'm beginning to get cross, Vera! Ach, damn it
all! Give me a leg up, Alyosha; I'll get in. You
are a naughty girl, nothing but a regular schoolgirl.
. . . Give me a hoist."

Puffing and panting, Laev gives him a leg up, and
Kozyavkin climbs in at the window and vanishes
into the darkness within.

" Vera! " Laev hears a minute later, " where are
you? . . . D—damnation! Tphoo! I've put my
hand into something! Tphoo! "

There is a rustling sound, a flapping of wings, and
the desperate cackling of a fowl.

" A nice state of things," Laev hears. " Vera,
where on earth did these chickens come from?
Why, the devil, there's no end of them! There's
a basket with a turkey in it. . . . It pecks, the
nasty creature."

Two hens fly out of the window, and cackling at
the top of their voices, flutter down the village
street.

" Alyosha, we've made a mistake! " says Kozyavkin in a lachrymose voice. " There are a lot of
hens here. . . . I must have mistaken the house.
Confound you, you are all over the place, you cursed
brutes! "

" Well, then, make haste and come down. Do
you hear? I am dying of thirst! "

"In a minute. . . . I am looking for my cape
and portfolio."

"Light a match."

"The matches are in the cape. . . . I was a
crazy idiot to get into this place. The cottages are
exactly alike; the devil himself couldn't tell them
apart in the dark. Aie, the turkey's pecked my
cheek, nasty creature!"

"Make haste and get out or they'll think we are
stealing the chickens."

"In a minute. . . . I can't find my cape anywhere. . . . There are lots of old rags here, and
I can't tell where the cape is. Throw me a match."

"I haven't any."

"We are in a hole, I must say! What am I to
do? I can't go without my cape and my portfolio.
I must find them."

"I can't understand a man's not knowing his own
cottage," says Laev indignantly. "Drunken beast.
. . . If I'd known I was in for this sort of thing
I would never have come with you. I should have
been at home and fast asleep by now, and a nice fix
I'm in here. . . . I'm fearfully done up and
thirsty, and my head is going round."

"In a minute, in a minute. . . . You won't
expire."

A big cock flies crowing over Laev's head. Laev
heaves a deep sigh, and with a hopeless gesture sits
down on a stone. He is beset with a burning thirst,
his eyes are closing, his head drops forward. . . .
Five minutes pass, ten, twenty, and Kozyavkin is
still busy among the hens.

"Petya, will you be long?"

" A minute. I found the portfolio, but I have lost it again."

Laev lays his head on his fists, and closes his eyes. The cackling of the fowls grows louder and louder. The inhabitants of the empty cottage fly out of the window and flutter round in circles, he fancies, like owls over his head. His ears ring with their cackle, he is overwhelmed with terror.

" The beast! " he thinks. " He invited me to stay, promising me wine and junket, and then he makes me walk from the station and listen to these hens. . . ."

In the midst of his indignation his chin sinks into his collar, he lays his head on his portfolio, and gradually subsides. Weariness gets the upper hand and he begins to doze.

" I've found the portfolio! " he hears Kozyavkin cry triumphantly. " I shall find the cape in a minute and then off we go! "

Then through his sleep he hears the barking of dogs. First one dog barks, then a second, and a third. . . . And the barking of the dogs blends with the cackling of the fowls into a sort of savage music. Someone comes up to Laev and asks him something. Then he hears someone climb over his head into the window, then a knocking and a shouting. . . . A woman in a red apron stands beside him with a lantern in her hand and asks him something.

" You've no right to say so," he hears Kozyavkin's voice. " I am a lawyer, a bachelor of laws— Kozyavkin—here's my visiting card."

" What do I want with your card? " says someone in a husky bass. "You've disturbed all my fowls, you've smashed the eggs! Look what you've done. The turkey poults were to have come out to-day or to-morrow, and you've smashed them. What's the use of your giving me your card, sir?"

"How dare you interfere with me! No! I won't have it!"

"I am thirsty," thinks Laev, trying to open his eyes, and he feels somebody climb down from the window over his head.

"My name is Kozyavkin! I have a cottage here. Everyone knows me."

"We don't know anyone called Kozyavkin."

"What are you saying? Call the elder. He knows me."

"Don't get excited, the constable will be here directly. . . . We know all the summer visitors here, but I've never seen you in my life."

"I've had a cottage in Rottendale for five years."

"Whew! Do you take this for the Dale? This is Sicklystead, but Rottendale is farther to the right, beyond the match factory. It's three miles from here."

"Bless my soul! Then I've taken the wrong turning!"

The cries of men and fowls mingle with the barking of dogs, and the voice of Kozyavkin rises above the chaos of confused sounds:

"You shut up! I'll pay. I'll show you whom you have to deal with!"

Little by little the voices die down. Laev feels himself being shaken by the shoulder. . . .

1885

AN AVENGER

AN AVENGER

SHORTLY after finding his wife *in flagrante delicto* Fyodor Fyodorovitch Sigaev was standing in Schmuck and Co.'s, the gunsmiths, selecting a suitable revolver. His countenance expressed wrath, grief, and unalterable determination.

"I know what I must do," he was thinking. "The sanctities of the home are outraged, honour is trampled in the mud, vice is triumphant, and therefore as a citizen and a man of honour I must be their avenger. First, I will kill her and her lover and then myself."

He had not yet chosen a revolver or killed anyone, but already in imagination he saw three bloodstained corpses, broken skulls, brains oozing from them, the commotion, the crowd of gaping spectators, the post-mortem. . . . With the malignant joy of an insulted man he pictured the horror of the relations and the public, the agony of the traitress, and was mentally reading leading articles on the destruction of the traditions of the home.

The shopman, a sprightly little Frenchified figure with rounded belly and white waistcoat, displayed the revolvers, and smiling respectfully and scraping with his little feet observed:

". . . I would advise you, M'sieur, to take this superb revolver, the Smith and Wesson pattern, the last word in the science of firearms: triple-action, with ejector, kills at six hundred paces, central sight.

Let me draw your attention, M'sieu, to the beauty of the finish. The most fashionable system, M'sieu. We sell a dozen every day for burglars, wolves, and lovers. Very correct and powerful action, hits at a great distance, and kills wife and lover with one bullet. As for suicide, M'sieu, I don't know a better pattern."

The shopman pulled and cocked the trigger, breathed on the barrel, took aim, and affected to be breathless with delight. Looking at his ecstatic countenance, one might have supposed that he would readily have put a bullet through his brains if he had only possessed a revolver of such a superb pattern as a Smith-Wesson.

"And what price?" asked Sigaev.

"Forty-five roubles, M'sieu."

"Mm! . . . that's too dear for me."

"In that case, M'sieu, let me offer you another make, somewhat cheaper. Here, if you'll kindly look, we have an immense choice, at all prices. . . . Here, for instance, this revolver of the Lefaucher pattern costs only eighteen roubles, but . . ." (the shopman pursed up his face contemptuously) ". . . but, M'sieu, it's an old-fashioned make. They are only bought by hysterical ladies or the mentally deficient. To commit suicide or shoot one's wife with a Lefaucher revolver is considered bad form nowadays. Smith-Wesson is the only pattern that's correct style."

"I don't want to shoot myself or to kill anyone," said Sigaev, lying sullenly. "I am buying it simply for a country cottage . . . to frighten away burglars. . . ."

" That's not our business, what object you have
in buying it." The shopman smiled, dropping his
eyes discreetly. " If we were to investigate the
object in each case, M'sieu, we should have to close
our shop. To frighten burglars Lefaucher is not
a suitable pattern, M'sieu, for it goes off with a
faint, muffled sound. I would suggest Mortimer's,
the so-called duelling pistol. . . ."

" Shouldn't I challenge him to a duel? " flashed
through Sigaev's mind. " It's doing him too much
honour, though. . . . Beasts like that are killed
like dogs. . . ."

The shopman, swaying gracefully and tripping to
and fro on his little feet, still smiling and chattering, displayed before him a heap of revolvers. The
most inviting and impressive of all was the Smith
and Wesson's. Sigaev picked up a pistol of that
pattern, gazed blankly at it, and sank into brooding.
His imagination pictured how he would blow out
their brains, how blood would flow in streams over
the rug and the parquet, how the traitress's legs
would twitch in her last agony. . . . But that was
not enough for his indignant soul. The picture of
blood, wailing, and horror did not satisfy him. He
must think of something more terrible.

" I know! I'll kill myself and him," he thought,
" but I'll leave her alive. Let her pine away from
the stings of conscience and the contempt of all
surrounding her. For a sensitive nature like hers
that will be far more agonizing than death."

And he imagined his own funeral: he, the injured
husband, lies in his coffin with a gentle smile on his
lips, and she, pale, tortured by remorse, follows the

coffin like a Niobe, not knowing where to hide herself to escape from the withering, contemptuous looks cast upon her by the indignant crowd.

"I see, M'sieu, that you like the Smith and Wesson make," the shopman broke in upon his broodings. "If you think it too dear, very well, I'll knock off five roubles. . . . But we have other makes, cheaper."

The little Frenchified figure turned gracefully and took down another dozen cases of revolvers from the shelf.

"Here, M'sieu, price thirty roubles. That's not expensive, especially as the rate of exchange has dropped terribly and the Customs duties are rising every hour. M'sieu, I vow I am a Conservative, but even I am beginning to murmur. Why, with the rate of exchange and the Customs tariff, only the rich can purchase firearms. There's nothing left for the poor but Tula weapons and phosphorus matches, and Tula weapons are a misery! You may aim at your wife with a Tula revolver and shoot yourself through the shoulder-blade."

Sigaev suddenly felt mortified and sorry that he would be dead, and would miss seeing the agonies of the traitress. Revenge is only sweet when one can see and taste its fruits, and what sense would there be in it if he were lying in his coffin, knowing nothing about it?

"Hadn't I better do this?" he pondered. "I'll kill him, then I'll go to his funeral and look on, and after the funeral I'll kill myself. They'd arrest me, though, before the funeral, and take away my pistol. . . . And so I'll kill him, she shall remain alive, and I . . . for the time, I'll not kill myself, but go and be arrested. I shall always have time to kill myself. There will be this advantage about being arrested, that at the preliminary investigation I shall have an opportunity of exposing to the authorities and to the public all the infamy of her conduct. If I kill myself she may, with her characteristic duplicity and impudence, throw all the blame on me, and society will justify her behaviour and will very likely laugh at me. . . . If I remain alive, then . . ."

A minute later he was thinking:

" Yes, if I kill myself I may be blamed and suspected of petty feeling. . . . Besides, why should I kill myself? That's one thing. And for another, to shoot oneself is cowardly. And so I'll kill him and let her live, and I'll face my trial. I shall be tried, and she will be brought into court as a witness. . . . I can imagine her confusion, her disgrace when she is examined by my counsel! The sympathies of the court, of the Press, and of the public will certainly be with me."

While he deliberated the shopman displayed his wares, and felt it incumbent upon him to entertain his customer.

" Here are English ones, a new pattern, only just received," he prattled on. " But I warn you, M'sieu, all these systems pale beside the Smith and Wesson. The other day—as I dare say you have read—an officer bought from us a Smith and Wesson. He shot his wife's lover, and—would you believe it?—the bullet passed through him, pierced the bronze lamp, then the piano, and ricochetted back from the piano, killing the lap-dog and bruising the wife. A magnificent record redounding to the honour of our firm! The officer is now under arrest. He will no doubt be convicted and sent to penal servitude. In the first place, our penal code is quite out of date; and, secondly, M'sieu, the sympathies of the court are always with the lover. Why is it? Very simple, M'sieu. The judges and the jury and the prosecutor and the counsel for the defence are all living with other men's wives, and it'll add to their comfort that there will be one husband the less in Russia. Society would be pleased if the Government were to send all the husbands to Sahalin. Oh, M'sieu, you don't know how it excites my indignation to see the corruption of morals nowadays. To love other men's wives is as much the regular thing to-day as to smoke other men's cigarettes and to read other men's books. Every year our trade gets worse and worse—it doesn't mean that wives are more faithful, but that husbands resign themselves to their position and are afraid of the law and penal servitude."

The shopman looked round and whispered: "And whose fault is it, M'sieu? The Government's."

"To go to Sahalin for the sake of a pig like that —there's no sense in that either," Sigaev pondered. "If I go to penal servitude it will only give my wife an opportunity of marrying again and deceiving a second husband. She would triumph. . . . And so I will leave *her* alive, I won't kill myself, *him* . . . I won't kill either. I must think of something more sensible and more effective. I will punish them with my contempt, and will take divorce proceedings that will make a scandal."

" Here, M'sieu, is another make," said the shopman, taking down another dozen from the shelf. " Let me call your attention to the original mechanism of the lock."

In view of his determination a revolver was now of no use to Sigaev, but the shopman, meanwhile, getting more and more enthusiastic, persisted in displaying his wares before him. The outraged husband began to feel ashamed that the shopman should be taking so much trouble on his account for nothing, that he should be smiling, wasting time, displaying enthusiasm for nothing.

" Very well, in that case," he muttered, " I'll look in again later on . . . or I'll send someone."

He didn't see the expression of the shopman's face, but to smooth over the awkwardness of the position a little he felt called upon to make some purchase. But what should he buy? He looked round the walls of the shop to pick out something inexpensive, and his eyes rested on a green net hanging near the door.

" That's . . . what's that? " he asked.

" That's a net for catching quails."

" And what price is it? "

" Eight roubles, M'sieu."

" Wrap it up for me. . . ."

The outraged husband paid his eight roubles, took the net, and, feeling even more outraged, walked out of the shop.

1887

THE JEUNE PREMIER

THE JEUNE PREMIER

YEVGENY ALEXEYITCH PODZHAROV, the *jeune premier*, a graceful, elegant young man with an oval face and little bags under his eyes, had come for the season to one of the southern towns of Russia, and tried at once to make the acquaintance of a few of the leading families of the place. " Yes, signor," he would often say, gracefully swinging his foot and displaying his red socks, " an artist ought to act upon the masses, both directly and indirectly; the first aim is attained by his work on the stage, the second by an acquaintance with the local inhabitants. On my honour, *parole d'honneur,* I don't understand why it is we actors avoid making acquaintance with local families. Why is it? To say nothing of dinners, name-day parties, feasts, *soirées fixes,* to say nothing of these entertainments, think of the moral influence we may have on society! Is it not agreeable to feel one has dropped a spark in some thick skull? The types one meets! The women! *Mon Dieu,* what women! they turn one's head! One penetrates into some huge merchant's house, into the sacred retreats, and picks out some fresh and rosy little peach—it's heaven, *parole d'honneur!* "

In the southern town, among other estimable families he made the acquaintance of that of a manufacturer called Zybaev. Whenever he remem-

bers that acquaintance now he frowns contemptuously, screws up his eyes, and nervously plays with
his watch-chain.

One day—it was at a name-day party at Zybaev's
—the actor was sitting in his new friends' drawing-
room and holding forth as usual. Around him
" types " were sitting in armchairs and on the sofa,
listening affably; from the next room came feminine
laughter and the sounds of evening tea. . . . Cross-
ing his legs, after each phrase sipping tea with rum
in it, and trying to assume an expression of careless
boredom, he talked of his stage triumphs.

" I am a provincial actor principally," he said,
smiling condescendingly, " but I have played in
Petersburg and Moscow too. . . . By the way,
I will describe an incident which illustrates pretty
well the state of mind of to-day. At my benefit
in Moscow the young people brought me such a
mass of laurel wreaths that I swear by all I hold
sacred I did not know where to put them! *Parole
d'honneur!* Later on, at a moment when funds
were short, I took the laurel wreaths to the shop,
and . . . guess what they weighed. Eighty
pounds altogether. Ha, ha! you can't think how
useful the money was. Artists, indeed, are often
hard up. To-day I have hundreds, thousands, to-
morrow nothing. . . . To-day I haven't a crust of
bread, to-morrow I have oysters and anchovies,
hang it all! "

The local inhabitants sipped their glasses de-
corously and listened. The well-pleased host, not
knowing how to make enough of his cultured and
interesting visitor, presented to him a distant rela-

tive who had just arrived, one Pavel Ignatyevitch
Klimov, a bulky gentleman about forty, wearing a
long frock-coat and very full trousers.

"You ought to know each other," said Zybaev
as he presented Klimov; "he loves theatres, and
at one time used to act himself. He has an estate
in the Tula province."

Podzharov and Klimov got into conversation. It
appeared, to the great satisfaction of both, that
the Tula landowner lived in the very town in which
the *jeune premier* had acted for two seasons in succession. Enquiries followed about the town, about
common acquaintances, and about the theatre. . . .

"Do you know, I like that town awfully," said
the *jeune premier,* displaying his red socks. "What
streets, what a charming park, and what society!
Delightful society!"

"Yes, delightful society," the landowner assented.

"A commercial town, but extremely cultured.
. . . For instance, er-er-er . . . the head master of
the high school, the public prosecutor . . . the officers. . . . The police captain, too, was not bad,
a man, as the French say, *enchanté,* and the women,
Allah, what women!"

"Yes, the women . . . certainly. . . ."

"Perhaps I am partial; the fact is that in your
town, I don't know why, I was devilishly lucky with
the fair sex! I could write a dozen novels. To
take this episode, for instance. . . . I was staying
in Yegoryevsky Street, in the very house where the
Treasury is. . . ."

"The red house without stucco?"

"Yes,   yes . . . without   stucco. . . . Close by, as I remember now, lived a local beauty, Varenka. . . ."

"Not Varvara Nikolayevna?" asked Klimov, and he beamed with satisfaction. "She really is a beauty . . . the most beautiful girl in the town."

"The most beautiful girl in the town! A classic profile, great black eyes . . . and hair to her waist! She saw me in 'Hamlet,' she wrote me a letter *à la* Pushkin's 'Tatyana.' . . . I answered, as you may guess. . . ."

Podzharov looked round, and having satisfied himself that there were no ladies in the room, rolled his eyes, smiled mournfully, and heaved a sigh.

"I came home one evening after a performance," he whispered, "and there she was, sitting on my sofa. There followed tears, protestations of love, kisses. . . . Oh, that was a marvellous, that was a divine night! Our romance lasted two months, but that night was never repeated. It was a night, *parole d'honneur!*"

"Excuse me, what's that?" muttered Klimov, turning crimson and gazing open-eyed at the actor. "I know Varvara Nikolayevna well: she's my niece."

Podzharov was embarrassed, and he, too, opened his eyes wide.

"How's this?" Klimov went on, throwing up his hands. "I know the girl, and . . . and . . . I am surprised. . . ."

"I am very sorry this has come up," muttered the actor, getting up and rubbing something out of his left eye with his little finger. "Though, of course . . . of course, you as her uncle . . ."

The other guests, who had hitherto been listening to the actor with pleasure and rewarding him with smiles, were embarrassed and dropped their eyes.

"Please, do be so good . . . take your words back . . ." said Klimov in extreme embarrassment. "I beg you to do so!"

"If . . . er-er-er . . . it offends you, certainly," answered the actor, with an undefined movement of his hand.

"And confess you have told a falsehood."

"I, no . . . er-er-er. . . . It was not a lie, but . . . I greatly regret having spoken too freely. . . . And, in fact . . . I don't understand your tone!"

Klimov walked up and down the room in silence, as though in uncertainty and hesitation. His fleshy face grew more and more crimson, and the veins in his neck swelled up. After walking up and down for about two minutes he went up to the actor and said in a tearful voice:

"No, do be so good as to confess that you told a lie about Varenka! Have the goodness to do so!"

"It's queer," said the actor, with a strained smile, shrugging his shoulders and swinging his leg. "This is positively insulting!"

"So you will not confess it?"

"I do-on't understand!"

"You will not? In that case, excuse me . . . I shall have to resort to unpleasant measures. Either, sir, I shall insult you at once on the spot,

or . . . if you are an honourable man, you will
kindly accept my challenge to a duel. . . . We will
fight!"

" Certainly!" rapped out the *jeune premier,* with
a contemptuous gesture. " Certainly."

Extremely perturbed, the guests and the host, not
knowing what to do, drew Klimov aside and began
begging him not to get up a scandal. Astonished
feminine countenances appeared in the doorway.
. . . The *jeune premier* turned round, said a few
words, and with an air of being unable to remain in
a house where he was insulted, took his cap and
made off without saying good-bye.

On his way home the *jeune premier* smiled contemptuously and shrugged his shoulders, but when
he reached his hotel room and stretched himself on
his sofa he felt exceedingly uneasy.

" The devil take him!" he thought. " A duel
does not matter, he won't kill me, but the trouble is
the other fellows will hear of it, and they know
perfectly well it was a yarn. It's abominable! I
shall be disgraced all over Russia. . . ."

Podzharov thought a little, smoked, and to calm
himself went out into the street.

" I ought to talk to this bully, ram into his stupid
noddle that he is a blockhead and a fool, and that
I am not in the least afraid of him. . . ."

The *jeune premier* stopped before Zybaev's house
and looked at the windows. Lights were still burning behind the muslin curtains and figures were
moving about.

" I'll wait for him!" the actor decided.

It was dark and cold. A hateful autumn rain was

drizzling as though through a sieve. Podzharov
leaned his elbow on a lamp-post and abandoned
himself to a feeling of uneasiness.

He was wet through and exhausted.

At two o'clock in the night the guests began coming out of Zybaev's house. The landowner from
Tula was the last to make his appearance. He
heaved a sigh that could be heard by the whole
street and scraped the pavement with his heavy
overboots.

"Excuse me!" said the *jeune premier,* overtaking him. "One minute."

Klimov stopped. The actor gave a smile, hesitated, and began, stammering: "I . . . I confess
. . . I told a lie."

"No, sir, you will please confess that publicly,"
said Klimov, and he turned crimson again. "I can't
leave it like that. . . ."

"But you see I am apologizing! I beg you . . .
don't you understand? I beg you because you will
admit a duel will make talk, and I am in a position.
. . . My fellow-actors . . . goodness knows what
they may think. . . ."

The *jeune premier* tried to appear unconcerned,
to smile, to stand erect, but his body would not obey
him, his voice trembled, his eyes blinked guiltily,
and his head drooped. For a good while he went
on muttering something. Klimov listened to him,
thought a little, and heaved a sigh.

"Well, so be it," he said. "May God forgive
you. Only don't lie in future, young man. Nothing
degrades a man like lying . . . yes, indeed!

You are a young man, you have had a good education. . . ."

The landowner from Tula, in a benignant,
fatherly way, gave him a lecture, while the *jeune
premier* listened and smiled meekly. . . . When it
was over he smirked, bowed, and with a guilty step
and a crestfallen air set off for his hotel.

As he went to bed half an hour later he felt that
he was out of danger and was already in excellent
spirits.   Serene and satisfied that the misunderstanding had ended so satisfactorily, he wrapped
himself in the bedclothes, soon fell asleep, and slept
soundly till ten o'clock next morning.

1886

A DEFENCELESS CREATURE

A DEFENCELESS CREATURE

In spite of a violent attack of gout in the night and the nervous exhaustion left by it, Kistunov went in the morning to his office and began punctually seeing the clients of the bank and persons who had come with petitions. He looked languid and exhausted, and spoke in a faint voice hardly above a whisper, as though he were dying.

"What can I do for you?" he asked a lady in an antediluvian mantle, whose back view was extremely suggestive of a huge dung-beetle.

"You see, your Excellency," the petitioner in question began, speaking rapidly, "my husband Shtchukin, a collegiate assessor, was ill for five months, and while he, if you will excuse my saying so, was laid up at home, he was for no sort of reason dismissed, your Excellency; and when I went for his salary they deducted, if you please, your Excellency, twenty-four roubles thirty-six kopecks from his salary. 'What for?' I asked. 'He borrowed from the club fund,' they told me, 'and the other clerks had stood security for him.' How was that? How could he have borrowed it without my consent? It's impossible, your Excellency. What's the reason of it? I am a poor woman, I earn my bread by taking in lodgers. I am a weak, defenceless woman . . . I have to put up with ill-usage from everyone and never hear a kind word. . . ."

The petitioner was blinking, and dived into her mantle for her handkerchief. Kistunov took her petition from her and began reading it.

"Excuse me, what's this?" he asked, shrugging his shoulders. "I can make nothing of it. Evidently you have come to the wrong place, madam. Your petition has nothing to do with us at all. You will have to apply to the department in which your husband was employed."

"Why, my dear sir, I have been to five places already, and they would not even take the petition anywhere," said Madame Shtchukin. "I'd quite lost my head, but, thank goodness—God bless him for it—my son-in-law, Boris Matveyitch, advised me to come to you. 'You go to Mr. Kistunov, mamma: he is an influential man, he can do anything for you. . . .' Help me, your Excellency!"

"We can do nothing for you, Madame Shtchukin. You must understand: your husband served in the Army Medical Department, and our establishment is a purely private commercial undertaking, a bank. Surely you must understand that!"

Kistunov shrugged his shoulders again and turned to a gentleman in a military uniform, with a swollen face.

"Your Excellency," piped Madame Shtchukin in a pitiful voice, "I have the doctor's certificate that my husband was ill! Here it is, if you will kindly look at it."

"Very good, I believe you," Kistunov said irritably, "but I repeat it has nothing to do with us. It's queer and positively absurd! Surely your husband must know where you are to apply?"

" He knows nothing, your Excellency. He keeps
on: 'It's not your business! Get away!'—that's
all I can get out of him. . . . Whose business is
it, then? It's I have to keep them all!"

Kistunov again turned to Madame Shtchukin and
began explaining to her the difference between the
Army Medical Department and a private bank.
She listened attentively, nodded in token of assent,
and said:

"Yes . . . yes . . . yes . . . I understand, sir.
In that case, your Excellency, tell them to pay me
fifteen roubles at least! I agree to take part on
account!"

"Ough!" sighed Kistunov, letting his head drop
back. "There's no making you see reason. Do
understand that to apply to us with such a petition
is as strange as to send in a petition concerning
divorce, for instance, to a chemist's or to the Assay-
ing Board. You have not been paid your due, but
what have we to do with it?"

"Your Excellency, make me remember you in
my prayers for the rest of my days, have pity on
a lone, lorn woman," wailed Madame Shtchukin;
"I am a weak, defenceless woman. . . . I am
worried to death, I've to settle with the lodgers
and see to my husband's affairs and fly round looking
after the house, and I am going to church every day
this week, and my son-in-law is out of a job. . . .
I might as well not eat or drink. . . . I can scarcely
keep on my feet. . . . I haven't slept all
night. . . ."

Kistunov was conscious of the palpitation of his
heart. With a face of anguish, pressing his hand

on his heart, he began explaining to Madame
Shtchukin again, but his voice failed him. . . .

"No, excuse me, I cannot talk to you," he said
with a wave of his hand. "My head's going round.
You are hindering us and wasting your time. Ough!
Alexey Nikolaitch," he said, addressing one of his
clerks, "please will you explain to Madame
Shtchukin?"

Kistunov, passing by all the petitioners, went to
his private room and signed about a dozen papers
while Alexey Nikolaitch was still engaged with Madame Shtchukin. As he sat in his room Kistunov
heard two voices: the monotonous, restrained bass
of Alexey Nikolaitch and the shrill, wailing voice of
Madame Shtchukin.

"I am a weak, defenceless woman, I am a woman
in delicate health," said Madame Shtchukin. "I
look strong, but if you were to overhaul me there is
not one healthy fibre in me. I can scarcely keep
on my feet, and my appetite is gone. . . . I drank
my cup of coffee this morning without the slightest
relish. . . ."

Alexey Nikolaitch explained to her the difference
between the departments and the complicated system of sending in papers. He was soon exhausted,
and his place was taken by the accountant.

"A wonderfully disagreeable woman!" said Kistunov, revolted, nervously cracking his fingers and
continually going to the decanter of water. "She's
a perfect idiot! She's worn me out and she'll ex-
haust them, the nasty creature! Ough! . . . my
heart is throbbing."

Half an hour later he rang his bell. Alexey Nikolaitch made his appearance.

"How are things going?" Kistunov asked languidly.

"We can't make her see anything, Pyotr Alexandritch! We are simply done. We talk of one thing and she talks of something else."

"I . . . I can't stand the sound of her voice. . . . I am ill. . . . I can't bear it."

"Send for the porter, Pyotr Alexandritch, let him put her out."

"No, no," cried Kistunov in alarm. "She will set up a squeal, and there are lots of flats in this building, and goodness knows what they would think of us. . . . Do try and explain to her, my dear fellow. . . ."

A minute later the deep drone of Alexey Nikolaitch's voice was audible again. A quarter of an hour passed, and instead of his bass there was the murmur of the accountant's powerful tenor."

"Re-mark-ab-ly nasty woman," Kistunov thought indignantly, nervously shrugging his shoulders. "No more brains than a sheep. I believe that's a twinge of the gout again. . . . My migraine is coming back. . . ."

In the next room Alexey Nikolaitch, at the end of his resources, at last tapped his finger on the table and then on his own forehead.

"The fact of the matter is you haven't a head on your shoulders," he said, "but this."

"Come, come," said the old lady, offended.

" Talk to your own wife like that. . . . You screw!
. . . Don't be too free with your hands."

And looking at her with fury, with exasperation,
as though he would devour her, Alexey Nikolaitch
said in a quiet, stifled voice:

" Clear out."

" Wha-at? " squealed Madame Shtchukin.
" How dare you? I am a weak, defenceless
woman; I won't endure it. My husband is a collegiate assessor. You screw! . . . I will go to Dmitri
Karlitch, the lawyer, and there will be nothing left
of you! I've had the law of three lodgers, and I
will make you flop down at my feet for your saucy
words! I'll go to your general. Your Excellency,
your Excellency! "

" Be off, you pest," hissed Alexey Nikolaitch.

Kistunov opened his door and looked into the
office.

" What is it? " he asked in a tearful voice.

Madame Shtchukin, as red as a crab, was standing in the middle of the room, rolling her eyes and
prodding the air with her fingers. The bank clerks
were standing round red in the face too, and, evidently harassed, were looking at each other
distractedly.

" Your Excellency," cried Madame Shtchukin,
pouncing upon Kistunov. " Here, this man, he
here . . . this man . . ." (she pointed to Alexey
Nikolaitch) " tapped himself on the forehead and
then tapped the table. . . . You told him to go
into my case, and he's jeering at me! I am a weak,
defenceless woman. . . . My husband is a collegiate assessor, and I am a major's daughter myself! "

"Very good, madam," moaned Kistunov. "I will go into it . . . I will take steps. . . . Go away . . . later!"

"And when shall I get the money, your Excellency? I need it to-day!"

Kistunov passed his trembling hand over his forehead, heaved a sigh, and began explaining again.

"Madam, I have told you already this is a bank, a private commercial establishment. . . . What do you want of us? And do understand that you are hindering us."

Madame Shtchukin listened to him and sighed.

"To be sure, to be sure," she assented. "Only, your Excellency, do me the kindness, make me pray for you for the rest of my life, be a father, protect me! If a medical certificate is not enough I can produce an affidavit from the police. . . . Tell them to give me the money."

Everything began swimming before Kistunov's eyes. He breathed out all the air in his lungs in a prolonged sigh and sank helpless on a chair.

"How much do you want?" he asked in a weak voice.

"Twenty-four roubles and thirty-six kopecks."

Kistunov took his pocket-book out of his pocket, extracted a twenty-five rouble note and gave it to Madame Shtchukin.

"Take it and . . . and go away!"

Madame Shtchukin wrapped the money up in her handkerchief, put it away, and pursing up her face into a sweet, mincing, even coquettish smile, asked:

"Your Excellency, and would it be possible for my husband to get a post again?"

"I am going . . . I am ill . . ." said Kistunov in a weary voice. "I have dreadful palpitations."

When he had driven home Alexey Nikolaitch sent Nikita for some laurel drops, and, after taking twenty drops each, all the clerks set to work, while Madame Shtchukin stayed another two hours in the vestibule, talking to the porter and waiting for Kistunov to return. . . .

She came again next day.

1887

AN ENIGMATIC NATURE

AN ENIGMATIC NATURE

ON the red velvet seat of a first-class railway carriage a pretty lady sits half reclining. An expensive fluffy fan trembles in her tightly closed fingers, a pince-nez keeps dropping off her pretty little nose, the brooch heaves and falls on her bosom, like a boat on the ocean. She is greatly agitated.

On the seat opposite sits the Provincial Secretary of Special Commissions, a budding young author, who from time to time publishes long stories of high life, or " Novelli " as he calls them, in the leading paper of the province. He is gazing into her face, gazing intently, with the eyes of a connoisseur. He is watching, studying, catching every shade of this exceptional, enigmatic nature. He understands it, he fathoms it. Her soul, her whole psychology lies open before him.

" Oh, I understand, I understand you to your inmost depths! " says the Secretary of Special Commissions, kissing her hand near the bracelet. " Your sensitive, responsive soul is seeking to escape from the maze of—— Yes, the struggle is terrific, titanic. But do not lose heart, you will be triumphant! Yes! "

" Write about me, Voldemar! " says the pretty lady, with a mournful smile. " My life has been so full, so varied, so chequered. Above all, I am unhappy. I am a suffering soul in some page of

Dostoevsky. Reveal my soul to the world, Voldemar. Reveal that hapless soul. You are a psychol-
ogist. We have not been in the train an hour together, and you have already fathomed my heart."

"Tell me! I beseech you, tell me!"

"Listen. My father was a poor clerk in the
Service. He had a good heart and was not without
intelligence; but the spirit of the age—of his envir-
onment—*vous comprenez?*—I do not blame my
poor father. He drank, gambled, took bribes. My
mother—but why say more? Poverty, the struggle
for daily bread, the consciousness of insignificance
—ah, do not force me to recall it! I had to make
my own way. You know the monstrous education
at a boarding-school, foolish novel-reading, the er-
rors of early youth, the first timid flutter of love.
It was awful! The vacillation! And the agonies
of losing faith in life, in oneself! Ah, you are an
author. You know us women. You will understand. Unhappily I have an intense nature. I
looked for happiness—and what happiness! I
longed to set my soul free. Yes. In that I saw
my happiness!"

"Exquisite creature!" murmured the author,
kissing her hand close to the bracelet. "It's not
you I am kissing, but the suffering of humanity.
Do you remember Raskolnikov and his kiss?"

"Oh, Voldemar, I longed for glory, renown, success, like every—why affect modesty?—every nature
above the commonplace. I yearned for something
extraordinary, above the common lot of woman!
And then—and then—there crossed my path—an
old general—very well off. Understand me, Volde-

mar! It was self-sacrifice, renunciation! You must
see that! I could do nothing else. I restored the
family fortunes, was able to travel, to do good.
Yet how I suffered, how revolting, how loathsome
to me were his embraces—though I will be fair to
him—he had fought nobly in his day. There were
moments—terrible moments—but I was kept up by
the thought that from day to day the old man might
die, that then I would begin to live as I liked, to give
myself to the man I adore—be happy. There is
such a man, Voldemar, indeed there is!"

The pretty lady flutters her fan more violently.
Her face takes a lachrymose expression. She goes
on:

"But at last the old man died. He left me something. I was free as a bird of the air. Now is the
moment for me to be happy, isn't it, Voldemar?
Happiness comes tapping at my window, I had only
to let it in—but—Voldemar, listen, I implore you!
Now is the time for me to give myself to the man
I love, to become the partner of his life, to help, to
uphold his ideals, to be happy—to find rest—but
—how ignoble, repulsive, and senseless all our life
is! How mean it all is, Voldemar. I am wretched,
wretched, wretched! Again there is an obstacle in
my path! Again I feel that my happiness is far,
far away! Ah, what anguish!—if only you knew
what anguish!"

"But what—what stands in your way? I implore you tell me! What is it?"

"Another old general, very well off——"

The broken fan conceals the pretty little face.

The author props on his fist his thought-heavy brow and ponders with the air of a master in psychology. The engine is whistling and hissing while the window curtains flush red with the glow of the setting sun.

1883

A HAPPY MAN

A HAPPY MAN

THE passenger train is just starting from Bologoe, the junction on the Petersburg-Moscow line. In a second-class smoking compartment five passengers sit dozing, shrouded in the twilight of the carriage. They had just had a meal, and now, snugly ensconced in their seats, they are trying to go to sleep. Stillness.

The door opens and in there walks a tall, lanky figure straight as a poker, with a ginger-coloured hat and a smart overcoat, wonderfully suggestive of a journalist in Jules Verne or on the comic stage.

The figure stands still in the middle of the compartment for a long while, breathing heavily, screwing up his eyes and peering at the seats.

"No, wrong again!" he mutters. "What the deuce! It's positively revolting! No, the wrong one again!"

One of the passengers stares at the figure and utters a shout of joy:

"Ivan Alexyevitch! what brings you here? Is it you?"

The poker-like gentleman starts, stares blankly at the passenger, and recognizing him claps his hands with delight.

"Ha! Pyotr Petrovitch," he says. "How many summers, how many winters! I didn't know you were in this train."

" How are you getting on? "

" I am all right; the only thing is, my dear fellow, I've lost my compartment and I simply can't find it. What an idiot I am! I ought to be thrashed! "

The poker-like gentleman sways a little unsteadily and sniggers.

" Queer things do happen! " he continues. " I stepped out just after the second bell to get a glass of brandy. I got it, of course. Well, I thought, since it's a long way to the next station, it would be as well to have a second glass. While I was thinking about it and drinking it the third bell rang. . . . I ran like mad and jumped into the first carriage. I am an idiot! I am the son of a hen! "

" But you seem in very good spirits," observes Pyotr Petrovitch. " Come and sit down! There's room and a welcome."

" No, no. . . . I'm off to look for my carriage. Good-bye! "

" You'll fall between the carriages in the dark if you don't look out! Sit down, and when we get to a station you'll find your own compartment. Sit down! "

Ivan Alexyevitch heaves a sigh and irresolutely sits down facing Pyotr Petrovitch. He is visibly excited, and fidgets as though he were sitting on thorns.

" Where are you travelling to? " Pyotr Petrovitch enquires.

" I? Into space. There is such a turmoil in my head that I couldn't tell where I am going myself. I go where fate takes me. Ha-ha! My dear fellow, have you ever seen a happy fool? No?

Well, then, take a look at one. You behold the happiest of mortals! Yes! Don't you see something from my face?"

"Well, one can see you're a bit . . . a tiny bit so-so."

"I dare say I look awfully stupid just now. Ach! it's a pity I haven't a looking-glass, I should like to look at my counting-house. My dear fellow, I feel I am turning into an idiot, honour bright. Haha! Would you believe it, I'm on my honeymoon. Am I not the son of a hen?"

"You? Do you mean to say you are married?"

"To-day, my dear boy. We came away straight after the wedding."

Congratulations and the usual questions follow.

"Well, you are a fellow!" laughs Pyotr Petrovitch. "That's why you are rigged out such a dandy."

"Yes, indeed. . . . To complete the illusion. I've even sprinkled myself with scent. I am over my ears in vanity! No care, no thought, nothing but a sensation of something or other . . . deuce knows what to call it . . . beatitude or something? I've never felt so grand in my life!"

Ivan Alexyevitch shuts his eyes and waggles his head.

"I'm revoltingly happy," he says. "Just think; in a minute I shall go to my compartment. There on the seat near the window is sitting a being who is, so to say, devoted to you with her whole being. A little blonde with a little nose . . . little fingers. . . . My little darling! My angel! My little poppet! Phylloxera of my soul! And her little foot! Good God! A little foot not like our beetle-crushers, but something miniature, fairylike, allegorical. I could pick it up and eat it, that little foot! Oh, but you don't understand! You're a materialist, of course, you begin analyzing at once, and one thing and another. You are cold-hearted bachelors, that's what you are! When you get married you'll think of me. 'Where's Ivan Alexyevitch now?' you'll say. Yes; so in a minute I'm going to my compartment. There she is waiting for me with impatience . . . in joyful anticipation of my appearance. She'll have a smile to greet me. I sit down beside her and take her chin with my two fingers. . . ."

Ivan Alexyevitch waggles his head and goes off into a chuckle of delight.

" Then I lay my noddle on her shoulder and put my arm round her waist. Around all is silence, you know . . . poetic twilight. I could embrace the whole world at such a moment. Pyotr Petrovitch, allow me to embrace you! "

" Delighted, I'm sure." The two friends embrace while the passengers laugh in chorus. And the happy bridegroom continues:

" And to complete the idiocy, or, as the novelists say, to complete the illusion, one goes to the refreshment-room and tosses off two or three glasses. And then something happens in your head and your heart, finer than you can read of in a fairy tale. I am a man of no importance, but I feel as though I were limitless: I embrace the whole world! "

The passengers, looking at the tipsy and blissful bridegroom, are infected by his cheerfulness and no longer feel sleepy. Instead of one listener, Ivan Alexyevitch has now an audience of five. He wriggles and splutters, gesticulates, and prattles on without ceasing. He laughs and they all laugh.

"Gentlemen, gentlemen, don't think so much! Damn all this analysis! If you want a drink, drink, no need to philosophize as to whether it's bad for you or not. . . . Damn all this philosophy and psychology!"

The guard walks through the compartment.

"My dear fellow," the bridegroom addresses him, "when you pass through the carriage No. 209 look out for a lady in a grey hat with a white bird and tell her I'm here!"

"Yes, sir. Only there isn't a No. 209 in this train; there's 219!"

"Well, 219, then! It's all the same. Tell that lady, then, that her husband is all right!"

Ivan Alexyevitch suddenly clutches his head and groans:

"Husband. . . . Lady. . . . All in a minute! Husband. . . . Ha-ha! I am a puppy that needs thrashing, and here I am a husband! Ach, idiot! But think of her! . . . Yesterday she was a little girl, a midget . . . it's simply incredible!"

"Nowadays it really seems strange to see a happy man," observes one of the passengers; "one as soon expects to see a white elephant."

"Yes, and whose fault is it?" says Ivan Alexyevitch, stretching his long legs and thrusting out his feet with their very pointed toes. "If you are not happy it's your own fault! Yes, what else do you suppose it is? Man is the creator of his own happiness. If you want to be happy you will be, but you don't want to be! You obstinately turn away from happiness."

" Why, what next! How do you make that out? "

" Very simply. Nature has ordained that at a certain stage in his life man should love. When that time comes you should love like a house on fire, but you won't heed the dictates of nature, you keep waiting for something. What's more, it's laid down by law that the normal man should enter upon matrimony. There's no happiness without marriage. When the propitious moment has come, get married. There's no use in shilly-shallying. . . . But you don't get married, you keep waiting for something! Then the Scriptures tell us that ' wine maketh glad the heart of man.' . . . If you feel happy and you want to feel better still, then go to the refreshment bar and have a drink. The great thing is not to be too clever, but to follow the beaten track! The beaten track is a grand thing! "

" You say that man is the creator of his own happiness. How the devil is he the creator of it when a toothache or an ill-natured mother-in-law is enough to scatter his happiness to the winds? Everything depends on chance. If we had an accident at this moment you'd sing a different tune."

" Stuff and nonsense! " retorts the bridegroom. " Railway accidents only happen once a year. I'm not afraid of an accident, for there is no reason for one. Accidents are exceptional! Confound them! I don't want to talk of them! Oh, I believe we're stopping at a station."

"Where are you going now?" asks Pyotr Petrovitch. "To Moscow or somewhere further south?"

"Why, bless you! How could I go somewhere further south, when I'm on my way to the north?"

"But Moscow isn't in the north."

"I know that, but we're on our way to Petersburg," says Ivan Alexyevitch.

"We are going to Moscow, mercy on us!"

"To Moscow? What do you mean?" says the bridegroom in amazement.

"It's queer. . . . For what station did you take your ticket?"

"For Petersburg."

"In that case I congratulate you. You've got into the wrong train."

There follows a minute of silence. The bridegroom gets up and looks blankly round the company.

"Yes, yes," Pyotr Petrovitch explains. "You must have jumped into the wrong train at Bologoe. . . . After your glass of brandy you succeeded in getting into the down-train."

Ivan Alexyevitch turns pale, clutches his head, and begins pacing rapidly about the carriage.

"Ach, idiot that I am!" he says in indignation. "Scoundrel! The devil devour me! Whatever am I to do now? Why, my wife is in that train! She's there all alone, expecting me, consumed by anxiety. Ach, I'm a motley fool!"

The bridegroom falls on the seat and writhes as though someone had trodden on his corns.

"I am un-unhappy man!" he moans. "What am I to do, what am I to do?"

"There, there!" the passengers try to console him. "It's all right. . . . You must telegraph to your wife and try to change into the Petersburg express. In that way you'll overtake her."

"The Petersburg express!" weeps the bridegroom, the creator of his own happiness. "And how am I to get a ticket for the Petersburg express? All my money is with my wife."

The passengers, laughing and whispering together, make a collection and furnish the happy man with funds.

1886

A TROUBLESOME VISITOR

A TROUBLESOME VISITOR

In the low-pitched, crooked little hut of Artyom, the forester, two men were sitting under the big dark ikon—Artyom himself, a short and lean peasant with a wrinkled, aged-looking face and a little beard that grew out of his neck, and a well-grown young man in a new crimson shirt and big wading boots, who had been out hunting and come in for the night. They were sitting on a bench at a little three-legged table on which a tallow candle stuck into a bottle was lazily burning.

Outside the window the darkness of the night was full of the noisy uproar into which nature usually breaks out before a thunderstorm. The wind howled angrily and the bowed trees moaned miserably. One pane of the window had been pasted up with paper, and leaves torn off by the wind could be heard pattering against the paper.

" I tell you what, good Christian," said Artyom in a hoarse little tenor half-whisper, staring with unblinking, scared-looking eyes at the hunter. " I am not afraid of wolves or bears, or wild beasts of any sort, but I am afraid of man. You can save yourself from beasts with a gun or some other weapon, but you have no means of saving yourself from a wicked man."

" To be sure, you can fire at a beast, but if you

shoot at a robber you will have to answer for it: you will go to Siberia."

"I've been forester, my lad, for thirty years, and I couldn't tell you what I have had to put up with from wicked men. There have been lots and lots of them here. The hut's on a track, it's a cart-road, and that brings them, the devils. Every sort of ruffian turns up, and without taking off his cap or making the sign of the cross, bursts straight in upon one with: 'Give us some bread, you old so-and-so.' And where am I to get bread for him? What claim has he? Am I a millionaire to feed every drunkard that passes? They are half-blind with spite. . . . They have no cross on them, the devils. . . . They'll give you a clout on the ear and not think twice about it: 'Give us bread!' Well, one gives it. . . . One is not going to fight with them, the idols! Some of them are two yards across the shoulders, and a great fist as big as your boot, and you see the sort of figure I am. One of them could smash me with his little finger. . . . Well, one gives him bread and he gobbles it up, and stretches out full length across the hut with not a word of thanks. And there are some that ask for money. 'Tell me, where is your money?' As though I had money! How should I come by it?"

"A forester and no money!" laughed the hunter. "You get wages every month, and I'll be bound you sell timber on the sly."

Artyom took a timid sideway glance at his visitor and twitched his beard as a magpie twitches her tail.

"You are still young to say a thing like that to

me," he said. " You will have to answer to God
for those words. Whom may your people be?
Where do you come from? "

" I am from Vyazovka. I am the son of Nefed
the village elder."

" You have gone out for sport with your gun.
. . . I used to like sport, too, when I was young.
H'm! Ah, our sins are grievous," said Artyom,
with a yawn. " It's a sad thing! There are few
good folks, but villains and murderers no end—
God have mercy upon us."

" You seem to be frightened of me, too. . . ."

" Come, what next! What should I be afraid
of you for? I see. . . . I understand. . . . You
came in, and not just anyhow, but you made the sign
of the cross, you bowed, all decent and proper.
. . . I understand. . . . One can give you bread.
. . . I am a widower, I don't heat the stove, I sold
the samovar. . . . I am too poor to keep meat or
anything else, but bread you are welcome to."

At that moment something began growling under
the bench: the growl was followed by a hiss.
Artyom started, drew up his legs, and looked enquiringly at the hunter.

" It's my dog worrying your cat," said the hunter.
" You devils! " he shouted under the bench. " Lie
down. You'll be beaten. I say, your cat's thin,
mate! She is nothing but skin and bone."

" She is old, it is time she was dead. . . . So
you say you are from Vyazovka? "

" I see you don't feed her. Though she's a cat
she's a creature . . . every breathing thing. You
should have pity on her! "

"You are a queer lot in Vyazovka," Artyom went on, as though not listening. "The church has been robbed twice in one year. . . . To think that there are such wicked men! So they fear neither man nor God! To steal what is the Lord's! Hanging's too good for them! In old days the governors used to have such rogues flogged."

"However you punish, whether it is with flogging or anything else, it will be no good, you will not knock the wickedness out of a wicked man."

"Save and preserve us, Queen of Heaven!" The forester sighed abruptly. "Save us from all enemies and evildoers. Last week at Volovy Zaimishtchy, a mower struck another on the chest with his scythe . . . he killed him outright! And what was it all about, God bless me! One mower came out of the tavern . . . drunk. The other met him, drunk too."

The young man, who had been listening attentively, suddenly started, and his face grew tense as he listened.

"Stay," he said, interrupting the forester. "I fancy someone is shouting."

The hunter and the forester fell to listening with their eyes fixed on the window. Through the noise of the forest they could hear sounds such as the strained ear can always distinguish in every storm, so that it was difficult to make out whether people were calling for help or whether the wind was wailing in the chimney. But the wind tore at the roof, tapped at the paper on the window, and brought a distinct shout of "Help!"

"Talk of your murderers," said the hunter, turn-

ing pale and getting up. "Someone is being
robbed!"

"Lord have mercy on us," whispered the forester, and he, too, turned pale and got up.

The hunter looked aimlessly out of window and
walked up and down the hut.

"What a night, what a night!" he muttered.
"You can't see your hand before your face! The
very time for a robbery. Do you hear? There is
a shout again."

The forester looked at the ikon and from the
ikon turned his eyes upon the hunter, and sank on
to the bench, collapsing like a man terrified by
sudden bad news.

"Good Christian," he said in a tearful voice,
"you might go into the passage and bolt the door.
And we must put out the light."

"What for?"

"By ill-luck they may find their way here. . . .
Oh, our sins!"

"We ought to be going, and you talk of bolting
the door! You are a clever one! Are you
coming?"

The hunter threw his gun over his shoulder and
picked up his cap.

"Get ready, take your gun. Hey, Flerka, here,"
he called to his dog. "Flerka!"

A dog with long frayed ears, a mongrel between
a setter and a house-dog, came out from under the
bench. He stretched himself by his master's feet
and wagged his tail.

"Why are you sitting there?" cried the hunter

to the forester. "You mean to say you are not going?"

"Where?"

"To help!"

"How can I?" said the forester with a wave of his hand, shuddering all over. "I can't bother about it!"

"Why won't you come?"

"After talking of such dreadful things I won't stir a step into the darkness. Bless them! And what should I go for?"

"What are you afraid of? Haven't you got a gun? Let us go, please do. It's scaring to go alone; it will be more cheerful, the two of us. Do you hear? There was a shout again. Get up!"

"Whatever do you think of me, lad?" wailed the forester. "Do you think I am such a fool to go straight to my undoing?"

"So you are not coming?"

The forester did not answer. The dog, probably hearing a human cry, gave a plaintive whine.

"Are you coming, I ask you?" cried the hunter, rolling his eyes angrily.

"You do keep on, upon my word," said the forester with annoyance. "Go yourself."

"Ugh! . . . low cur," growled the hunter, turning towards the door. "Flerka, here!"

He went out and left the door open. The wind flew into the hut. The flame of the candle flickered uneasily, flared up, and went out.

As he bolted the door after the hunter, the forester saw the puddles in the track, the nearest pine-trees, and the retreating figure of his guest lighted up by a flash of lightning. Far away he heard the rumble of thunder.

"Holy, holy, holy," whispered the forester, making haste to thrust the thick bolt into the great iron rings. "What weather the Lord has sent us!"

Going back into the room, he felt his way to the stove, lay down, and covered himself from head to foot. Lying under the sheepskin and listening intently, he could no longer hear the human cry, but the peals of thunder kept growing louder and more prolonged. He could hear the big wind-lashed raindrops pattering angrily on the panes and on the paper of the window.

"He's gone on a fool's errand," he thought, picturing the hunter soaked with rain and stumbling over the tree-stumps. "I bet his teeth are chattering with terror!"

Not more than ten minutes later there was a sound of footsteps, followed by a loud knock at the door.

"Who's there?" cried the forester.

"It's I," he heard the young man's voice. "Unfasten the door."

The forester clambered down from the stove, felt for the candle, and, lighting it, went to the door. The hunter and his dog were drenched to the skin. They had come in for the heaviest of the downpour, and now the water ran from them as from washed clothes before they have been wrung out.

"What was it?" asked the forester.

"A peasant woman driving in a cart; she had got off the road . . ." answered the young man, struggling with his breathlessness. "She was caught in a thicket."

"Ah, the silly thing! She was frightened, then. . . . Well, did you put her on the road?"

"I don't care to talk to a scoundrel like you."

The young man flung his wet cap on the bench and went on:

"I know now that you are a scoundrel and the lowest of men. And you a keeper, too, getting a salary! You blackguard!"

The forester slunk with a guilty step to the stove, cleared his throat, and lay down. The young man sat on the bench, thought a little, and lay down on it full length. Not long afterwards he got up, put out the candle, and lay down again. During a particularly loud clap of thunder he turned over, spat on the floor, and growled out:

"He's afraid. . . . And what if the woman were being murdered? Whose business is it to defend her? And he an old man, too, and a Christian. . . . He's a pig and nothing else."

The forester cleared his throat and heaved a deep sigh. Somewhere in the darkness Flerka shook his wet coat vigorously, which sent drops of water flying about all over the room.

"So you wouldn't care if the woman were murdered?" the hunter went on. "Well—strike me, God—I had no notion you were that sort of man. . . ."

A silence followed. The thunderstorm was by now over and the thunder came from far away, but it was still raining.

"And suppose it hadn't been a woman but you

shouting ' Help I ' ? " said the hunter, breaking the
silence. " How would you feel, you beast, if no one
ran to your aid? You have upset me with your
meanness, plague take you I "

After another long interval the hunter said:

" You must have money to be afraid of people!
A man who is poor is not likely to be afraid. . . ."

" For those words you will answer before God,"
Artyom said hoarsely from the stove. " I have no
money."

" I dare say! Scoundrels always have money.
. . . Why are you afraid of people, then? So you
must have! I'd like to take and rob you for spite,
to teach you a lesson! . . ."

Artyom slipped noiselessly from the stove, lighted
a candle, and sat down under the holy image. He
was pale and did not take his eyes off the hunter.

" Here, I'll rob you," said the hunter, getting up.
" What do you think about it? Fellows like you
want a lesson. Tell me, where is your money
hidden? "

Artyom drew his legs up under him and blinked.

" What are you wriggling for? Where is your
money hidden? Have you lost your tongue, you
fool? Why don't you answer? "

The young man jumped up and went up to the
forester.

" He is blinking like an owl! Well? Give me
your money, or I will shoot you with my gun."

" Why do you keep on at me? " squealed the
forester, and big tears rolled from his eyes.
" What's the reason of it? God sees all! You
will have to answer, for every word you say, to

God.   You have no right whatever to ask for my money."

The young man looked at Artyom's tearful face, frowned, and walked up and down the hut, then angrily clapped his cap on his head and picked up his gun.

"Ugh! . . . ugh! . . . it makes me sick to look at you," he filtered through his teeth.   "I can't bear the sight of you.   I won't sleep in your house, anyway.   Good-bye!   Hey, Flerka!"

The door slammed and the troublesome visitor went out with his dog. . . . Artyom bolted the door after him, crossed himself, and lay down.

1886

AN ACTOR'S END

AN ACTOR'S END

SHTCHIPTSOV, the "heavy father" and "good-hearted simpleton," a tall and thick-set old man, not so much distinguished by his talents as an actor as by his exceptional physical strength, had a desperate quarrel with the manager during the performance, and just when the storm of words was at its height felt as though something had snapped in his chest. Zhukov, the manager, as a rule began at the end of every heated discussion to laugh hysterically and to fall into a swoon; on this occasion, however, Shtchiptsov did not remain for this climax, but hurried home. The high words and the sensation of something ruptured in his chest so agitated him as he left the theatre that he forgot to wash off his paint, and did nothing but take off his beard.

When he reached his hotel room, Shtchiptsov spent a long time pacing up and down, then sat down on the bed, propped his head on his fists, and sank into thought. He sat like that without stirring or uttering a sound till two o'clock the next afternoon, when Sigaev, the comic man, walked into his room.

"Why is it you did not come to the rehearsal, Booby Ivanitch?" the comic man began, panting and filling the room with fumes of vodka. "Where have you been?"

Shtchiptsov made no answer, but simply stared at

the comic man with lustreless eyes, under which there were smudges of paint.

"You might at least have washed your phiz!" Sigaev went on. "You are a disgraceful sight! Have you been boozing, or . . . are you ill, or what? But why don't you speak? I am asking you: are you ill?"

Shtchiptsov did not speak. In spite of the paint on his face, the comic man could not help noticing his striking pallor, the drops of sweat on his forehead, and the twitching of his lips. His hands and feet were trembling too, and the whole huge figure of the "good-natured simpleton" looked somehow crushed and flattened. The comic man took a rapid glance round the room, but saw neither bottle nor flask nor any other suspicious vessel.

"I say, Mishutka, you know you are ill!" he said in a flutter. "Strike me dead, you are ill! You don't look yourself!"

Shtchiptsov remained silent and stared disconsolately at the floor.

"You must have caught cold," said Sigaev, taking him by the hand. "Oh, dear, how hot your hands are! What's the trouble?"

"I wa-ant to go home," muttered Shtchiptsov.

"But you are at home now, aren't you?"

"No. . . . To Vyazma. . . ."

"Oh, my, anywhere else! It would take you three years to get to your Vyazma. . . . What? do you want to go and see your daddy and mummy? I'll be bound, they've kicked the bucket years ago, and you won't find their graves. . . ."

"My ho-ome's there."

" Come, it's no good giving way to the dismal
dumps. These neurotic feelings are the limit, old
man. You must get well, for you have to play
Mitka in ' The Terrible Tsar ' to-morrow. There
is nobody else to do it. Drink something hot and
take some castor-oil? Have you got the money for
some castor-oil? Or, stay, I'll run and buy some."

The comic man fumbled in his pockets, found a
fifteen-kopeck piece, and ran to the chemist's. A
quarter of an hour later he came back.

" Come, drink it," he said, holding the bottle to
the " heavy father's " mouth. " Drink it straight
out of the bottle. . . . All at a go! That's the
way. . . . Now nibble at a clove that your very soul
mayn't stink of the filthy stuff."

The comic man sat a little longer with his sick
friend, then kissed him tenderly, and went away.
Towards evening the *jeune premier,* Brama-Glinsky,
ran in to see Shtchiptsov. The gifted actor was
wearing a pair of prunella boots, had a glove on his
left hand, was smoking a cigar, and even smelt of
heliotrope, yet nevertheless he strongly suggested a
traveller cast away in some land in which there were
neither baths nor laundresses nor tailors. . . .

" I hear you are ill? " he said to Shtchiptsov,
twirling round on his heel. " What's wrong with
you? What's wrong with you, really? . . ."

Shtchiptsov did not speak nor stir.

" Why don't you speak? Do you feel giddy?
Oh well, don't talk, I won't pester you . . . don't
talk. . . ."

Brama-Glinsky (that was his stage name, in his
passport he was called Guskov) walked away to the

window, put his hands in his pockets, and fell to gazing into the street. Before his eyes stretched an immense waste, bounded by a grey fence beside which ran a perfect forest of last year's burdocks. Beyond the waste ground was a dark, deserted factory, with windows boarded up. A belated jackdaw was flying round the chimney. This dreary, lifeless scene was beginning to be veiled in the dusk of evening.

" I must go home ! " the *jeune premier* heard.

" Where is home ? "

" To Vyazma . . . to my home. . . ."

" It is a thousand miles to Vyazma . . . my boy," sighed Brama-Glinsky, drumming on the window-pane. " And what do you want to go to Vyazma for ? "

" I want to die there."

" What next ! Now he's dying ! He has fallen ill for the first time in his life, and already he fancies that his last hour is come. . . . No, my boy, no cholera will carry off a buffalo like you. You'll live to be a hundred. . . . Where's the pain ? "

" There's no pain, but I . . . feel . . ."

" You don't feel anything, it all comes from being too healthy. Your surplus energy upsets you. You ought to get jolly tight—drink, you know, till your whole inside is topsy-turvy. Getting drunk is wonderfully restoring. . . . Do you remember how screwed you were at Rostov on the Don? Good Lord, the very thought of it is alarming! Sashka and I together could only just carry in the barrel, and you emptied it alone, and even sent for rum afterwards. . . . You got so drunk you were catching devils in a sack and pulled a lamp-post up by the roots. Do you remember? Then you went off to beat the Greeks. . . ."

Under the influence of these agreeable reminiscences Shtchiptsov's face brightened a little and his eyes began to shine.

" And do you remember how I beat Savoikin the manager? " he muttered, raising his head. " But there! I've beaten thirty-three managers in my time, and I can't remember how many smaller fry. And what managers they were! Men who would not permit the very winds to touch them! I've beaten two celebrated authors and one painter! "

" What are you crying for? "

" At Kherson I killed a horse with my fists. And at Taganrog some roughs fell upon me at night, fifteen of them. I took off their caps and they followed me, begging: ' Uncle, give us back our caps.' That's how I used to go on."

" What are you crying for, then, you silly? "

" But now it's all over . . . I feel it. If only I could go to Vyazma! "

A pause followed. After a silence Shtchiptsov suddenly jumped up and seized his cap. He looked distraught.

" Good-bye! I am going to Vyazma! " he articulated, staggering.

" And the money for the journey? "

" H'm! . . . I shall go on foot! "

" You are crazy. . . ."

The two men looked at each other, probably because the same thought—of the boundless plains, the unending forests and swamps—struck both of them at once.

" Well, I see you have gone off your head," the *jeune premier* commented. " I'll tell you what, old man. . . . First thing, go to bed, then drink some brandy and tea to put you into a sweat. And some castor-oil, of course. Stay, where am I to get some brandy? "

Brama-Glinsky thought a minute, then made up his mind to go to a shopkeeper called Madame Tsitrinnikov to try and get it from her on tick: who knows? perhaps the woman would feel for them and let them have it. The *jeune premier* went off, and half an hour later returned with a bottle of brandy and some castor-oil. Shtchiptsov was sitting motionless, as before, on the bed, gazing dumbly at the floor. He drank the castor-oil offered him by his friend like an automaton, with no consciousness of what he was doing. Like an automaton he sat afterwards at the table, and drank tea and brandy; mechanically he emptied the whole bottle and let the *jeune premier* put him to bed. The latter covered him up with a quilt and an overcoat, advised him to get into a perspiration, and went away.

The night came on; Shtchiptsov had drunk a great deal of brandy, but he did not sleep. He lay motionless under the quilt and stared at the dark ceiling; then, seeing the moon looking in at the window, he turned his eyes from the ceiling towards the companion of the earth, and lay so with open eyes till the morning. At nine o'clock in the morning Zhukov, the manager, ran in.

" What has put it into your head to be ill, my

angel?" he cackled, wrinkling up his nose. "Aie, aie! A man with your physique has no business to be ill! For shame, for shame! Do you know, I was quite frightened. 'Can our conversation have had such an effect on him?' I wondered. My dear soul, I hope it's not through me you've fallen ill! You know you gave me as good . . . er . . . And, besides, comrades can never get on without words. You called me all sorts of names . . . and have gone at me with your fists too, and yet I am fond of you! Upon my soul, I am. I respect you and am fond of you! Explain, my angel, why I am so fond of you. You are neither kith nor kin nor wife, but as soon as I heard you had fallen ill it cut me to the heart."

Zhukov spent a long time declaring his affection, then fell to kissing the invalid, and finally was so overcome by his feelings that he began laughing hysterically, and was even meaning to fall into a swoon, but, probably remembering that he was not at home nor at the theatre, put off the swoon to a more convenient opportunity and went away.

Soon after him Adabashev, the tragic actor, a dingy, short-sighted individual who talked through his nose, made his appearance. . . . For a long while he looked at Shtchiptsov, for a long while he pondered, and at last he made a discovery.

"Do you know what, Mifa?" he said, pronouncing through his nose "f" instead of "sh," and assuming a mysterious expression. "Do you know what? You ought to have a dose of castor-oil!"

Shtchiptsov was silent. He remained silent, too,

a little later as the tragic actor poured the loathsome oil into his mouth. Two hours later Yevlampy, or, as the actors for some reason called him, Rigoletto, the hairdresser of the company, came into the room. He too, like the tragic man, stared at Shtchiptsov for a long time, then sighed like a steam-engine, and slowly and deliberately began untying a parcel he had brought with him. In it there were twenty cups and several little flasks.

"You should have sent for me and I would have cupped you long ago," he said, tenderly baring Shtchiptsov's chest. "It is easy to neglect illness."

Thereupon Rigoletto stroked the broad chest of the "heavy father" and covered it all over with suction cups.

"Yes . . ." he said, as after this operation he packed up his paraphernalia, crimson with Shtchiptsov's blood. "You should have sent for me, and I would have come. . . . You needn't trouble about payment. . . . I do it from sympathy. Where are you to get the money if that idol won't pay you? Now, please take these drops. They are nice drops! And now you must have a dose of this castor-oil. It's the real thing. That's right! I hope it will do you good. Well, now, good-bye. . . ."

Rigoletto took his parcel and withdrew, pleased that he had been of assistance to a fellow-creature.

The next morning Sigaev, the comic man, going in to see Shtchiptsov, found him in a terrible condition. He was lying under his coat, breathing in gasps, while his eyes strayed over the ceiling. In his hands he was crushing convulsively the crumpled quilt.

" To Vyazma ! " he whispered, when he saw the comic man. " To Vyazma."

" Come, I don't like that, old man ! " said the comic man, flinging up his hands. " You see . . . you see . . . you see, old man, that's not the thing ! Excuse me, but . . . it's positively stupid. . . ."

" To go to Vyazma ! My God, to Vyazma ! "

" I . . . I did not expect it of you," the comic man muttered, utterly distracted. " What the deuce do you want to collapse like this for ? Aie . . . aie . . . aie ! . . . that's not the thing. A giant as tall as a watch-tower, and crying. Is it the thing for actors to cry ? "

" No wife nor children," muttered Shtchiptsov. " I ought not to have gone for an actor, but have stayed at Vyazma. My life has been wasted, Semyon ! Oh, to be in Vyazma ! "

" Aie . . . aie . . . aie ! . . . that's not the thing ! You see, it's stupid . . . contemptible indeed ! "

Recovering his composure and setting his feelings in order, Sigaev began comforting Shtchiptsov, telling him untruly that his comrades had decided to send him to the Crimea at their expense, and so on, but the sick man did not listen and kept muttering about Vyazma. . . . At last, with a wave of his hand, the comic man began talking about Vyazma himself to comfort the invalid.

" It's a fine town," he said soothingly, " a capital town, old man ! It's famous for its cakes. The cakes are classical, but—between ourselves—h'm !— they are a bit groggy. For a whole week after

eating them I was . . . h'm! . . . But what is fine
there is the merchants! They are something like
merchants. When they treat you they do treat
you!"

The comic man talked while Shtchiptsov listened
in silence and nodded his head approvingly.

Towards evening he died.

1886